UNSHACKLE

PAM GODWIN

Cover Designer: Pam Godwin
Interior Designer: Pam Godwin

Content Warning

Visit my website at pamgodwin.com

The books in the DELIVER series are stand-alones, but they should be read in order.

DELIVER (#1)
VANQUISH (#2)
DISCLAIM (#3)
DEVASTATE (#4)
TAKE (#5)
MANIPULATE (#6)
UNSHACKLE (#7)
DOMINATE (#8)
COMPLICATE (#9)

Dedicated to my college English Lit professor for accusing me of plagiarism.

When I defended my original work, you lambasted me, claiming the writing was too good to be my own.

After that class, it took me fifteen years, a degree in Computer Science, and a career in finance to realize…

I'm a writer.

Thank you for that rude lesson.

ONE

A man with soulless eyes shoved a hood over Luke Sanch's head, blocking out the private airplane hangar and spiking his heart rate. The stifling fabric allowed in no light. Just pitch goddamn darkness.

He was officially past the point of no return.

One could argue he'd passed that point the night he woke in Van Quiso's attic, naked and shackled. But unlike that brutal, defining moment, he'd put himself in *this* situation willingly.

The hood had been expected. What would follow, however, was anyone's guess.

Beside him, his roommate and close friend, Tomas Dine, received the same treatment. They'd worked numerous jobs together, alongside their vigilante team. Jobs that put them neck and neck with vile human sex traffickers. This operation was no different.

Except this time, he and Tomas were going in alone.

The tread of soft-soled shoes approached from

behind, circled ominously, and paused a few inches before Luke.

"Welcome, John Smith." The man's voice drawled beneath the weight of a nasally Latino accent. "Your luggage has been searched and transferred. I trust you had no complications during your travels?"

The flight had been over-the-top luxurious—one of the perks of having a Colombian cartel *jefe* on their vigilante team. Matias Restrepo was funding this entire operation, which included flying Luke and Tomas on an untraceable private jet from Mexico to this hangar outside Orange County, California.

To meet with La Rocha Cartel.

The most aggressive, most organized, most violent cartel in existence.

Sharing the same air with these men made Luke's knees twitch, threatening to weaken his stance. Saliva gathered in his mouth. He felt sick. Surrounded. Overpowered. Horrifyingly out of his league.

Whether these homicidal terrorists bought his story or intended to kill him was yet to be determined. Survival depended on his ability to maintain his carefully crafted ruse over the next few days or weeks.

"The flight was adequate." He slipped the tips of his fingers into the pockets of his designer suit pants. "And you are?"

"I'm John Smith," the voice deadpanned. "My colleague here… He's John Smith, too. As are the men at your back, who are currently aiming high-caliber guns at you and your bodyguard."

Funny guy. A blade in the motherfucker's gullet would be funnier. And oh-so-satisfying. His hands clenched.

Finesse, Luke. Find it and wield it. Don't be a moron.

Posing as his bodyguard, Tomas didn't make a sound. The hoods provided a reprieve, hiding involuntary facial tics. They'd been trained for covert operations by Cole Hartman, a retired military, secret agent, whatever-he-was operative. But weeks of lessons hadn't miraculously turned them into seasoned professionals.

Where they lacked undercover experience, they made up for in vicious determination. Or was it stubborn recklessness?

Or just plain stupidity?

"I expect nothing less." Luke injected a cocky smile into his voice. "I followed your instructions. We're unarmed, and all electronic devices were left behind."

No bugs or tracers. No way for his team to track his movements beyond this hangar. His neck tightened with unease.

"We appreciate your cooperation, Mr. Smith," the man said. "And you'll understand the necessity of being searched before we depart."

"Make it quick." Luke grunted. "And mind the suit. It's worth more than the lives of your men."

Arrogance. That was one of the character traits he donned as John Smith. Along with greed, cruelty, and a few other unsavory qualities that would befit the sort of man who shopped for sex in the slave trade.

Several hands fell upon him, thoroughly patting down every inch of his fit frame. They untucked his shirt, dug around in his pants, and lifted his nuts to prod beneath.

Fucking hell. He gritted his teeth as fingers breached the crack of his ass. Then they moved on to his socks, shoes, and other less invasive areas. A growling sound beside him indicated Tomas underwent a similar body search.

That done, they were led to a waiting car. He straightened his suit, blindly ducked into an air-conditioned cabin, and slid across leather seats.

"Right behind you, sir," Tomas said, confirming they hadn't been separated.

The doors shut, and the vehicle rolled into motion.

Stretching out, Luke felt his way around the configuration of seats. A limousine.

No surprise. He was masquerading as a powerful businessman with the wealth of Bill Gates and the ethics of Lucifer. The cartel wanted his business, his *money,* and would wine and dine him until he splurged on their product.

He would have his pick of any of their high-priced, stolen girls.

"The hoods remain on until we arrive. Protocol, you understand." The man from the hangar spoke from an adjacent seat, his accent unnervingly cultured for a cutthroat cartel gangster. "To offset the inconvenience, I have something to make the ride more enjoyable. This one's on the house."

Luke tensed as someone shifted across from him. Body heat brushed his legs. Small hands molded around his knees and traveled up his thighs. Female hands.

He cringed beneath the hood. God only knew how old she was. Or how willing.

Going undercover for this job meant he would have to do things that violated his moral principles. Vile things, like forcing his dick inside girls who weren't in a position to consent.

He wasn't here to rescue them. Not directly. His assignment was to locate Vera Gomez, glean her involvement in the human trafficking syndicate, and finish the job that his roommates, Martin and Ricky, had started during their undercover stint in Jaulaso Prison.

His friends hadn't failed in Jaulaso. They'd just, rather unexpectedly, fallen in love with Hector La Rocha's daughter, Tula Gomez.

Tula's intel on the cartel was marginal at best. Hector hadn't fully trusted her with his secrets, and rightfully so. In the end, she'd killed the cartel capo and passed along everything she'd learned about the trafficking operation in his cartel.

She wanted to find Vera, her missing half-sister. Luke wanted to take down her father's operation and annihilate everyone involved. If the sister wasn't as innocent as Tula adamantly claimed, he didn't know if he could keep his promise to show mercy.

The female hands, now sliding over his groin, could very well belong to the missing sister. A sick part of him hoped for that. He'd memorized her face in the old pictures Tula had provided.

Vera's photographic beauty attached itself to the fingers currently stroking Luke's hardening cock. He strained against the fabric of his trousers, cursing the confinement but also grateful for it.

Hector La Rocha's dying confession had painted Vera as the enemy. Add to that her track record with the cartel, and Luke had a good idea about what he was dealing with.

Beneath the hood, he closed his eyes and gripped the slender arms on his lap, ruthlessly squeezing the delicate bones. "I don't fuck what I can't see."

"I assure you," his cartel escort growled, "she's every man's fantasy."

"I'll be the judge of that." He shoved her away.

"Very well."

A tense moment passed, coiling with the hum of tires on pavement. Their destination might have only been five minutes from the hangar, but he wouldn't put it past the cartel to drive around for an hour to safeguard the compound's location.

Without warning, a small body straddled his lap and lifted the hood to his forehead. His vision filled with a flash of Tomas' leg beside him, the opulent interior of the limo, and the girl's face an inch away from his own.

Not Vera. But no less gorgeous. Christ, her eyes alone made his skin heat and shiver. Huge, gray, and feathered with thick lashes, they blinked at him with gut-hardening vacancy. Innocence. She couldn't have been older than sixteen.

A seductive, practiced smile stole across her features but didn't touch her gaze. Not even a little. She was probably drugged. And brainwashed.

Holding the hood to his brow, she reached between them and unbuckled his belt.

Most trafficked victims came from homes with little supervision and even less love. A distinguished, wealthy stranger could saunter into an impoverished town and lure neglected teenagers with a silver tongue and mouthful of lies. Promises of a new home, money, loving attention, education, and above all, passage to the United States turned desperate kids into easy prey.

Luke would know. Eight years ago, he'd been one of them. Hard-up, naive, and broke as fuck, he'd fallen right into Van Quiso's trap.

It had been eight years since his life irrevocably changed. Nine years for Tomas. Even longer for Ricky and Camila. In total, they were nine ex-slaves, collected one by one, sexually trained, abused, and united in misery.

Luke was damn proud of what they'd become. Vigilantes. Freedom fighters. An inseparable family. The only family he had, and he would take a bullet for every single one of them.

Beyond the tinted windows, luxurious estates dominated the Orange County landscape. The limo headed east, away from the coastline and commercial clusters.

Canting his head, he locked onto the man sitting across from him.

"Is she too cooperative for you?" Dark aura and oily eyes—the desperado scowled at Luke's grip on the girl's arms. "You like them to fight? Is that it?"

"I forwarded my specifications." Luke pushed her away. "You know what I want."

She returned to her seat without argument, and the hood fell back in place, blinding him. On instinct, he reached up to lift it.

"Leave it." The man clucked his tongue. "When we arrive, you'll be pleased with the selection. We have exactly what you requested."

Early twenties, brown eyes, black hair, slender build, golden complexion. Luke didn't have a type, but those were the attributes that had been sent to the cartel because they matched Vera Gomez.

Best case, she was enslaved at the compound and available for purchase. He would buy her and get her the hell out of there.

But he was prepared for the worst.

Unbeknown to the cartel, Van Quiso had made this meeting possible. Van, the notorious slave trader from Texas. Van, the dead man who had been shot by his partner, Liv Reed, six years ago.

Only those connected to the Freedom Fighters knew he'd survived. Over the past month, Van had dug up some connections from his old trafficking life and reinserted himself into the underground network as an interested buyer named John Smith.

Within days, La Rocha Cartel had taken the bait.

They'd vetted and trusted the information Van fed them. And why not? Van had contacts that could only be obtained by powerful, scum-sucking rapists.

Because Van had been one of them.

He'd done a lot of atoning since then. Enough to make him seem almost… Empathetic? Accountable? *Human.*

It was strange to admit—no one ever said it aloud—but Van had become a trusted friend among them. A Freedom Fighter. Family.

The bastard was still a cocky prick. But Luke no longer held a grudge for the unspeakable weeks he'd been raped and tortured as Van's captive. If he were honest, Van had done him a favor.

Luke had a purpose now, a reason to fight. Many reasons. He had friends who cared about him. Because of Van, he'd escaped a lonely, meaningless, dead-end life.

Because of Van—and the obscene down payment wired to the cartel—he was on this blindfolded ride to an unknown destination, where he would be expected to sample the merchandise and purchase a stolen girl.

For a wealthy, sexually depraved monster, it was a dream vacation.

For Luke, it was a chance to exact justice.

Silence thrummed for nearly an hour. The hood eliminated eye contact and the awkward need to make conversation, but the tension mounted. It was coming from him, knotting in his shoulders and making every second unbearable. Reality setting in.

He was on his way to La Rocha Cartel's secret compound. Without a weapon. Without a tactical team of Delta operatives. Without federal agents who did this shit for a living. It was just him and Tomas, working outside the boundaries of the law.

If they succeeded, Hector La Rocha's four sons and their despicable operation would be eliminated. Vera would be returned to her sister, and countless slaves would be freed.

If they failed, he and Tomas would be gutted, dismembered, and never seen or heard from again.

You volunteered for this. Trained for it. You know what you're doing.

It wasn't working. His heart refused to abandon its frantic sprint around his ribcage.

Eventually, the limo slowed, motoring in stops and starts, presumably through gated entrances manned by armed guards. Then the engine shut off.

"Have a look, Mr. Smith." His escort shifted, creaking the seats as the doors opened.

Luke dragged off the hood and caught Tomas' expressionless stare before turning his attention beyond the windows.

Parked in a massive, extravagantly landscaped courtyard, they were surrounded by opulence and money. A lot of fucking money.

Stone archways and monolith columns supported red-tile roofs that stretched between Mediterranean-style buildings. The compound formed a sprawling, symmetrical circle around him. A towering, open-air fortress, broken up by breezeways and multilevel turrets to create individual living spaces with wrought-iron balconies and stucco exteriors.

The travertine driveway snaked through a portico and curved out of sight. Patterned pavers drew walkways in every direction, leading under covered arches to smaller courtyards, lush gardens, fountains, and pools.

Less conspicuous, but no less excessive, was the security detail. Cameras and guards covered every corner and entry point. Weapons weren't in view, but they were there, hidden under oversize jackets. Anything else would've made guests uncomfortable.

This was a resort designed to entertain depravity. A compound built on indulgence and the blood of innocents.

The limo emptied, leaving him to exit last. The unforgiving California heat baked into his black suit as he stepped out and joined Tomas. His gaze landed on the row of cars in the courtyard.

A Ferrari FXX-K, Lamborghini Centenario, and holy shit, that was goddamn Pagani Huayra. He blinked. And blinked again. One of only a few hundred in the world, that hypercar had taken over two years to build by hand. *Look at all the carbon fiber.* Complete with gull-wing doors, red leather upholstery, and a 720hp AMG Mercedes engine. Un-fucking-real.

He dragged his eyes away only to choke at the sight of the Koenigsegg Agera parked next in the line. Sexiest goddamn thing he'd ever seen. And *fast.* The rear wing adjusted at the push of a button for optimal speed. Not that it needed the help. It held the production car speed record of 278 mph.

His fingers twitched. *Damn.* This was the closest he'd ever come to touching one.

Back in Texas, he'd taken up mechanic work to pass the time between vigilante jobs. He'd learned the trade. Self-taught. Motorcycles mostly. But he'd always had a deep appreciation for fast cars.

More Ferraris and Lambos filled his view, forming a glimmering, drool-worthy panorama of rolling works of art. Every hypercar here was worth over a million dollars. Some valued at three to four mil. Whoever owned this collection was a car enthusiast, someone who shared his obsession and had the money to buy the rarest, most expensive models in the world.

There would be other guests on the property, slave buyers like him. But they would've been escorted here in the limo, wearing hoods. These cars belonged to someone who could come and go freely.

"If you're good with a stick, my brother will let you test drive one of his toys around the property."

The sultry feminine voice turned his head. The click of approaching heels drew his gaze. Long, shapely legs hewed his breath. Sun-kissed skin for miles.

His insides drew taut as he took in the sinuous lines of hips in the simple black dress. Early twenties, brown eyes, black hair, slender build, golden complexion. *Exquisite.*

She stepped right up to him, too fucking close for someone he didn't know, and dragged red-painted fingernails along the curve of his bicep. He dug through a swirl of potent perfume and male arousal and found his brain.

"Your brother owns these cars?" Prying her off his arm, he set her away. "Who is he?"

"Marco La Rocha."

The eldest son. Of course.

According to Hector, he'd fathered four sons and one daughter. While in prison, Tula Gomez saw the paternity test that confirmed her unsavory bloodline. Hector La Rocha was her father. *Gomez* was her mother's surname.

So who was *this* woman?

Dread sloshed through his veins.

"Welcome to *Casa de La Rocha*, John Smith," she said with a sensual, south-of-the-border accent. Then she drifted back into his space and hooked an arm around his elbow, turning him toward the main entrance. "Except we both know that's not your real name, handsome. Perhaps that's what I'll call you. *Handsome*."

"What do I call you?"

"I… I think…" She touched her chin to her shoulder, peering up at him with a coy smile. "When you turn those arresting green eyes on me, you can call me whatever you want." She cleared her throat and looked away, guiding him forward. "To everyone else, I'm Vera. Vera Gomez."

Fuck.

TWO

It was no secret that Luke loved women. Graceful legs, voluptuous asses, small tits, pouty lips, skinny, curvy, tall, and petite… He appreciated all shapes, sizes, and ethnicities. But more than that, he admired the female inner strength. The stronger her mind and spirit, the more he wanted her.

Lucky for him, women gravitated to him. Because he had a handsome face? A full head of auburn hair? Those were the only good things he'd inherited from the addicts who'd brought him into this world.

Years of dedication in the gym lent him a honed physique and the stamina of a horse. But he lived a dangerous life, had a deplorable past, a crass disposition, and he didn't know a damn thing about relationships. Unless it involved his voracious libido.

Yeah, that was what he had to offer.

Sex.

Orgasms.

Hours of unadulterated, mutually satisfying pleasure.

He could coax an explosive release from anyone, anywhere, anytime, with only his mouth. A skill that had been ruthlessly enforced upon all Van Quiso's captives.

But Luke wasn't here to worship the sexy minx on his arm.

He was going to destroy her.

That made him the best man for this operation. He could separate sentiment from logic, extinguish every ounce of compassion, and get his hands dirty without losing focus.

By the end of this, his hands would be covered in blood.

Vera Gomez's blood.

She wasn't enslaved. She wasn't chained in a cage, beaten into submission, and awaiting an unspeakable fate. Her confident steps escorted him into the yawning foyer, her painted lips curving into a soft smile.

What was her purpose here? Hostess? Liaison? Kinky party planner? Did she fuck the guests? Or hold down the victims while they were violated and abused?

Glancing over his shoulder, he exchanged a look with Tomas. On the surface, his friend wore the unflinching, alert demeanor of a bodyguard. That alertness was real. While Luke played the megalomaniac pervert role with the cartel, Tomas would discreetly scope out the lay of the land.

On Tula's last day in Jaulaso Prison, a dying inmate had choked out, *C-C-Calaaa.* An attempt to tell her where to find her sister. Now, six months later, Luke was in California with Vera literally in his grasp. But where in California was he exactly?

Beyond the open windows, acres of land

stretched out in every direction. At the farthest perimeter, a fortification of walls enclosed the compound, providing protection against the cartel's enemies. It also prevented guests on the inside from identifying any landmarks around them.

What was out there? Desert? Suburbia? One of the edge cities in Orange County?

It was Tomas' job to find out, as well as gather intel on the cartel's security guards, weapons, and technology. Once he uncovered something useful, they faced the task of transmitting it to the Freedom Fighters, who waited on standby in Orange County. Their friends would come, armed to the teeth, the moment they knew the location.

Tomas' expression didn't confess their agenda. Nor did it show his outrage at seeing Vera Gomez greeting them with a smile. Tula had been so certain her sister wasn't involved. Even now, Luke didn't want to believe what was right in front of him.

He planted his shoes on the tile, bringing Vera to an abrupt halt. Startled, she whirled on him, her mouth opening to speak. He didn't give a fuck what she had to say.

Knocking her hand off his arm, he grabbed her throat and yanked her against him. The force of his strength caused her to wobble in the heels.

Two men stepped forward, reaching for hidden weapons. She held out a hand, staying them, and he used that opportunity to angle her neck and put her left ear near his mouth.

"Never," he breathed, cold and calculated, "ever touch me without my permission."

At odds with his cruel tone, he tenderly curled her shoulder-length hair behind her ear. A gesture meant to confuse her as he imperceptibly exposed the skin behind her earlobe.

And there it was, exactly where Tula said it would be. A small black flower tattoo.

Fucking fuck.

The proof of her identity sank into his bones like burning ash. Disgusted, he stepped away, strolling ahead without waiting.

The click of her heels sounded, giving chase.

"Your rooms are this way." She passed him, veering right, shoulders back, and chin raised. No eye contact. Probably because she couldn't hide that butthurt look in her pinched expression. *Good.*

She guided him through arched doorways designed to let breezes flow through the estate. High ceilings added to the open-air concept, but his stifling unease didn't abate.

Voices drifted from unseen rooms. Deep rumbles. Feminine titters. Sounds of flirtation and foreplay. He hardened himself against it, bracing for the hours and days to come.

Other than Vera, the women within these walls weren't here of their own volition. They didn't want rotten, horny, old men touching them. But before the night was over, Luke would shed the last of his humanity and become one of their tormentors.

Through passageways and common areas, Vera narrated the function of each space. With flicks of a hand, she rattled off directions to the indoor gym, spa, main pool, and communal dining room.

He focused on what she didn't point out. Cameras in the ceilings of every room and corridor. Weapons beneath the shirts of every cartel member. Vacancy in the eyes of every young female.

They were all young. As in *not* legal. Not legal age or citizenship. The half-dressed girls milled about carrying drink trays, mopping floors, and entertaining the guests.

A white-haired man in a suit sat on the veranda with a snake-skinned boot propped on the coffee table. An oil baron? Texan rancher? Probably a greasy politician. A topless Asian girl perched on his lap, staring at nothing as he fondled her breasts.

In the pool beyond, another girl bent over the side, moaning half-heartedly while an obese man plowed into her from behind.

At the end of the hall, a petite brunette sat on the floor of a sunlit library, playing with a menagerie of plastic animal figurines. *Toys.* She wore two curly pigtails and a frilly pink sundress that bunched around her waist. A child's dress.

She was physically small enough to be prepubescent, but her profile revealed a woman in her twenties. A creepy dichotomy, made worse by the tinkling octave of her childlike voice singing in Spanish.

He slowed in the doorway, morbidly captivated as she spread her legs and licked the long neck of a plastic giraffe. Her hand went between her thighs, exposing herself, and the figurine followed, repurposed as a different sort of toy.

Nothing wrong with age play in a safe environment. But this place wasn't safe. Who knew how long she'd been enslaved here? Likely captured at a young age, the girl needed a loving home. *And therapy.* Not a sex resort for pedophiles.

"Como este, papá?" She worked the giraffe in and out of her body like a dildo, groaning a hollow giggling sound.

"Yes, babygirl. Just like that." A masculine voice rasped from around the corner. "Fuck that juicy cunt for your daddy."

Heat simmered across Luke's skin, and he quickened his gait. But he couldn't look away as he passed the room, locking onto a middle-aged, average-looking man sprawled in the chair a few feet from her.

There was nothing normal or average in his eyes. The son of a bitch viciously face-fucked another girl while watching the one on the floor.

Sex charged the air, humming and writhing on the breeze. Luke felt it in his pores, sizzling his blood, and tightening his trousers. It made him itchy. Restless. Primed to sink into hot, wet pussy.

Christ, he was surrounded by temptation. Perfect bodies, soft mouths, doll-like eyes, irresistible feminine beauty, and it was all his for the taking. The wrongness of it swelled his cock, thickening with violent need.

What a sick, twisted fuck.

He dragged a hand down his face and looked away, catching Tomas' blank stare behind him. At least one of them seemed to be unaffected.

Everything about this place stank of sin, awakening suppressed urges, tantalizing him, and they hadn't even scratched the surface. These girls were just the entertainment, the docile ones who had been beaten out of their wild state and made tractable. Usable. Stripped of all hope and will.

There would be others hidden somewhere on the property—the untouched virgins who were freshly captured, full of fight, and caged like livestock. They were the forbidden flesh. The highest price tags. The ones who would be sold and sent home with guests.

Despite Luke's filthy dark appetite for sex, he

only wished to free them. But that wasn't his purpose here.

His target was Vera.

Why would she want any part of this? Didn't she miss her sister? He knew her background, her education, her life story. She hadn't been raised in an abusive household or neglected by an unloving family. What was her motivation to be here? Money? Power? Or was she in trouble? Maybe she was being blackmailed, and her participation was all smoke and mirrors?

After surviving his own captivity and learning the tragic truth behind his captors, Van and Liv, he knew that not everything was as it seemed. The quickest way to the truth was to get close to this woman and coax her to talk.

She waited a few paces ahead, studying her fingernails as if the scene in the library had no effect on her. Maybe it didn't, but he needed to test her.

A pretty Latina emerged in the hallway, carrying a stack of towels. Eyes directed at the floor, she strode by without looking up.

He grabbed her arm, halting her. "How old are you?"

"Whatever age you want me to be." Her mousy voice matched the downward gaze.

"Show me."

She set the towels on a chair behind her and reached for the neckline of her simple maid frock. A zipper ran down the front, which she pulled to the hem, fully opening the dress and revealing nothing beneath. *Designed for easy access.*

Stepping into him, she set her feet shoulder-length apart and put her hairless cunt next to his hand at his side. He only needed to twitch his fingers to feel her heat, tease her open, and sink inside.

He should do it. Make it look like he was interested. It was exactly what was expected of him.

But her age was questionable, and that doubt dumped ice water in his veins, holding him immobile.

"If it pleases Mr. Smith," Vera said, nudging the girl back, "you'll be sent to his room later. Go on now. Finish your work."

The girl grabbed the towels and made a soundless, obedient exit. He kept his eyes on Vera, watching for something, anything, that might betray her thoughts.

She met his gaze with an unreadable expression. Impenetrable brown eyes. The stare-off stretched for a few seconds too long. Then her lips parted. A flush rose on her neck. Lashes fluttered, and her gaze pulled down and to the side.

Submissive. Aroused. Yeah, she definitely found him attractive. If he snapped his fingers, would she lower to her knees and service his cock?

"That girl wouldn't please me." He lifted her chin with a knuckle, guiding her eyes to his. "She's too young. Too…passive."

"Noted." She turned on her heels and exited the breezeway, stepping into the foyer of a connecting building.

He followed at a leisurely stroll, admiring the way her ass swayed. As Tomas trailed, Luke refrained from stealing another glance at his friend. Too many exchanged looks would invite suspicion from whomever monitored those cameras.

"Here we are." She stopped at the first door and inserted a key card.

The lock buzzed open.

Subtle hostility stiffened her movements. Was she jealous of his interaction with the girl? Annoyed? Tired of men hitting on her? No woman looked as good as she did without constant male attention. Especially not in this haven for perverts.

He played the part, leaning in and letting his breath brush her cheek. "What about you?"

"What about me?"

"You're neither too young nor too passive. It would please me to have you sent to my room later."

"Handsome *and* direct." She pushed through the doorway and into a large private sitting room. "Two bedrooms. Kitchenette. Only one bathroom, but its ample size should be sufficient to share with your assistant."

"Bodyguard."

"You don't need those services here."

Tomas ambled away to investigate the rooms. Standing in the entrance, Luke already spotted multiple cameras. Probably equipped with microphones. The guests had no privacy, and the cartel wasn't even trying to hide it.

She launched into a spiel about the amenities. Room service, personal butler, spa, unlimited alcohol, computer, cell phone, and Internet.

"Communication with outside parties is allowed on our devices." She led him into the enormous bathroom. "What do you do exactly? For work?"

"I'm a silent investor."

"And you invest in…?"

"Emphasis on *silent*."

"Very well. I advise using that same discretion if you conduct business here. Every message you send and receive, every call you make, will be monitored to ensure the safety of our guests and organization."

"In other words, you're recording everything I do, from the women I fuck to the transactions I make on-line. That's your insurance, yeah? If I piss you guys off, you'll use whatever dirt you have on me as blackmail."

"You're paying attention." She smiled.

"Do you give your little warning to all the guests?"

"Yes. It comes with the down payment."

The outrageous down payment bought him all the luxuries of an all-inclusive resort. Only here, the massages came with happy endings, and the whiskey was served with a side of cocaine. Pampering the guests was a small cost to the cartel, considering the amount of money they received at the end.

The going rate for a sex slave? Upper six digits.

Eight years ago, a buyer had paid close to a million dollars for Luke. When Liv had delivered him to the sadist, he'd stared straight into the man's gaze, knowing he was seconds from being handed off and forced to spend the rest of his life doing more than just sucking the fucker's cock. In that defining moment, shackled in the grip of those heartless eyes, he saw the place where the souls of evil were punished and tormented. He saw the face of hell and the terrifying power it held.

With a hard blink, he squared his shoulders and locked down the memory.

He needed a shower.

Prowling through the bathroom, he counted only one camera. Tomas would check every shadow, crack, and corner to verify that.

The wet room went on forever. At least three times the size of the bedroom he no longer had in Texas. The Freedom Fighters recently sold that house and moved to the Restrepo Cartel headquarters in Colombia. It was safer for them there, luxuriously furnished, and closer to the trafficking operations Camila was targeting.

But it wasn't home. He'd never really had a place to call home. Before Van, he'd never experienced the comfort of money. He had plenty of it now. Over six-hundred-thousand dollars. All Van's slaves had received a cut from his operation when he shut it down and grew a conscience.

Multiple floating vanities and countless jets and shower heads jutted from the bathroom walls. A modern, freestanding tub sat at the center, surrounded by a sleek use of white stone materials, giving the room a rich, clean look.

"Did you read the specifications I sent?" He began to undress, toeing off his shoes and draping his clothes neatly over a white settee.

"Yes." Her breathing quickened as she inched toward the door. "I'll just let you—"

"Turn around." Stripped down to his pants, he approached her on bare feet and angled her to face one of the full-length mirrors. "Tell me what I want."

"Early twenties, brown eyes, black hair, slender build…" Her mouth pinched into a line as she regarded her reflection, which embodied the specifications.

"I requested *you*."

"You requested a Latina. There are plenty here to choose from."

He wanted to say her sister's name and watch her reaction. But exposing his connection would be suicide.

Vera was one of them.

"How much for you?" He edged closer, his chest touching her back as he met her gaze in the mirror.

"I'm not for sale."

"Everything has a price. Who do I speak to about your ownership?"

Her nostrils widened with a sharp inhale. "No one owns me."

"Not yet." He unbuckled his belt and opened his zip, noting her flush at the sounds of him undressing. "When I want something, I take it. I'm very good at that—taking, consuming, *fucking*. You'll learn this soon enough, whether you're watching me with another or riding me yourself. Which will it be?"

"I've seen it all, handsome. Not interested."

"You're going to swallow those words, right along with the load I shoot down your pretty throat. *After* you beg for it."

She shivered, ruining her attempt at indifference.

With a smirk, he let his breath trickle against her neck. She made a small noise, and he stepped back, shedding the last of his clothes. Then he ambled to the far wall and turned on the shower heads.

"Dinner and entertainment begin at seven on the veranda." She spun away, heading for the exit.

"Vera."

She kept walking, face forward, and vanished around the corner.

He'd scared her. Shaken her. Sent her running right out the door.

Damn, that was easy.

Too easy.

THREE

Warm water blasted Luke's body, washing away the long day of traveling. Slowly, his muscles unclenched, releasing knots he hadn't realized were there.

To think, he'd only been at the compound for an hour. This job could last days. Weeks. He wasn't leaving until it was finished.

Amid the rising steam, Tomas entered the wet room, his gaze darting, sweeping for hidden technology. Luke left him to it, closing his eyes and running soap through his hair.

Until something screeched across the floor. A loud crash followed. What the—?

He turned as Tomas set down a heavy chair, which had apparently just been swung at the camera in the ceiling. Plastic pieces crunched beneath Tomas' boot. Pulverized. That must've been the only camera. Tomas wasn't looking anywhere but at his mechanical watch. Checking the time.

The cartel would come, and the speed of their arrival would indicate how closely they were monitoring them. With so many cameras on the property, there would be a security room with multiple eyes on dozens of screens. It would also have views of the surrounding landscape so they could see a threat approaching before it arrived.

Access to that room would reveal the location of the compound.

Tomas strode toward him, and he stepped out of the fall of water so his friend wouldn't get wet.

"Twelve cameras with microphones in the other rooms." Tomas gripped Luke's neck, pulling him close to speak at his ear. "They shouldn't hear us over the water."

"Any revelations so far?"

"She's nice to look at. Grade *A* tit-to-ass ratio. Don't deny it. You want to fuck her."

"Who wouldn't?"

"Rein that shit in. You can't trust her."

"Sex and trust. Two things I've always kept separate."

"So what's your plan?" Tomas leaned back just enough to lob a surly scowl. "Make her jealous? Then what?"

It was a gamble. Women were smart, resourceful, and underestimated only by fools. But they shared a common weakness. He'd seen it time and again, the way they rallied together in support of one another. Until they didn't.

Too often, they let men come between them. Especially the narcissistic assholes who slept around and committed to no one.

"Put a good-looking bachelor in a house full of women, and what happens?" Luke asked.

"Reality TV?" Tomas twitched his lips. "They

turn on one another, plotting and competing to be the one who ensnares him."

"Exactly."

He couldn't blame them. It was animal instinct. Find the mightiest male in the herd, mate with him, and breed the strongest offspring. Vera might not consider herself part of the female selection here, but her biology said otherwise.

Men were simpler, like trees in a field, with the urge to spread their seeds far and wide to ensure they take root in as many diverse and distant places as possible.

Survival, stripped down to its crudest, most basic denomination.

"Okay..." Tomas squinted, giving Luke's nude body a once-over before meeting his eyes. "From what I've seen of the guests, you're the only attractive dickhead here."

Not exactly true. Tomas turned heads without trying. Beauty had been the primary requirement in Van's selection process. Their entire vigilante team looked like they'd walked off the set of *Baywatch*.

But Tomas' sex appeal suffocated beneath the cloud of fuck-off vibes he wore like a pressed suit. Luke trusted his friend without hesitation, but there were moments when he detected something sinister—in Tomas' glare, in his voice—that sent a chill through the bones. For that reason, as well as Tomas' shadowed role as a bodyguard, it was unlikely that Vera would take an interest in him.

"You make her nervous." Tomas glanced at his watch. "She's clearly attracted to you. Maybe that scares her."

"Maybe."

But Luke meant what he'd told her. She wasn't meek. Once she saw him with another woman, her primal nature would claw to get out.

If she made the mistake of falling into his bed, it was game over. He was trained in the art of sexual pleasure. Add to that his insidious brand of dominance, and she was as good as his. Her heart. Her trust. Whatever he wanted.

In theory.

A knock sounded on the exterior door, and the hinges creaked, opening without waiting for an answer.

"Four-minute response time." Tomas raised his eyes from his watch and moved to the far wall.

Luke returned to the warm spray, giving his visitors a full-frontal view as they stormed in. Two armed guards led the intrusion, their eyes instantly locating and assessing the broken camera.

Vera swept in behind them and anchored her hands on her hips. "Damaging property is not—"

"My boss," Tomas said, crossing his arms, "doesn't need an audience while taking a shit."

"But you're welcome to stay while I finish my shower." He arched a brow. "Or join me."

Her gaze dropped to his half-hard cock and skittered away. "No, I..." She coughed. "I don't play with the guests."

He shouldn't derive this much pleasure from her discomfort. He wanted to like her. Pity her, even. She was Tula's half-sister, for fuck's sake. But beyond his appreciation of her physical attributes, he felt nothing for her. No chemistry. No interest in learning why she was a human trafficking bitch.

The sooner he rid the world of her and this operation, the better.

"Then stop wasting my time." He turned off the shower, giving her his back.

"If you break another camera—"

"My being here doesn't mean my business stops running out there. I require a secure space to discuss confidential details with my right-hand man." He nodded at Tomas. "This room will serve as my private meeting space. If I learn that your organization is eavesdropping on the business dealings of my organization while I'm in this room, I will take you down with every connection I have."

"La Rocha doesn't tolerate threats or damage to their property."

"Put it on my tab and go fuck yourself on the way out."

Her gasp filled him with sick satisfaction. As she vanished out the door, he squeezed his fist, imagining it crushing the bones in her neck. It wasn't rage that pumped through his veins. It was focus, clarity, all thoughts aligning on the path ahead.

He twisted to find the same determination in Tomas' hard eyes.

Martin and Ricky wouldn't have been able to finish this job. They loved Tula too much to hurt her sister. In fact, they might never forgive him for the things he was about to do.

"I'm gonna take a walk and do some reconnaissance." Tomas pushed off the wall. "Try not to get yourself killed while I'm gone."

FOUR

Dinner included lamb chops with balsamic reduction, crispy Hasselback potatoes, carrot soufflé, and superficial chitchat with five disgustingly wealthy slave buyers. Appetite long gone, Luke slid his fork away, fighting the impulse to repeatedly stab them with it.

"Best lamb I had in ages." Lester, with his snake-skinned boots and Texan drawl, leaned back from his empty plate and lit a cigar. "Wouldn't you agree, John?"

"No. My whore of a mother cooked better than this slop." Luke lied through smiling lips, prompting a ripple of laughter around the table.

He'd lied about his name, his mansion in Tahoe, his trophy wife, and his undefeated golf game at the country club. They all lied, and they all knew they were spouting canards to one another. It was the most pointless, fucked-up dinner conversation in history.

Maybe this was a game to them, to see who could spout the most bullshit without getting called out. After two hours of table talk, he still didn't know their real names, real occupations, or anything genuine or useful.

They were master manipulators. Whatever powerful positions they held—CEOs, politicians, investment moguls—they hadn't achieved their success honestly.

They were bad men, the sort who fraternized with a cartel and fucked underage girls. Someday their sins would catch up to them. If he moved quickly enough, he could be the one to deliver what they deserved.

Tomas ate alone on the other side of the veranda, ever the scowly, unapproachable bodyguard. He wasn't the only *plus one*. Most of the guests had brought along a male attendant. They probably couldn't function without their personal servants wiping their asses.

Without looking, Luke marked Vera's footsteps in and out of the dining area. She hadn't eaten with them, hadn't sat down long enough to join the conversation. If he didn't know better, he'd think she was avoiding him.

La Rocha guards loitered in the periphery. Cantina girls, dressed in corsets and garters, kept the food and drinks coming. Hector's sons had yet to make an appearance, and no one seemed to care.

Except Luke. He wanted to see the faces of his primary targets.

"Are you betting on the fight tonight?" Ted, a wrinkly old man with sharp eyes and a frail body, met his gaze across the table.

"Fight?" He took a swig of peated whiskey, swallowing the smoky burn with a trickle of dread.

"Oh, yeah." Ted gestured at the grassy area beyond the veranda's railing. "It'll start out there any minute. I have a hundred grand riding on it."

A hundred grand? On what? A cockfight? Dog fight? Knowing the cartel, it would be any manner of cruelty, and he wanted nothing to do with it.

Lester flicked the ash from his cigar. "Putting your money on the girl, old man?"

"Are you kidding?" Ted laughed. "I saw what she's up against. She won't last the first round."

"Human girl?" Luke yawned, pretending a blithe disregard. "Or something else?"

"They say she's human, but I hear she looks and fights like an animal."

"Well, hell." Twisting in the chair, Lester motioned at one of the half-dressed servants. "I'm in. Might even bet against you, Ted."

More laughter and Luke feigned a moderate chuckle. Maybe the girl was a trained fighter, someone they brought in and paid for a harmless night of entertainment.

But he knew better.

"Gentlemen." Vera approached the table, smothering his senses in a cloying fog of perfume. "If you're ready to move to the railing, the show will begin shortly."

The table emptied as everyone grabbed their drinks and ambled toward the long bar that overlooked the lawn. Everyone but Luke.

"I didn't get a chance to tell you about the fight." She stepped closer, her breasts rising over the low neckline of her dress. "It's not too late to place a bet."

"Who or what is the girl fighting?"

"I don't want to ruin the surprise."

"Will it be a fair fight?"

She shrugged.

He couldn't bet against a dead girl. "I'll sit this one out."

"Suit yourself." She scanned the room as if

looking for an excuse to move away from him. "Did you enjoy your dinner?"

"I prefer a private meal with a beautiful woman. Tell me something." He reclined, resting his fingers on the arms of the chair. "What do you get out of this?"

"This?"

"You deal in sex but blush when you're propositioned."

"No, I—"

"You keep dangerous company but run from the smallest confrontation."

Her face turned crimson. "I do not—"

"There's that blush. Listen, I'm sure La Rocha pays you well. And not just that. They give you security. Protection. You're loyal to them because they stand between you and whatever it is you fear."

"You don't know what you're talking about," she said, her accent thick beneath her breath as her gaze flicked through the room.

"I can give you everything they give you and more."

"This conversation is—"

"I'll buy your freedom. As far as they're concerned, I'll own you. But the moment we walk out of here, you're free. I'll pay you a salary and provide all the security money can buy."

"And what do you get out of it, handsome?" She cocked a hip and stared down at him.

"Your willing cunt."

"Willing?" Her gaze lingered on his before hardening and snapping away. "I've had enough—"

"Honey, one night with me is never enough."

She laughed, a strained cackle of disbelief.

Yeah, he was laying on the douchery nice and

thick. He didn't have a choice. There were cameras and ears everywhere. Decent men didn't come here. Not that he ever claimed decency.

"Do you leave this property? Are you allowed?" At her silence, he stroked a knuckle, light as a feather, along her exposed thigh beneath the hem. "Where are you from?"

"We're not doing this." She jerked her leg away from his touch.

"Oh, come on. I'm not the first man to make you an offer. But I'll pay a lot of money to be the last."

She blinked, and her eyebrows pulled in, knitting grooves across her forehead.

This could be so easy for her. She only needed to agree. He would buy her from the cartel. Fly her ass to Colombia. Put her in an interrogation room at the Restrepo compound and pry every answer he needed to finish the job. She would have Tula in her corner, so the torture would be minimal. Far less painful than the alternative.

Solar lights flickered like torches, illuminating the perimeter in a glow of amber against nightfall's backdrop. The guests gathered at the railing, their murmurs rising in volume as they watched whatever was unfolding on the well-lit lawn.

"No." She straightened. "While you're not accustomed to taking *no* for an answer, ignoring my objection will have severe consequences." Pivoting, she strolled toward the fight.

Well, he tried the easy way. Her funeral.

Drinks refilled. Voices rose, and excitement intensified among the guests. But he remained seated, reluctant to join them.

Until Tomas bent over his shoulder and growled

in his ear. "Your contempt is showing. Get over there and prove to the bloodthirsty pigs that you're one of them."

His friend paced to the far end of the railing, which provided views of the fight and the entire veranda.

Tomas was right, of course. Sitting here alone helped no one. But watching an innocent girl die while pretending to enjoy it? Luke had limits, and that one sat firmly at the top.

He listened for the sounds of a feral dog barking or the wild flap of fowl wings. When he heard neither, his nerves wrung tighter, his imagination making it worse. So he crossed the porch and found an empty spot at the railing away from the guests.

Just beyond the covered veranda, a grassy cockpit glowed in a ring of solar garden stakes. A woman stood at the edge, fisting her hands at her sides.

Greasy strings of hair hung in her face and twisted around gaunt shoulders. Not an ounce of fat on her sharp, protruding bones. But the little meat she did have looked hard. Honed from strife.

Long muscles wrapped her arms and legs. A tight t-shirt molded around the small curves of breasts. Frayed denim shorts clung to narrow hips and thighs. She was a tiny thing. Almost a foot shorter than his six-three height and at least a hundred pounds lighter.

Who was she? A trafficked girl? A cartel dissenter? The kidnapped daughter or wife of an enemy? One thing was certain, she didn't want to be here.

Angry red welts encircled her wrists and ankles. Layers of grime stained her torn clothing. Tangles of unwashed hair hid her face, but her eyes glowed through the knots. Dark eyes. Ferocious. Possessed with seething hatred.

She directed her fiery gaze across the ring, and from the shadows, a man stepped into the pit. If he could be called a man. The thug had barely grown into his baggy jeans, his swarthy face too young to take his thin goatee seriously.

Tattooed symbols scattered his bare chest and arms. The markings of a kid who was desperate to prove himself. He couldn't have been older than eighteen. Yet he had about forty pounds on the woman.

The woman he intended to fight.

Luke's stomach sank.

Another man sidled up against her back, gripping her shoulders and whispering in her ear. She stiffened, as if to reject the touch, but didn't pull away.

"I knew you wouldn't miss this." Vera leaned against the railing at his side, all glossy lips and shiny black hair.

Stunning woman.

Unfeeling eyes.

"It's a favorite attraction among the guests." A hint of annoyance clipped her tone.

"Who's the girl?"

"One of my brothers' whores."

"You mean Hector's sons? They're your brothers?"

"They're my family."

Not her biological family. Very few outside of the cartel knew Hector had a daughter, and that daughter was Tula Gomez, who was safe in Colombia with Martin and Ricky.

Tula and Vera shared the same mother. Different fathers. Vera couldn't have been related to Hector's sons. Unless she considered them stepbrothers? As far as he knew, they hadn't grown up together. Tula didn't even know she had brothers until a few months ago. He couldn't ask Vera about any of this because he wasn't supposed to know Tula existed.

"Omar!" Ted thrust out his glass, sloshing the contents over the railing. "Quit sweet-talking the bitch and throw her in there!"

Omar. Hector's second-oldest son.

"Fight to the death!" Omar snatched a fistful of her hair and shoved her toward her opponent.

To the death.

He'd expected as much, but as reality sank in, he couldn't calm his breathing. This girl was going to die, and there wasn't a damn thing he could do about it.

FIVE

Without preamble, the fighters crashed together in a burst of punches, missing and hitting with brute speed. Luke half-expected a knockout in the first minute, but the girl surprised him.

Blood spurted from a powerbomb that landed across her mouth. She dodged the next blow and caught the kid in the solar plexus with her knee. Once. Twice. He staggered backward, sneered, and attacked again.

Hit. Crunch. Smash. Grunt. The crescendo of brutality spiked Luke's pulse. The harder she fought, the more invested he became. Every strike she delivered confessed her will to live. Every ruthless shot she received hardened her jaw, promising retaliation.

Outmatched in strength and skill, she had zero chance of winning. But she didn't give up. Didn't show signs of slowing. As if she'd discovered a way to block out the pain, she limped, boxed, and snarled through bleeding injuries.

Her technique wasn't disciplined. Nothing about her performance indicated she'd been trained in combat sports. She fought with her heart. Like she had nothing to lose. *Like an animal.*

Even with the odds stacked against her, she possessed more bravery in one finger than the combined assembly of tycoons yelling from the veranda.

"Hit her good! Make it hurt!" Ted shouted and gulped back his drink.

"Stay on your feet!" Omar roared, shaking his fist from the sidelines. "If he gets you on your back, he'll fuck you in half. Is that what you want, cunt? You wanna bleed out on his dick?"

Gobsmacked, Luke couldn't look away. Couldn't move. Christ, he wanted to be in that pit, his instinct to defend her riding him hard. Every part of his being rooted for her, his muscles vehemently locked, his mind spinning, grasping for a way she could survive this.

Too late, he remembered himself and realized Vera had inched closer, studying his reactions.

"What are the rules?" Ordering his hands to unclench from the railing, he schooled his expression.

"No rules. It ends when she kills him, or he fucks her. If he manages to hold her down long enough to bury his prick, well…" She lifted a shoulder. "*Then* he can end her life."

Pressure built at the base of his skull, spreading and numbing until he couldn't feel his legs. "What if he kills her first?"

"He loses." She wrinkled her nose. "That's how they make it fair. He might be stronger, but he has to complete those two things in the right order. She only has to kill him to claim victory."

It wasn't what she said, but *how* she said it. No compassion. Not a trace of humanity. She didn't even flinch as the girl took a pounding of rapid-fire fists to the face.

The merciless beating sent her careening across the lawn, where she lay in a pile of twitching limbs.

Luke froze, breathless, seconds from leaping over the railing.

Get up. Come on, goddammit, get up!

Slowly, she climbed to her feet, staggering, swaying. With a wet growl, she spat a wad of blood on the ground and leaped back into the fight.

The guests exploded in cries of approval, voices growing hoarse in their fervor. Dressed in their expensive suits, smoking their fancy cigars, they laughed and applauded while a young girl fought for her life.

This wasn't any different than the Romans and their Colosseum. Crowded against the railing, they elbowed and shoved, trying to steal a better look and smell the blood.

"What's wrong?" Vera brushed her arm against his, drawing his gaze. "You don't approve?"

"Do you?"

"I asked first."

"All right." He finished off the whiskey, his eyes on the fight. "When a man has it all—money, women, power—he grows bored, appreciates nothing, and soon, the only thing that moves him is the pleasure in controlling and abusing others."

"Is that supposed to be a revelation?"

"Not at all. What strikes me is how we try to normalize the barbaric behavior." He gestured around them. "The formal clothing, fine dining, soft music, classy cocktails, and let's not forget this…" He tapped the black steel railing built to withstand a mob. "This keeps us safely on the side of superiority, separated from the subhumans fighting below. As long as we keep to this side and surround ourselves with expensive things, we can remain desensitized to what's actually happening."

He glanced at the throng of desensitized monsters who trafficked innocents, bet on blood sports, and grew hard at the prospect of rape and murder.

Returning to Vera, he waited for something to click in her eyes—a softening, a hint of agreement—but it didn't come. Maybe he'd said too much, given too much away, but he needed to know if there was anything worth salvaging in Tula's sister.

"If you have a point…" She crossed her arms. "Make it."

"You entertain powerful guests, but if any of them stepped into that pit, their money, influence, power—none of it would save them."

"Same could be said for you."

"Wrong, darling. I'd win."

"Really?" She sniffed, incredulous. "Because you keep yourself fit?"

"Sure."

It was more than that. He and his entire team underwent extensive training. They knew how to shoot, fight, and fuck, among other skills they practiced on an on-going basis. He wanted her to know he wasn't like her other guests, and not just because he had a pretty face. He needed her to walk away from this conversation thinking about everything he said until it consumed her.

Messing with her head was just another way to control her.

"Yet here you are," she said, "standing on the

safe side while casting hypocritical judgment on your peers."

"Hypocrisy is the least of my sins." He turned his attention back to the fight, his tone stoic and bored. "Put me in there. I'll prove it."

"It's not allowed."

Of course not. He would end the fight. The girl wouldn't die, and all bets would be off. Where was the fun in that?

"Who's the male opponent?" he asked.

"A new recruit."

His chest constricted.

New cartel members were required to do all sorts of horrific things as part of their initiation. He'd heard of capos forcing initiates to eat children's hearts to prove their loyalty. Talk about desensitizing a person.

If the kid lost this fight, he wouldn't just lose his chance at joining the cartel. He would be shot dead.

Good riddance. One less enemy to deal with.

But from the kid's perspective, the stakes were high. Too high to have any last-minute scruples about killing a girl.

Rivers of red dripped from her hair and face, staining her shirt. She managed to stay on her feet, but her balance was shit. Probably a concussion. She favored her left side, where she'd been hit in the ribs too many times.

The next strike sent her tumbling to the ground, and instead of regaining her stance, she rolled to her side and coughed a scarlet spray across the lawn.

Luke tensed, leaning over the railing as sweat gathered on his brow. She wasn't getting up.

Time moved in slow motion, and a hush fell over the spectators, producing ringing in his ears.

The kid climbed over her and tackled the fly on her shorts. She slapped at his hands and tried to squirm away, her movements clumsy. But not defeated. She was still fighting, her growls loud and short of breath.

He wrestled the denim down her thighs, and she twisted, crawling on her stomach along the perimeter of garden lights. Keeping his grip on her shorts, he yanked them off and went for her underwear.

It would only take seconds to rip that flimsy barrier out of the way. He wrestled with her flailing limbs, eyes wild and teeth bared before he flipped her face-up and wrenched open her legs.

Luke seethed but managed to keep his posture relaxed.

You're not here to help that girl.

Don't expose your cover.

You.

Cannot.

Help.

Her.

Vera said something, her voice snatched away by the pounding in his head. His fists balled to the point of pain, but he held himself still, battling raging impulses.

The girl's hand reached blindly for a solar light. Not the one closest to her. She stretched her fingers for the one above her head. What was she doing? They were staked in hard dirt and impossible to—

She pulled it out. As if seated in butter, the metal stake glided smoothly from the ground. He held his breath.

"Oh my God." Vera's hand came down on the railing next to his.

In a blink, the girl thrust the stake, impaling the sharp end through the kid's throat and out the back of his neck.

"Nooooo!" Ted yelled from the veranda.

Her opponent crumpled, the flow of blood too great. A gurgle sounded, a final gasp, and just like that, it was over.

Unfuckingbelivable. She did it. She fucking won.

Stunned silence strangled the guests, rendering them as motionless as Luke.

A snarl sounded beside him, and Vera stormed away. Fuck her. How she could've wished for a different outcome was beyond him. He couldn't remember the last time he felt this goddamn relieved.

As the guests lost interest and wandered back to the table, he remained at the railing, his gaze glued to the injured girl.

Omar tried to haul her up, but she wasn't coherent enough to stand. He yanked her harder, lugging her out of the ring.

Motherfucker. Luke maintained a neutral expression even as his blood boiled to dangerous levels. What were their plans for her? Would they kill her? Rape her? Make her fight another night?

He swiped a hand down his face. She wasn't his mission.

As Omar dragged her off the lawn and out of view, Luke kept his feet planted and cleared her from his mind.

"Gentlemen." Vera stood on the far side of the veranda, clinking a knife against a glass. "We've arrived at the part of the evening where you can bid on who you want to spend the next twenty-four hours with. As you can see, we have an irresistible selection tonight. Nothing but the best for our guests."

Her sugary sweet voice grated on his nerves as a

line of half-dressed girls paraded through the dining area. Some he recognized from his walk-through earlier, all of them young and beautiful. Beauty-queen faces. Flawless bodies. As if they'd been grown in a lab and plucked at perfect ripeness.

The ones who smiled made the attempt look wooden. Others didn't bother, their downward gazes failing to look shy. Timidness came from self-preservation and worry. These girls were long past that. The mind could only withstand so much suffering before it shut down.

The bartering began, and one by one, Vera auctioned off humans like property. He didn't move to join in, knowing his reluctance only delayed the inevitable.

Tomas watched him from across the veranda, his eyes hard with wordless commands. Annoyed, Luke gave him his back and studied the remaining girls.

It didn't matter who he selected. They were all submissive, emotionless, broken in… Broken in general. The redhead or the Latina or the black-skinned beauty over there… He could take any one of them to his room, and she wouldn't put up a fight.

That only made the task harder to stomach.

He didn't fuck gently. Didn't know how to be intimate without fire and passion. When he entered a woman, he did it with his entire body, every sinew, organ, and nerve ending engaged.

Sure, he could go through the motions. But could he make it look believable? Could he maintain an erection with someone who just lay there, eyes glazed over and mind shattered? Could he bring a damaged girl back from the dead?

He was good, but maybe not that good.

Where were the lively ones? The girls who would claw, bite, and scream with murderous passion? If he was going to do this, he needed someone who would hit him, try to reject him, and remind him that he was here for a job, not for his own depraved pleasure.

"Vera." He caught her gaze and crooked a finger.

She pulled herself into a taller stance, her nostrils flaring on a deep inhalation. Then she crossed the room, approaching him.

"Do you see something you like, handsome?" Her smile didn't reach her dark, narrowed eyes.

"Where are you hiding the quality selection? The freshly picked gems?"

"We like to give the guests some time to—"

"Be watched by your cameras? To make sure I'm not a narc? Don't waste my time, Vera. I came here to make a purchase. Show me what I'm buying."

She flinched. Cleared her throat. Looked around the room. As her gaze passed over a camera in the ceiling, she gave it an extra blink before skipping away.

"Fine." Straightening, she turned toward the exit. "Follow me."

SIX

As Luke followed Vera's swishing backside through the compound, he wracked his brain for a way to tie her up and sneak her out without getting shot. But every furtive glance she gave the passing cameras was a reminder he would never get her alone.

She tried in vain to maintain several paces ahead of his long-legged gait. He allowed it a few times, because hey, he was a guy, and the view of her ass didn't suck. But each time she lengthened her strides, deliberately shoving distance between them, he didn't know whether to be annoyed or pleased.

He affected her. Why? Was it fear? Unwanted attraction? Or something else?

"I make you nervous." He strolled along, hands folded at his back, listening to Tomas' footsteps behind him.

"I don't know why you would think that. Turn here."

He stepped into another breezeway. "Your body language writhes with discomfort."

"I do not *writhe*."

"Pity." He trailed her into a connecting building, separate from the main compound.

"Do you analyze everyone you meet?"

"Yes."

She paused in a large foyer with shiny tiles and no furniture. No windows. Just a bay of double metal doors and a key reader.

With a swipe of her card, the elevator opened. They took it down one floor—the only option—and stepped into a dimly lit underground corridor. It led back toward the estate, ending somewhere beneath the guest quarters.

He was instantly aware of how different the ambiance felt down here. The floors, walls, ceiling—everything was drab concrete. No paint. No decor or embellishments. It reeked of gloom and cold imprisonment.

Like a dungeon.

His palms slicked with sweat. Cameras hung from the corners, always watching, so he quelled the urge to look at Tomas.

Relaxing into his apathetic mask, he measured his breaths and followed Vera through the tunnel.

A steel door greeted them at the end. Another card reader. Only those with access could enter. *And exit.*

"Do you bring all your guests down here?" He leaned a shoulder against the wall.

"Yes." She glanced at him sidelong. "We prefer to do it on the day of their departure."

Like a souvenir shop at the end of a tourist attraction. After they admired the art and enjoyed the rides, they took a walk through the shop and purchased a parting keepsake. A memento in the form of a sex slave.

"You haven't tried very hard to spruce up this part of the attraction. That's intentional, isn't it? If a man can't handle a walk down a crude hallway, he won't be able to deal with what waits on the other side of that door."

"You seem to be coping just fine."

"I appreciate beauty in its rawest form. Unrefined. Wild. When you strip away the savagery of nature, polish it up, and make it behave, it loses its appeal."

"You say that while looking rather polished and well-behaved in your dapper suit."

"I assure you, Vera, I'm unapologetically primitive beneath the threads." He leaned in. "Open the door."

Her lips parted on a soft intake of air, her gaze fixed on his.

He'd give anything to know her thoughts, her secrets. Christ, if he just knew the coordinates of this rotten place, he would make an excuse to leave. They would blindfold him and transport him back to the hangar, where he could call in his team and tell them where to attack.

But if he had to guess, not even Vera knew how to find her way back to this corner of hell.

She opened the door.

The din of a television reached his ears, playing a commercial with a catchy jingle in Spanish. Otherwise, the room within lay quiet. The sort of eerie quiet that sent a chill along his scalp, at odds with that happy jingle.

He didn't want to enter, but he forced his feet

forward, grateful for Tomas at his back.

The space was vast and empty, except for an old couch in the corner and a hard-looking man perched upon it. A small flat-screen TV hung lopsided on the wall, holding the man's attention.

He didn't even spare a glance at Vera as she strode past and poked her head into a dark doorway.

"Marco?" She jumped back. "Oh! There you are."

A tall man emerged from the shadowed depths, his brown eyes instantly locking onto Luke.

Splatters of blood stained his collared shirt. That would've been disturbing on its own, yet everything about Hector's oldest son radiated violence, from his menacing stare and tense jaw to his hard-set shoulders and wordless greeting.

"This is John Smith and his assistant." Vera gave them a nod. "He's ready to make a purchase."

"Are you leaving tonight?" Marco spoke around the cigarette dangling from his lips, his accent straight out of Mexico.

"Just looking." Luke ambled forward, speaking confidently through the lie. "If you don't have what I want, then yes. I'm leaving tonight."

"You don't enjoy the accommodations? Not having a good time?"

Oh, how he wanted to voice exactly what he thought about the disgusting operation. With Hector dead, he stood toe to toe with the new capo of La Rocha, a man who wore his authority in the harsh lines of his face. This was an opportunity the cartel's enemies could only dream about.

But.

There was always a *but.*

Marco only needed to twitch a finger, and an

army of guards would pour into the room. Luke had no power here. His next breath depended on the whim of this heartless slave trader.

He would be lying if he said he wasn't on tenterhooks, waiting to be gunned down any moment. The tension strung so tightly in the air he didn't dare move.

Mexican cartels were a distrusting lot, as they should be. They had more adversaries than allies, and as a result, they treated everyone like a threat. Including their guests.

"I'm a busy man, Mr. La Rocha." Luke expelled a bored breath as if he weren't sweating from neck to balls. "If you have something more interesting to sell than the mannequins you're parading around up there, show me. Otherwise, I think we're finished here."

Marco choked on a sharp grunt of disbelief. His eyes flared, shooting his brows to his black hairline. He huffed again and looked around, maybe to see if anyone else shared his shock. But there was only Vera, and she gave no reaction.

"Mannequins?" Marco tugged at his rolled-up sleeves. "What does this mean?"

Whiskers darkened his jaw, making his forty-something face look harsher. His tailored black pants showed wet smudges. Probably blood. The stained shirt hung open at the collar, revealing tanned skin beneath. If he'd been wearing a jacket and tie, both were now gone. What remained of his attire had been loosened and adjusted to do whatever nefarious thing he'd been up to beyond that doorway.

"He wants a lively one." Vera looked anywhere but at Luke. "One he can break himself."

"Of course." No smile from Marco. Not a hint of

satisfaction or trust.

Not good.

"You want a struggle? A resistant *niñita*?" The capo stepped out of the doorway and motioned Luke through. "Have a look. Tell me which pussy you like, and we'll discuss a price. Or choose more than one. We'll work something out."

A hot ember sat in Luke's throat. He let it fester there. No swallowing. No twitchy movements. Expressionless, he strode past Marco and into the darkness.

The doorway led to a corridor that veered sharply around a corner. Another tunnel—this one lined with rooms. Eight chambers on each side. No doors or gates.

The overhead bulbs, spaced too far apart, provided little light. Some flickered erratically, sparking trepidation down his spine.

He knew what he would find in those rooms, and given the fresh blood on Marco's clothing, it wouldn't be easy. Even more difficult was the looming task of choosing a girl to purchase and rape.

Any compassion he would've felt was stifled. Fucking a girl was part of the plan, a necessary evil to maintain his cover. So he would pick a strong one, drag her upstairs—by a collar and leash if necessary—and use her to fuck with Vera.

Glancing over his shoulder, he expected to find his cartel escort. But only Tomas had followed him into the corridor. Didn't mean he could let his guard down. Cameras were everywhere.

No more delaying, he made his way to the first doorway.

Inside the cement cell, a dark-haired girl curled up on the grimy floor. She jumped at the sight of him, rattling the chains that connected to hooks in the wall.

"What do you want?" A sob erupted past her trembling lips. "Why am I here? I just want to go home. Please, take me back!"

"How old are you?"

"F-f-fourteen. Are you here to help me? Please!"

"Too young." He said it for the cameras and ordered his feet to move to the next doorway.

Same story. Same torment.

Room after room, girls cried in shackles, pleading, spitting, and demanding to be freed. Some answered his questions. Others angrily refused to acknowledge him. Many didn't speak English.

All of them wore street clothes—jeans, shorts, tattered dresses, whatever they'd had on when they'd been abducted. Ages ranging from thirteen to eighteen, they'd come from Mexico, South America, the United States, and several parts of Asia.

Sixteen girls in all.

None appeared to have life-threatening injuries. Bruises and cuts marred their skin from rough handling. But no visible blood.

He backed out of the last room and stood in the dim corridor, listening to their screams. His presence had stirred every chamber into a frenzy of keening sobs and gutting pleas.

His rage stretched on the brink of snapping, but he kept it bottled.

"Might I suggest the one in there?" Tomas pointed at the room two doors down. "She seems the best fit for you."

The pretty black American girl with blazing eyes and a fuming temper.

At eighteen, she was the oldest. She also

appeared to be the strongest, physically and mentally. Even now, her voice rang out above the rest.

"Motherfucker!" she shouted. "Bring your sorry ass back here and let me go! Swear to God, I will find you and cut you for chaining up girls!"

Yeah, she was the best choice. If she held onto that fire, she had the best chance of emotionally surviving what he would do to her.

At least, that had been his own experience. Van had broken his body, repeatedly violating him in ways he'd never imagined or wanted a man to touch him. But, week after week in that attic, he never stopped fighting. Never let his mind surrender or give up.

If he could survive Van Quiso, that girl could survive him.

"Yes, I agree she's…" He went still, certain he'd heard something in the distance. "Do you hear that?"

Tomas cocked his head, eyes narrowed at the unlit bend in the corridor, where they hadn't ventured. "Are there more rooms?"

There were no lights beyond where they stood. But there was definitely something…or *someone* down there.

"Help." The voice trickled into a weak moan, coming from nowhere and everywhere. "Help me."

Tomas straightened. "Another girl?"

Luke held up a finger as a frail cry whispered around them, so soft, so fucking strained with pain. His stomach hardened. His heart pounded, and every muscle turned to stone.

He followed the sound.

The whimpers rose in volume, growing closer as he reached the bend in the pitch black. Tomas touched his back, guiding, pushing him forward. With every step, his legs felt heavier, laden with dread.

As his vision adjusted to the absence of light, the stench of rot and fear invaded. The tunnel opened to a room, the shadows so dense he couldn't breathe.

His head filled with sounds of slapping flesh, his lips cracked and crusted with blood. He heard Van's voice. Demanding. Lustful. Chains clanked. A haunting nightmare.

An omen.

He saw it now. Watching as an outsider, he saw his silhouette hanging in a cage without sunlight. Except the dangling dark shape wasn't him. Not this time. It was something else. Someone was there, only a few feet away. It moved.

And cried.

"Please." The pale whisper dissolved into mewling murmurs too weak to vibrate vocal cords.

He blinked, the thud of his heart hot and viscid. Urgency moved him toward the wall, his fingers sliding over gritty concrete, searching. "Where's the fucking light?"

"Here." Tomas bumped his hand, locating a switch.

An overhead bulb buzzed to life, casting the room in filmy yellow. He squinted through the glow, and his eyes came into focus.

He stopped breathing.

A young blonde girl hung from the rafters by one leg.

By a fucking meat hook.

"Sweet mother of God," Tomas whispered behind him.

The S-shaped hook went through her thigh and suspended her several feet above the floor. Her other leg had been broken in multiple places, the skin flayed, exposing white splintered bones.

His fist flew to his mouth as he cataloged countless stab wounds, purple contusions, and missing appendages. Fucking Christ, this girl was missing fingers, parts of her ears, and a goddamn foot.

The leg impaled by the hook had been sawed off at the ankle. Not a clean amputation. No tourniquet. Nothing to slow the flow of blood except gravity.

"Please." Her mouth moved, coughing on a dry gasp. "Kill me."

No.

Fuck no.

He couldn't.

But he couldn't leave her like this, either. She wouldn't survive the wounds unless she saw the inside of an emergency room soon. That wouldn't happen. Not in the next few minutes. Not ever.

She didn't even try to move, her body too weak and wracked with pain. She could barely cry, and even then, it wasn't enough to produce tears.

"Sir." Tomas touched his elbow, guiding his attention to the wall where they entered.

Another girl.

She sat on the floor, legs stretched out before her. No crying from this one. No tears of anguish. But she wasn't without injuries.

Tangled black hair framed her bloodied, bruised face. More blood soaked her shirt and denim cutoffs.

Lifting her head, dark brown eyes collided with his.

Ferocious, familiar eyes.

The fighter.

SEVEN

"You." Luke opened his mouth to say more, but all that came out was a scathing exhale.

His first thought? *She did this.* The vicious scrapper tortured this young girl and hung her by a hook.

But no, that didn't make sense at all.

The blood on Marco's shirt, the shackles on the fighter's arms and legs, and the fact that she couldn't stand after the fight… She was as much a victim as the others. Perhaps more so. She'd been thrown into the dark with a dying girl, forced to listen to her shallow cries for help.

"End this." The blonde's fractured voice pulled him back. "Kill…me."

His blood shivered, and denial banged in his skull. Again, he took inventory of her injuries, searching for a sign of hope, anything that might save her.

Rust and dirt coated the hook through her leg. Infection would set in soon. The amount of blood on the floor beneath her was more than a human could lose.

She wouldn't survive this, and every minute she lived was a cruelty she didn't deserve.

"Why is she in here with you?" He glanced at the fighter.

She glared back, a hostile, rancorous glare that promised death to him and everyone if she broke free.

"What's your name?" he asked.

She slowly raised a hand, dragging the chain across her lap, and extended her middle finger.

The blonde moaned, choking out another plea for death. Her cries thickened with distress, producing a change in the fighter's expression.

For a fleeting moment, those savage eyes softened. Grief, compassion, whatever it was sank into the grooves of her battered, swollen face, blurring her gaze in a sheen of moisture.

Then she blinked, and the tenderness vanished, replaced with red-hot fury.

Do it. Her eyes demanded.

A camera hung in the doorway. Would they try to stop him? Shoot him for interfering?

Fuck it.

Fuck the cartel. Fuck his dead parents. Fuck Van Quiso. Fuck every injustice he'd ever gone up against. None of it owned him.

But this? This he couldn't walk away from.

As the blonde continued to cry, he blocked everything out—Tomas, the fighter, the mission. He put one foot before the other and did the only thing he could do.

He stood behind her inverted body, wrapped a large hand over her nose and mouth, and smothered her air.

She struggled, an involuntary reaction as her

mutilated body fought to breathe. His other hand held the crown of her head, his fingers hidden by her crusty hair, discreetly massaging, stroking her scalp. The only comfort he could offer.

As interminable seconds passed, he felt chunks of his soul rip away. He was breaking inside. Battling hardwired convictions. Roaring on his knees. Dying with this girl.

Dying.

Dying.

Make it end. God almighty, I can't do this.

But he did. He finished it, holding her against him as she fell limp.

Lifeless.

Gone.

Fucking God, help me. What have I done?

He'd killed men before. Vile men. But never with his bare hands. Never a woman.

Never an innocent.

His chest squeezed so tightly he thought his heart stopped working. But no, it was still beating, pulsing strenuously, yet… Altered. Twisted into something nastier. Stiffer. Thorny. No longer human.

Raising his head, his gaze caught on the fighter. She watched him, motionless, her expression iced over with suspicion and horror, but deeper, closer, he glimpsed gratitude.

He hadn't done it for her. He hadn't done it for himself, either, and he would live with the cold, stricken guilt for the rest of his life.

She and Tomas hadn't been the only witnesses to his heinous crime. Marco and Vera stood in the doorway, clotting the room with displeasure.

Pure scum of the earth. Neither of them deserved

to breathe, let alone stand there in a snit of condemnation. Marco had butchered a young girl, strung her up like slaughtered meat, and left her to die.

Luke's vision turned red. Adrenaline charged, and wrath fired on all cylinders.

Kill him.

Gut him.

Make him pay.

He would. Goddammit, he would exterminate all of them. But to do that, he had to become a man that no one fucked with.

Make them cower.

Earn their horror and respect.

Beat them at their own game.

With his hands still wrapped around the dead girl's head, he showed them a monster that all monsters feared.

"Look what you made me do." He hauled the corpse upward so that he could stare into the dead eyes. "Sniveling little cunt. We could've played so well together, but you just…wouldn't…shut up." He shook the body, punctuating every word before shoving it away. "What a waste."

His stomach cramped. Saliva gathered around his gums. He was going to puke.

"This is unexpected." Marco lumbered into the room, head tilted. "You killed her… Because she was crying? That will cost you—"

"She was half-dead." He wiped off his hands on a clean scrap of her shirt. "I'm not paying for broken goods. Besides, I know which one I want."

He prowled a circuit around Marco and paused before the fighter, staring down at her with a malicious smile.

Realization burst behind her eyes, and she went wild, spitting a string of Spanish and bucking in her restraints.

Across the room, Tomas shot him a look that said he didn't agree with the turn of events.

Too bad. Luke refused to leave the girl chained in the dark with a corpse.

"This one," he announced to the room.

"No." Marco folded his arms over his chest. "She belongs to me."

"And your brothers." Vera scowled.

"I see. And those hypercars out front?" Luke clasped his hands behind him, head down, with his back to Marco. "They belong to you, too?"

"Of course."

"Of course." He glanced over his shoulder. "When I arrived, Vera promised I could test drive one of your toys around the property."

Her eyes widened. "I didn't promise—"

"Shh." Marco's hand slashed through the air, and he held Luke's gaze, deadly captivated. "Is that right?"

"Yes. Perhaps you can appease me another way." Luke straightened his suit jacket and turned to face the capo. "Sell me the Pagani Huayra."

Marco laughed, a shocked sound, and sobered abruptly. "Not in a million lifetimes."

"What's her name?"

"The Huayra?"

"The whore." Luke met her livid stare.

"Who cares?" Marco grunted. "She's a whore."

"Which do you value more? The Huayra or the whore?"

"There are only a few hundred Huayras in existence."

"I'm aware. Yet I'm only asking to test drive a common whore."

"Ah." A humorless grin underscored Marco's wagging finger. "I see what you're doing." Then he went still, thoughtful. "Just a test drive?"

"Give me a week with her. I'll keep her in working, *fighting* condition. At the end of the week, if she still holds my attention, we'll discuss a more permanent arrangement. If not, I'll pay for the mileage I put on her and make another selection."

Marco's eyebrows pulled tight, his gaze narrowed on the thrashing fighter, considering her worth.

"Why *her?*" Vera fisted her hands, the snarl of her lips baring white teeth. "Omar will not allow—"

"Cállate!" Marco returned fire, spitting a mouthful of Spanish before thrusting a finger at the door. *"¡Vete!"*

With an enraged glower at Luke, Vera spun and stormed out of the room.

"I'll gladly test drive Ms. Gomez, instead." Luke ogled at her retreating backside, angling his neck and making a show of it.

She slammed to a stop, just long enough to shoot daggers over her shoulder before vanishing around the corner.

"No, no, no." Marco shook his head, chuckling. "I will not share that one."

"Because she's your sister?"

"Because she's *mine.*" With that unnerving announcement, the man removed a key from his pocket and held it up. "I give you a week with the whore. But I warn you. Watch the grill." He gestured at his mouth. "She bites."

"I look forward to it." He grabbed the key and squatted before the seething girl.

Woman.

Hard to be sure with her face banged up, but her eyes confessed her maturity. Mid-twenties? Possibly older. Jaded beyond her years.

She hadn't stopped kicking and bucking in the shackles, her anger so intense it foamed from her mouth. He couldn't fault her for the tantrum, but all that straining couldn't be good for a concussion.

Marco left without another word. Luke waited for the heavy thud of footsteps to fade in the distance. Then he addressed the woman now in his charge.

"You can fight me." He caught her swollen jaw in his hand and squeezed, making her eyes burn hotter. "Kick and scream and wear yourself out. It only makes me harder. *Hungrier.* But if you cause serious harm to my bodyguard or me, or if you run and make us chase you, I will find another girl and hurt her worse than this one." He tilted his head at the dangling corpse. "I'll make her beg for death, and there will be no mercy next time. No escape from the agony. And you'll watch every second of it, knowing you caused it. Nod your head if you understand."

Her eyes flashed, but her head didn't move.

The point was to scare her with threats instead of his fists. She didn't know he would never follow through. Only it wasn't working. He didn't detect a trace of fear in the air.

Maybe she didn't speak English?

No, there was too much comprehension in her expression. Too much stubbornness. She understood him perfectly.

He yanked her up by her long black hair, hauling

her body against his, and grazed his teeth across her swollen cheek, the corner of her mouth, and bit her ear. "Nod your goddamn head."

Her lashes fluttered against his face, and her breath came in rapid gusts. Then she nodded.

He unlocked her restraints.

When she didn't move to stand, he scooped her up and cradled her to his chest. She weighed nothing but felt as strong as hell. Compact muscle. Sturdy bones. It would require a lot of effort to really hurt her.

He hoped he was right about that, for both their sakes.

"Should I bring the shackles?" Tomas asked.

"No." His threat would suffice.

As he carried her out, the pull to look back at the dead girl slowed his steps. He wanted nothing more than to bow his head and give her a moment of respect. He needed to tell her he would never forget.

He'd stolen her life, and he didn't even know her name.

How would he ever redeem himself? Ever forgive himself for what he'd done? Or what he was about to do?

Pushing forward, he felt like he was wading through ice, every step a perilous obstacle, every breath a frigid stab in his chest.

Vera waited at the exit, holding the door open to the final tunnel. Marco had already left.

"I want a medical kit." He strode past her, tightening his grip on the injured woman. "Ice packs. Food. High-calorie, nutritional food. And a bottle of your best whiskey."

"Tequila." The fighter buried her nails into his nape, deliberately breaking skin.

"And tequila." His lips quirked. "Make sure it's in my room within the hour."

"I'm surprised." Vera hurried after him, eyes on her phone, presumably passing along his demands. "There are sixteen untouched girls back there, and you choose a whore who can't even walk. She's been thoroughly used up by all four of my brothers. This very moment, their come is leaking down her legs."

His jaw hardened, and he almost lost his footing. But the rage inside him didn't compare to that of the woman in his arms. She exploded in a fit of slashing claws, reaching toward Vera's face while shouting in Spanish.

He wrangled her back, using more strength than he wanted to restrain her against his chest. Then he threw a withering glare at Vera.

"Oh, you didn't know?" She swiped her key card and opened the elevator. "Marco and Omar tag teamed her after the fight."

Raped.

If he'd acted sooner and followed Omar down here, he could've prevented that.

"Why do you care?" He stepped onto the lift with Tomas at his heels.

"I just think… You can do better."

"Better, as in… You? Have you reconsidered my offer?"

Her gaze slid to the woman in his arms, and a malevolent drum of energy electrocuted the space between them. A hatred so rancid and sticky it raised the hairs on his arms.

"The two of you have a story." He looked from one to the other, back and forth, before pausing on the woman he held. "How long have you been here?"

"Too long," they snarled in chorus.

"Are you related?"

"God, no." Vera laughed.

Similar brown eyes, black hair, and tawny skin. Both had Mexican accents, like many of the girls here. But their likeness ended there. Where Vera held herself with sophistication and reserve, the fighter was feral and impulsive. Vera had grown up in a loving home, until her mother died of heart disease.

The common thread between them was Hector's sons. The brothers prized the woman in his arms, whether for sex or blood sports. But the nature of Vera's relationship with them wasn't clear.

Was she jealous of the fighter? Because Hector's sons showed interest in another woman? Or because Luke showed interest in her?

The elevator opened, and Vera sashayed away, leaving Luke standing there holding an unsolved puzzle.

She entered a breezeway in the opposite direction of his rooms and paused, glancing at him before scowling at the fighter. "Have fun with that."

"Have no doubt." He headed the other way, placing his full attention on the woman he was about to become intimately acquainted with. "Tell me your name."

Stubborn silence.

He growled, "This will go much easier if you give me that."

"Easier for you?" Her accent dripped with vitriol while somehow retaining a seductive quality that made his balls tighten. "I'm not giving you shit."

"We'll both have fake names then. I'm John, and you're Gina." At her thinned stare, he clarified. "Gina

Carano. The hottest female fighter of all time. At least, she was until I saw you defeat that kid tonight."

She clamped her busted lips into an angry slash and looked away.

Why had he said that? He was supposed to scare her, not charm his way into her panties.

Old habits.

"Tell me what happened in the basement with the girl."

"Go to hell." She shoved at his chest with a shocking force of strength. "Put me down."

He constricted his grip, which only spurred her to push harder. In the next breath, she went wild, flailing and cursing in Spanish.

After spending years with Camila, Matias, and Ricky, he understood common words. Mostly slang. Too little to hold a conversation.

Not that this woman was interested in talking.

She aimed her mouth toward his, her eyes promising teeth and blood. He dodged her, wrapped her up, and still, she kept fighting.

The little heathen needed boundaries, and now was as good a time as any to set them.

He opened his arms.

She dropped. Her legs buckled, and her rear hit the floor. The woman had been hit so many times in the head tonight she couldn't keep her eyes focused. She was in no state to stand, and they both knew it.

"Let's go." He took three steps toward the room and stopped with his back to her. "Start walking, Gina, or I will rip off your pants and blister your ass."

Tomas stood off to the side, his expression blank. No one moved.

He set a toe behind the opposite heel, pivoted,

and stalked toward her. With her legs sprawled and chest heaving, she thrust up her chin. It was all she could do before he was on her.

Flipping her to her stomach, he set a knee on her back and shoved a hand beneath her waistband.

A button flew. The zipper broke, and the thin cutoffs ripped like tissue paper. Her panties followed, and he tossed the shreds aside.

Nude from the waist down, she clenched a firm, round, tanned backside.

Lust hit his circulation like a crackle of fireworks, lighting him up from the inside out. But he couldn't enjoy this. He shouldn't.

That was the real bitch of it. He had to behave as if spanking and touching and fucking this woman was pure goddamn bliss without taking real pleasure in it. Without becoming the monster he pretended to be.

She'd been violated and abused in unspeakable ways. No matter what he did with her, *to her*, he couldn't forget that.

So as his hand came down on her ass, he made her feel it without feeling it himself. He wailed on her, avoiding her injuries smoothly enough that she didn't notice the mercy. He hit her just enough to make her fear him, and she took the punishment without making a sound.

When he was sure his point was made, he threw her over his shoulder and hauled her to his room.

She didn't cry or struggle, didn't try to hide her red backside from the men he passed. But she didn't just hang there, either. Her muscles contracted against him, bracing for war, biding time.

She was plotting a way out of this. If she wasn't, she fucking well should've been.

Tomas opened the door with his key reader, and Luke carried her directly to the bathroom.

Placing a chair beside the tub, he dropped her there and got in her face. "Don't move."

She gave him an unblinking stare, looking pissed and miserable beneath all those bruises.

He cranked the faucet for the bath, tested the water, and let it run. Then he strode behind her, out of her range of sight.

Tomas joined him at the vanity across the room, monitoring her as Luke doused cold water on his face. In the mirror, he watched her, too, stealing glimpses between splashes of water.

His hands were shaking.

Shoving them under the faucet, he tried to calm himself. Except he didn't feel nervous. No panic or dread. Could've been the lingering effects of adrenaline. But there was something else. He felt different. Dazed. Empty.

"I'm losing myself," he whispered.

I killed an innocent girl.

Tomas leaned in while keeping his golden eyes laser-focused on the woman's back.

She couldn't hear them, not over the water spraying from multiple faucets.

"You're still you." Tomas gripped the tie at Luke's throat, loosening and removing it.

"I feel numb. Cold. Really fucking cold."

"It's temporary. Embrace it for just a little longer." With steady hands, Tomas unbuttoned Luke's collar and spoke in his ear. "I know it doesn't feel right, but you're doing a good thing. Focus on the big picture, the end goal, and remember, I'm here. If you fall too deep, I'll pull you back."

Too late.

Luke shrugged out of his jacket and rolled up his sleeves, his movements wooden.

Tomas placed a supportive hand on his neck and gave him a look that had been forged in trauma, friendship, and solidarity.

"You're John Smith. A slave buyer." Tomas shored up his grip, squeezing painfully. "Act like it."

"Done." He knocked the hand away and shed the remains of Luke Sanch.

Then he turned toward his newly acquired slave.

EIGHT

Her lower half was naked, but she hadn't consciously registered that detail until his eyes latched onto her in the mirror. Green eyes, glowing like toxic fire as they licked across her battered body.

With her back to him, she didn't need to turn around. The full-length mirror near the door hung at a convenient angle, giving her a direct view of him with his bodyguard. And what a strange bromance they shared.

First off, why were they both so damn good-looking? That wasn't normal. Not in this cesspool of pervy sadists. In the years she'd been imprisoned here, she'd never seen an attractive guest.

It was surface-level bullshit anyway. Every man here was hideous at his core.

But what struck her was the way these two interacted. A moment ago, the golden-eyed bodyguard seemed to console his boss, whispering sternly while helping him undress.

The boss—a sickeningly gorgeous redhead who

called himself John – certainly didn't look like he needed comfort. Especially not now as he swung his searing gaze around the damage splotching her skin.

God, she hurt. Her head pounded, and her face felt like an overinflated basketball. Her mouth and cheeks throbbed, so hard and swollen she couldn't even scowl. Or cry.

The pain in her ribs indicated more bruising. Last year, they'd cracked during a fight and hadn't felt the same since. Then there were the degrading welts on her ass, which burned each time she shifted. He'd enjoyed that particular torment. No noticeable bulge in his pants, but his eyes had dilated the moment he'd hit her.

He didn't take those eyes off her now as he prowled closer, all hard angles and long, muscled legs, eating up the distance. He hadn't known she'd been watching him with his employee and didn't look happy about it. Whatever. It didn't change her outcome.

She knew why she was here and what he expected from her. If she fled, he would punish another girl. Even if she could physically run to the outside perimeter, Marco's men would capture her, drag her back to the basement, and torture another captive.

Like today.

That poor, innocent girl. Viciously butchered and killed. Because of her.

Every time she closed her eyes, she relived that horror. She still couldn't believe John had the balls to end the girl's life. Despite what he'd said, he hadn't done it out of cruel annoyance. Marco might've bought the act, but the conflict in John's eyes hadn't lied. He'd hated doing it and suffered for it.

Circling her chair, he stopped before her and laid his gaze boldly on hers. He didn't move, didn't blink, as if caught in a trance. Or maybe she was the one entranced. His stare wasn't a stare. It was a labyrinth. All high walls, dark corners, and confusing dead ends.

No way out.

She spent a week in the maze of his eyes. At least, that was how long it felt before he released her and shifted his attention to her lap.

He lingered on the shallow gashes, the dirt caking her knees and feet, and the patch of trim black hair between her legs. Despite the conversation in the elevator, he wouldn't find a drop of come on her body.

Marco and Omar usually fucked her after a fight. But tonight, they'd punished her in the worst way possible.

Her chest squeezed, and a thousand needles stabbed the backs of her eyes. She would mourn the nameless girl who'd bled for her. But not now, not here. She couldn't let the sorrow cripple her.

Anger was her only friend. "What are you looking at?"

"A repulsive mess. Grubby fingernails, filthy clothes, a fucked-up face…" His American accent penetrated her senses, cold and ravaging. He shut off the water. "I can't decide if you're hiding anything pretty beneath the bruises or something even more abhorrent."

She flinched and pulled in a slow breath to conceal it. They were just words. Harmless cruelty. She'd endured much, much worse.

"Remove your shirt." He stepped around her, casting a smothering shadow over her back.

The shirt was the only clothing she wore. Whether she liked it or not, it was coming off. But she wouldn't make it easy.

Crossing her arms, she trapped the bloodstained cotton against her chest.

He didn't say a word. Not a sound for the longest minute.

With a deep shaky breath, she twisted around and looked up into the greenest, wickedest, most terrifying pair of eyes she'd ever seen.

Oh, God. She turned back.

Would he strike her? Throw her across the room? Rip away the fabric?

He took his time wringing out her nerves, and when he finally moved, she didn't hear or see him. But she sensed him all around her. His body heat against her skin, his breath on her neck, and his chilling patience like a collar on her throat.

"Do you feel the walls pressing in around you? Restricting your movements? Strangling your air?" He brushed his nose against her ear. "That's me, Gina. The more you defy me, the closer and meaner I get."

"Don't call me that."

"Do you prefer whore? Slave?" He held her motionless without touching her. "How about cunt?"

A fist pounded on the door, prompting Golden Eyes to exit the bathroom. She welcomed the distraction, knowing food had arrived. When was the last time she'd had an actual meal?

Confusion edged in, fogging her vision. The thought of eating made her sick. She needed sleep. Just a few moments to close her heavy eyelids. But that was dangerous. And impossible.

The night had only just begun.

As voices drifted from the main room, he shoved a hand between her legs. It happened so fast she wasn't prepared. The iron bar of his arm caught her across the chest, pinning her to the chair. His other hand hooked around her waist, his fingers seeking and finding the hood of her clit.

Before she could blink, he had the bundle of nerves exposed and held captive between his finger and thumb. A sharp, ruthless tweak wrenched a shriek from her throat. He did it again, pinching and twisting with unholy pressure. The agony was more than she could bear.

"Stop!" She thrashed, screeching the chair on the tiles. "No! Please! No more, no more, oh, God. Please stop!"

He squeezed harder, yanking the raw bud so aggressively it felt as though he was ripping it from her body.

With him behind her, she couldn't land a punch or kick. Her fingernails proved useless against the steel cage of his arms, and her efforts quickly exhausted her.

Tears swarmed her eyes. Her throat swelled with wet cries. God help her, she couldn't stop screaming, which only made her face hurt that much more.

"Okay, okay, I'll do it!" She tried to tear her shirt from beneath his arm. "Let go, goddammit, and I'll do what you said!"

He freed her, and she doubled over, groaning in misery as blood rushed to her clit. Nausea raged, and the pain in her skull grew claws. She breathed through it, waiting for the rampage to subside. Then she clumsily pulled off the last of her clothes.

Golden Eyes entered, pushing a cart full of covered plates, liquor, and medical supplies and closed the door behind him. Before the scent of food reached her nose, John scooped her up and dumped her into the bathtub.

Warm water rose to her chin and stung her wounds, finding lacerations and open sores she didn't even know she had. But once the shock wore off, relief seeped into her bones. She lay her head back on the ledge and sighed.

"When was the last time you had a bath?" John dragged the chair closer and lowered into it.

When she didn't answer, he sank a hand in the water and grabbed her inner thigh. It was a promise, not a threat. He would hurt her again.

What was the point in remaining silent? She wouldn't win.

"A week, I think." She met his stony eyes. "There are no bathrooms in the basement."

"When do they let you out? When you fight?"

"When I behave. I have my own room away from the main house."

Not really. She slept in a garage filled with old cars and lawn equipment, but no one bothered her there. It was her solace in hell.

Golden Eyes carried over a container of soaps and stood off to the side.

"Tell me about the girl and the hook." John lathered up his hands and started cleaning her arms.

The foam turned pink as he scrubbed dried blood from her skin. She marveled at the gentleness of his fingers, so contradictory to the agony they'd inflicted just moments ago.

"I tried to escape last night." She let him lift her leg from the water, wincing at the movement.

"Relax." He held her weight, massaging soap around damaged muscles. "Was it your first attempt?"

"No. But when they caught me this time, they made sure I'd never try again."

"The girl." His hand paused on her calf, his gaze locked on hers. "They butchered her to teach you a lesson."

"Yeah. Lovely friends you have. I guess birds of a feather really do flock together."

He yanked hard on her foot and hauled her along the bottom of the tub. The sudden motion pulled her head beneath the water. Panic rose, and her legs cartwheeled as the memory of his hand over the blonde's mouth flooded her brain.

She flailed, shot up, and gulped for air. "Fuck you!"

"I'll be the one doing the fucking. Hold still." He resumed his lathering before she'd even caught her breath.

"I can wash myself."

"No. Explain your relationship with Vera Gomez."

Homicidal rage spiked through her, quivering her muscles. "We have no relationship."

"If your face wasn't broken, I'd see a vein bulging in your forehead just at the mention of her name."

There was so much she wanted to say, but she couldn't. If she thought today's punishment was unbearable, it was nothing compared to what they would do if she told her secrets.

But if she didn't give him something, he would just keep pushing. Keep hurting her.

"I've been here as long as that bitch." She tilted her head back to locate the cameras and found none. Then she spotted a hole in the ceiling. "What—?"

"I'm a very private man, and I don't appreciate *anyone* recording my personal activities."

So he tore out the only camera? What about the

other rooms? The cartel would never allow that.

He followed her gaze to the doorway and shook his head. "This is the only room that isn't monitored."

"They can't hear us in here?

"Only when you scream," Golden Eyes said without emotion.

"You and Vera came here…" John inched the chair toward her head and washed her hair. "When?"

"Nine-hundred and fifty-eight days ago."

Almost three years. It felt like three decades.

"You arrived together?" he asked.

How much could she tell him? Maybe the cartel wasn't listening right now, but could she really take that chance?

"Not together. The compound had just been built." She closed her eyes and wiped at the stream of bubbles running from his hands. "She hated me from the beginning."

"Why?"

So many reasons, and none that she could disclose. So she settled on another truth. "Why does La Rocha abduct, rape, and sell girls? They're evil. *She* is pure fucking evil."

He seemed so perplexed by this with his brows all knitted and his lips clamped together. Of course, he didn't get it. He associated with the Mexican cartel. Hell, he was a goddamn slave buyer.

Except… He didn't fit the mold. Not exactly. Something was weirdly off about him.

He finished shampooing and moved on to conditioner. "Was she ever a captive here?"

"Are you kidding? This place is her brainchild. Her pride and joy. She built it from the ground up." She squinted at him. "Why are you so interested in her?"

"She's fucking gorgeous." He licked the corner of his mouth and put his face in hers. "You're jealous."

Yeah, right. Beautiful women grew on trees around here, and she never wanted to be one of them. Which was why she welcomed every fight, hoping the beatings would make her less desirable.

He fell quiet as he rinsed her hair, seemingly lost in thought.

Then he finished the rest of her. Somehow, he managed the intimate task without making it sexual. His gaze touched her nudity without being creepy. His hands glided over her breasts and between her legs without trying to violate her.

He couldn't have made it more obvious that something strange was going on.

Maybe it was her appearance? She didn't need a mirror to imagine how grotesque she looked. *Good.* If a puffy face killed his boner, she might consider punching herself to maintain the swelling all week.

But if her looks turned him off, why had he chosen her?

"How many times have you been pimped out to the guests?" He pulled the drain and let the water out.

"You're the first."

He winged up an auburn eyebrow, an expression that made him look younger. Almost playful.

"You're not special." She slid her knees to her chest, shivering in the draining water. "If I hadn't won so many fights for the cartel, they would've killed me a long time ago. I'm a flight risk who's outlived her value, and you said you wouldn't pay for broken goods." She laughed hollowly. "You've been duped, Johnny Boy."

"You're not only wrong. You're scared." He bent in and wrapped a hand around her throat, holding her gaze. "Scared shitless, because you know that when your bruises fade, I'm going to like what I see. When I taste you, I'm going to savor that, too. What you may not know, but will soon discover, is that when I'm inside you, you'll come on such a violent tailspin of pleasure that my cock will be the only one that ever matters. Then, now, and forever."

"Hate to burst your bubble, but women don't get off when they're raped."

He grabbed a towel and lifted her from the tub, his voice the texture of velvet. "We'll see about that."

NINE

Her mysterious captor was right about one thing. She was scared. How could she not be? As traumatizing as it was to be fucked into the dirt by the four top dogs of La Rocha Cartel, sex with them was always predictable, routine, and over quickly.

This man promised none of that.

She lay on a settee in the wet room, swaddled in a towel, watching him and his bodyguard gather supplies. They worked effortlessly together, anticipating each other's movements, communicating without words. She was horrifyingly captivated.

How many times had they done this? How many women had they raped? Killed?

They didn't need to pay for sex. Not with those sculpted faces. But it wasn't uncommon for serial killers to charm women into their beds.

These guys had more than just charisma, with their powerfully honed physiques, the intelligence behind their eyes, determination in the set of their shoulders, and they smelled good. Sweet Jesus, the room reeked of clean, woodsy, virile masculinity.

Potent males.

Gorgeous.

They looked like fashion models, not corrupt businessmen. But to be invited here, John must be tremendously wealthy. Or in debt up to his pretty green eyeballs.

"During the fight tonight…" He perched on the settee beside her hip and loaded a toothbrush with paste. "You knew which solar light would pull free."

"It was a lucky guess." She reached for the toothbrush.

He drew it away. "Don't lie to me."

"Fine. Last time I walked through the yard, I dug up the stake and loosened the hole."

He took her hand and caressed his thumb across her palm. She shivered, waiting for him to do something mean. But he just kept the pad of that thumb moving in featherlight circles.

Tingles of sensation licked through her, unlike anything she'd ever felt. It made her uncomfortable. Nervous. She knew how to battle pain. But affection? Kindness? She liked it too much. More than liked it, and that put her at a disadvantage.

"Don't." She yanked her hand from his grip.

"You're not in a position to make objections."

"Oh, buddy, I can and *will* refuse you. Isn't that what you wanted? A whore who will kick and scream and wear herself out? It makes you hard and hung—"

He shoved the toothbrush in her mouth, and she choked on the glob of mint.

"Asshole." Her garbled, foamy insult lit up his eyes with a devilish gleam.

It was almost a smile. A beautiful one, unfortunately. He really was so nice to look at, with his red hair glinting like metallic copper in the overhead light. Though he kept it short, it curled at the ends, giving him a relaxed, tousled look.

Wide across the shoulders and narrow through the waist, he had the *V* thing that she'd only ever seen on porn sites. Like in the male on male videos, and the macho men with big cocks, oh, and the naked solo amateur guys, stroking themselves for the camera… God, she used to love watching those.

She used to love sex.

There had been a time when she loved having a boyfriend, too. A guy she could talk to and kiss whenever the impulse struck. She missed the comfort in connecting with another person, even when they turned mean and tried to smack her around.

Someday, if she escaped this place with her mind and body intact, she would find a decent partner, someone to love, and just maybe, she wouldn't feel so alone.

As she brushed her teeth and spat in a cup, John watched her as fixedly as a predator with eyes on his prey. A wolf in a suit. She could admire his impossible beauty and even hold a conversation with him, but it didn't change the fact that he was going to rape her. If not her, then someone else.

Golden Eyes crouched beside her head with a medical kit and reached for her face. She jerked away.

"Be still." John bent over her and fingered her wet hair. "He's going to treat your wounds while we talk."

"Why bother?"

"If you're as smart as I think you are, you'll figure it out."

The quiet man stared at John in a scolding way. Like they were… Equals? Friends? Family?

What were they hiding?

"Do you have a fake name, too?" she asked the bodyguard.

"Tomas."

"Rhymes with dumbass." John pitched a scowl at the man. Then he held up one of her spirally black locks, studying it. "This wasn't curly before."

"It wasn't clean before."

The girls in the main house straightened it the last time she washed it. Sometimes, she let them play dress-up with her, looking for any excuse to eavesdrop on their gossip.

Since they had more freedom to roam the property, they knew things she didn't, such as who was coming and going, which guards were on patrol, how many guests were in-house, and when the next shipment of girls would arrive.

His fingertips ran down her breastbone and loosened the knot on the towel. She dropped the toothbrush and stopped him from descending farther.

He smiled down at her. No humor. All heat.

"No." She wasn't ready. She would never be ready.

"Fight me." His voice slid over her with silken confidence. A voice that could carry brutal commands over the length of a dark, oppressive dungeon.

"Fuck you."

He ripped away the towel.

"No! Stop!" She shrieked, scrambling to pull it back.

But he'd already tossed it away, chuckling blackly. So she kneed him in the chin. Hard.

His head snapped back, and the crook of his mouth kicked up. Not a hint of surprise on his face.

He'd let her have that shot.

"That's the only one you get tonight." He captured her legs and pinned them down. "Your coordination is getting worse. Are you dizzy?"

"Eat a dick."

"You'll be doing exactly that if you don't answer the question."

"Yes, John, the room is spinning."

Nausea, headache, sleepiness, blurred vision, ringing in her ears… She had a concussion. But that wasn't the only reason she was pinned down. Every punch she'd thrown at him had been easily dodged and redirected. He knew how to neutralize an attacker.

"You've had training." She wrapped an arm over her bare chest and a hand between her legs, covering her nudity. "Combat sports."

"It's a hobby of mine, along with weights and cardio. You'll work out with me once you're fed and rested."

By *work out*, he didn't mean jogging.

He blatantly inspected her naked body while Tomas cleaned the cuts on her face.

Antibiotic ointment was applied. Her eyes were pried open and checked. Then her teeth, ears, and nose. That done, Tomas ran his hands over every inch of her scalp, searching for hidden wounds. The scrupulous efficiency in his work suggested he'd done this before.

"Are you a bodyguard or a doctor?" she asked him.

"I've treated a lot of wounds."

"Your boss must toss all his beaten slaves your way."

John splayed a large hand over her hipbone, his fingers stretching nearly around her waist. "Why are you so thin?"

"It's called intermittent fasting. If you want to shed extra pounds, you have to feel the pangs of hunger every day."

He narrowed his eyes, not buying a single word.

"They say fasting also helps you live longer." She shrugged.

"If you're concerned about longevity, you wouldn't be breaking through a wall patrolled by heavily armed guards. You're lucky they didn't shoot you."

"How did you know I breached the wall?"

"I didn't until you just told me."

Fuck, fuck, fuck. Her lungs emptied of air.

His eyes darkened, half-hooded by thick copper lashes that did nothing to conceal the intellect blazing there. "Tell me what you saw on the other side."

No way. That was *her* secret. She'd barely convinced Marco she hadn't seen anything. She sure as fuck couldn't trust this man. What would stop him from running straight to Marco and ratting her out?

"It was nighttime." She swallowed her rising panic. "I couldn't see my hands in front of my—"

"Shut up." He climbed over her and straddled her waist.

With his knees astride her hips, he held his weight off her while lowering his upper body, chest to chest, and arms bracketing her head. His mouth hovered so close she tasted his breath. Peated whiskey, hot and smoky, like the blood burning through her veins.

"I know you're lying." His lips grazed hers, shooting unwanted frissons across her skin. "If you tell me what you saw outside the perimeter, they'll kill you.

And me, as well." His gaze darted to the closed door. "We'll discuss it another time."

Like never.

There was only one reason he'd be interested in what lay beyond the wall. He wanted the location of the compound.

Some guests felt paranoid and isolated here and didn't like the cartel monitoring their external communications. They knew if something happened to them, no one would ever find them. Last year, a government agent had disguised himself as a buyer and infiltrated the estate. The cartel discovered his identity quickly, and the man was never seen again. His bones were undoubtedly buried somewhere on the property.

Whether John was a narc, military operative, or just another paranoid dipshit, she needed to stay clear of the crossfire.

"They're starving you." He swept his fingers over her ribs and raised his body to stare down the length of hers. "What's the purpose in that?"

"Have you ever seen a pit bull in a fighting ring? Or a greyhound on a racetrack? Those malnourished, neglected animals are worked to the bone and kept only to make their owners money. When they're no longer useful, they're put down." Her eyes closed without her permission. "I'm just a dog on death row."

He cleared a bit of hair off her cheek, prompting her to look up at him. "You're more than that to them. How many in the cartel have fucked you?"

"If you wanted a virgin—"

"I want information about the woman I'm paying for." His hand captured her nape, fingers closing around her hair, restraining her as he breathed his threatening words against her lips. "We can go round and round, but eventually, you'll tell me what I want to know."

"No one touched me tonight."

"But Vera—"

"Is a goddamn liar. They raped the girl on the hook instead."

An anguished look stole across his handsome face. Didn't he know that any show of emotion would get him killed?

He didn't belong here. Which begged the question… Who the hell was he?

"How many times have they forced you to fight?" His hands held her so firmly against him her neck smarted.

"I don't know. Maybe a dozen."

"You've never lost."

"You know the rules. If I lose, I'm dead."

"How do you rig every fight?"

"Shoestring and fishing line in my pocket make good garrotes. Same with a belt. Then there's the stolen switchblade I buried in the dirt. A hidden nail file works well in the eye socket. Sometimes, I'm just lucky."

Damn lucky she was still alive.

He released her and shifted down her body. "I want the names of every man who raped you."

For what reason? To avenge her?

Just like that, she was a wishful, simple-minded teenager again. *Oh, that pathetic girl.*

The cynical, realistic woman knew better. He simply wanted to know the state of her used-up pussy before he shoved his dick in it.

"Their names," he said.

"Marco, Omar, Miguel, and Alejandro." She

turned her head, refusing to look at him.

The cartel brothers had been passing her between them for almost three years. They never fucked her at the same time, but they shared her, nonetheless.

John was so quiet she thought he would push her away with disgust. She waited, hoping he would. Concussion or not, she just wanted to sleep.

When she finally dared a sideways glance, he was ready with one of those ice-cold expressions.

"Hector's sons kept you to themselves?"

"Until tonight."

Maybe they were finally done with her. Maybe John was, too.

"Are you going to send me back to them?" she asked.

"Should I?"

"Don't care."

His jaw turned rigid. "You watched them butcher a girl."

"Still don't care." She knew what she was getting with the cartel.

This guy had a mouth on him. Full, pillowed lips that would wrench ungodly screams until he wore her out. Screams of pain were one thing. They fueled her hatred and kept her focused. But she feared they would be screams of pleasure. Then she would only hate *herself.*

"Roll over." He shifted lower, straddling her knees.

So we're doing this.

Go directly to anal. Do not pass go.

Her stomach hardened. "I want tequila first."

"No." He smacked her thigh so hard it sent shock waves down her leg.

Was this a battle worth fighting? Unfortunately, no. Sex from behind was impersonal and would be a thousand times easier than looking this man in the eyes.

She flipped over gingerly and tried to relax her sphincter. There were worse things than being plowed in the ass.

Like watching a girl get her foot sawed off.

Tomas passed a tube of ointment to John, and she focused on her breathing. In. Out. In—

A lubed finger pressed against her rectum. "They fuck you here?"

"Every time." She clenched, unbidden. "Use a condom."

"I'm clean."

"They're not. Use a fucking condom."

She didn't have an STD, but she couldn't trust John's claim about himself. Not that he'd listen to her demand.

He adjusted his weight on the backs of her legs. A wet squirt belched from the tube, and she held her breath.

Make it hurt.

Make me want to gut you.

His hands came down on her buttocks, soft and sticky and warm. *Oh, God.* She tensed. Not from pain. No, his touch was pure heaven.

The sensual slide of palms, the hypnotic rhythm of his caress, and the sinful friction of skin on skin made her pulse sing and belly quiver.

Talented fingers kneaded her flesh, working antibiotic ointment—not lube—into her welts. Trickles of bliss crept up from her toes, melting her joints and turning her bones to sludge.

She'd never had a massage but imagined this one

exceeded every touch ever set upon the human body. She felt heavy, hot, and under attack. He lay siege to her senses, wrecking her ability to think as his hands parted ways, dividing and conquering the length of her.

His touch was everywhere, gliding over curves and wrapping around achy muscles. Each caress imparted authority, ordering her flesh to heat, commanding her nerve endings to dance, and teaching her body to crave.

He knew where to stroke her, how much pressure to use, and precisely which spots would make her sigh. And sigh she did, open-mouthed and collecting drool. Never had she felt this relaxed.

Until he lowered his head and curled his tongue along her spine.

TEN

"What are you doing?" Her blood spun hot at the shocking, wet caress along her back.

The sensation couldn't have been produced by his mouth. She twisted her neck to see behind her, and *holy fuck.* His firm lips were right there, his kiss gliding up her backbone.

From the moment he'd flipped her to her stomach, she hadn't anticipated anything remotely pleasurable nor half as sensual as the swirling possession of his hands and tongue.

Fear was always a glaring partner when she was alone with the brothers. But never arousal. Never *this.*

This destructively alluring man made her want more than a *hurry-up-and-finish* encounter. She wanted hours of him doing this. Touching, kissing, hungering… She didn't want him to stop.

What the hell was wrong with her? She couldn't accept this. Not from a slave-buying rapist.

"Stop that." She tried to jerk free. "Don't touch me."

His teeth clamped down, holding her in place as effectively as his intimidating gaze.

With her chin to her shoulder, she stared back, scrambling to find footing in the stellar depths of his eyes. "Quit toying with me, and just do what you're going to do."

He licked her bitten skin defiantly. "I'm responsible for the care and feeding of my woman."

"I'm not your woman, and unless I'm mistaken, you're feeding yourself."

"You're mine for a week, and tonight, I eat first."

He trailed his lips toward the curves of her ass, just as seductively as before, staring down at her nudity with those long thick lashes fanning over his cheeks. Then he glanced up, delivered another diabolical sweep of his tongue, and looked pointedly at Tomas.

His bodyguard nodded and paced off toward the door. When he opened it, he didn't leave and instead took up a watchful position on the threshold.

What was happening?

John returned to his torture, sucking, tonguing, and nipping her backside. The delicious incursion pulled her insides this way and that. She thrashed beneath his greedy mouth, gasping at the overload of stimulation.

No one had ever taken time to warm up her body. It had been so long since she'd experienced anything akin to foreplay she'd forgotten it was even a thing people did.

The worst part? She was enjoying it. Allowing it to happen. Imagining other parts of her that would tingle and heat beneath his lips. Would he find her as hot and wet, as lush and needy as his wicked mouth?

Not possible. She didn't get wet. Not anymore.

His affection was so fucking wrong it was cruel.

With renewed clarity, she met his gaze. He rolled his tongue, and her stomach seized up.

"Enough!" She exploded out of her skin.

Twisting to her back, she let her fist fly. Missed his face by an inch. Swung a left hook. Missed that one, too. Fuck!

"You're off-balance, Gina." He wrapped a hand around her neck and easily immobilized her.

"Release me!" She writhed on her back, kicking uselessly as he settled between her legs.

The pressure on her throat tightened. Dots blurred her vision, and she clawed frantically at his arms, his hands.

"You're only hurting yourself." He loosened his grip just enough to allow breath. "Surrender."

"Never!" She coughed, gulping for air.

"Easy. I promise you'll enjoy this. You might even thank me."

"I'll blow the devil in hell before I thank you for anything!"

"I *am* the devil, and while your offer is tempting, I don't want your mouth." He released her throat. "Unless, of course, you use it to scream."

"I hate you."

The look he gave her was arched and dismissing. His attention lowered to his shirt, his fingers opening the buttons. Then it was off, and her heart stuck somewhere between one breath and the next.

He bent over her, his torso as arresting as his face, strong and powerful, enough to cause serious ruination to her mental health.

Every nerve in her body thrummed as he lowered his mouth to her breast, the harsh lines of his face unsoftened by the tenderness in his kiss.

She tried to push herself upright only to be shoved down by his forearm, the flex of muscle bulging against her throat. He radiated such an intense fusion of beauty and menace it sucked her breath. But that didn't stop her from sinking beneath the tangled warmth that spiraled from the tongue against her nipple.

His lips moved from one breast to the other, kissing and suckling until she burned beneath the quickening rush of his exhales. Hot mouth. Expert tongue. He licked her in a way she'd never dreamed.

From neck to hips, he dealt relentless strokes, slowly, steadily, inch after inch down her body. Her fingers caught his hair, pushing, pulling, knuckled against his scalp.

When had she started trembling? Jesus, she'd lost count of how many times she'd gulped down a moan.

"It's too much." Another gulp lodged in the back of her throat. "Stop!"

Kneeling between her legs, he straightened and stared down at her, eyes glinting with cold sparks of lightning. Then he lifted her knees and forced them to her shoulders, spreading her wide for his gaze.

And his mouth.

"No." She shook her head frantically, fighting the steely grip of his hands on her thighs.

"Tell me. Are you not the least bit passive in bed?" he asked. "Truthfully."

"When it's consensual, you mean? Like with a man I *want* to be with?"

"Yes."

She contemplated her answer as his mouth took a meandering stroll along her ankle.

"I don't remember." She tried to kick his face and

hit air. "Are you?"

"No." He moved on to her foot, warming the arch with an open-mouthed kiss. "You don't want a passive man."

"I don't want a man. Period." She thrashed and swung her arms, going nowhere. "Let me go!"

"Your body betrays you." His gaze dipped, bringing attention to the moisture chilling in the air against her folds.

No. How could that be? She didn't want this. "Don't—"

He buried his mouth between her thighs.

She bowed off the cushion and tried to roll away, but he stopped her. With his hands on her thighs, he ravished her pussy, plundering, conquering, until she was hoarse from screaming and dizzy with fatigue.

They'd been dueling in this position long enough for both of them to be covered in a sheen of sweat. She didn't want to straddle his shoulders anymore. Didn't want his tongue buried inside her. But there was no evading him. No interrupting that merciless mouth. No part of her left unexplored, unlicked.

Faster and hungrier, he ate, groaning against her, building the rhythm, and dragging her with him on a spiraling, breathless descent south of heaven.

Death would be waiting. At the bottom of the fall. At the end of his tongue. If she orgasmed, it would break her.

Every skilled touch felt like a sledgehammer crashing into her carefully erected shields. She wouldn't be able to stop the flood of pleasure much longer.

If she harmed him, he'd said he would hurt another girl. But would he, really? After the mercy he'd shown the blonde in the basement and the peculiar adoration he was giving her body now, his threat didn't hold true.

She decided to take a chance. A last-ditch effort of strength.

Balling a fist at her side, she swung and connected with the side of his head. *Yes!*

He grunted, reared back, and swiped at the moisture on his lips.

Oh, God. If looks could kill… There was no mistaking the haughty brows, tense mouth, and hawkish glare. He struck an impressive figure when he was calm. But when he was pissed, he was terrifying.

She couldn't pull air into her lungs.

"Tomas." He inclined his head, motioning his bodyguard forward. When his order was obeyed, he said in a wintry tone, "Pull out your cock."

"What?" Her breath released in short, hard pants. "No!"

John clapped a hand over her mouth as Tomas unzipped. It took a moment for the man's full length to spring free. Then it was there, semi-hard, growing harder, really goddamn hard to miss.

She choked at the sight of him, abandoning her fight to utter horrified shock. John removed his hand from her face, but she still couldn't breathe. She'd never seen a man hung like that. Maybe in porn, but sweet Jesus, never in person. It couldn't be real.

The girth, the length, the sheer fucking size… And it was still lengthening, thickening substantially in the fist of his slow, lazy strokes.

"I don't need to hurt another girl when I have a solution right here." John slid a finger between her legs and pressed farther back, testing the give of her tightest hole. "You can struggle and scream, but I promise, little fighter, if you strike my face again, Tomas will impale that monster in your ass, and you'll feel all ten of those inches."

Fully erect, Tomas stared down at her with absolute intent in his eyes. John wore the same expression. No lust. No smiles. Just single, unified purpose.

They weren't fucking around.

The bitter taste of defeat filled her mouth. She swallowed, turned her head away, and ordered her body to relax.

"Hold down my arms." She didn't trust her impulses.

Tomas zipped up his fly and stood somewhere above her with his hands shackling her wrists. Then John pressed his mouth to the inside of her thigh. She shuddered.

He took his time edging his way back to her center. She whimpered as he explored, gasped as he bit, and sighed as he grazed on her flesh.

By the time he reached her pussy, she was strung out and panting. His finger was the first to sink inside, and her body jolted. He pumped that thick digit in and out, surging a torrent of honeyed lava through her system, sizzling, consuming, and rocking her through the invasion.

Her voice produced sounds she'd never heard, sobs of forced pleasure as he strained forward, thrust harder, and joined his tongue with his fingers.

"You taste like sin." His hands trembled against her, his breathing erratic. "Fucking addictive."

She liquefied, bones dissolving, and tears swarming her eyes. Raw, sexual heat flamed her skin. He probed deeper, licked her faster, and her whole body caught fire. She gripped Tomas' wrists, digging fingernails into muscle and shaking from head to toe.

"You look like a warrior goddess." John made a toe-curling lap around her clit. "Mottled with battle wounds and writhing on my tongue. So damn hot."

If anything, she felt remarkably weak and pathetic. But the urgent demand of his mouth couldn't be denied. He raided her senses and kept taking and taking until every muscle and bone in her body was spent.

Sliding a hand between his lips and her drenched flesh, he assaulted her anew. Hard to tell what he was doing, but the intersecting stimulation of his tongue gliding around and through his caressing fingers made everything slip together wetly, erotically. It was beyond arousing, turning her into a quivering, moaning puddle, and soon, she was screaming.

His lips drove savagely against her clit, his tongue a hot weapon of destruction, burrowing deep as if seeking the limits of her resistance. Swirling, tasting, owning, he built her release, climbed higher, faster, and carried her to the peak.

A starlit bomb detonated in her core, exploded outward, and crackled across her skin. Euphoria spasmed through her, arching her back, skyrocketing her voice, and flashing vivid color behind her eyelids.

"There she is." With a vibrating groan, he made a final, wet revolution with his tongue, teasing out the remnants of sensation.

"Stop." She panted breathlessly, twitching with lingering convulsions. "Please, stop."

His auburn head rose, and his body shifted up, up, up until he hovered above her face, gazing thoughtfully down at her. The lushness of his mouth glistened with her come. Then he licked it clean.

Ashamed to the pit of her stomach, she turned away.

He caught her nape, careful to avoid the bruises on her jaw, and hauled her close, his lips feathering against hers, touching… Or not touching? She wasn't sure. The heat of his mouth was so close her breath stuttered. Her nostrils flared. He smelled too good and felt too hard, his chest a pressing wall of burning muscle against her.

Why was he in her face, his parted mouth on hers, but not? He was just breathing against her lips, aggressively so, as if holding himself back from kissing her.

Please, don't kiss me.

"I've never witnessed anything more beautiful, and I haven't even seen your face yet." His words fell like a kiss over her gaping mouth. "Thank you for giving me your submission."

Her head reeled, and her heart stumbled into a strange, fitful rhythm. "I didn't—"

He pressed lips lightly against hers. "Don't ruin it."

Self-preservation was the first law of nature. In the presence of this man, she felt that law in the marrow of her bones.

"Tomas." Pushing to his feet, he opened his pants. "Move the food to my room."

She closed her legs and curled up on her side, knowing full well he wasn't finished with her.

"Hold these on your face." Tomas pressed two ice packs into her hands. Then he pushed the cart out of the bathroom.

John stripped off his pants and briefs and faced

her with his fists on his hips. He just stood there, head cocked, as if he didn't have a huge, raging erection jutting between them.

"Get those on your face." He nodded at the ice packs numbing her fingers.

She blinked, thunderstruck, and slowly raised the cloth-wrapped pads to her cheeks. Before she could form a question, he strode to the wall of shower heads and yanked on the faucet.

With his back to her, she found her gaze drawn to the perfect form of his body. The strong column of his neck, slope of broad shoulders, chiseled torso, well-muscled legs… She swallowed, drinking in his dangerous masculinity.

He leaned toward the wall, head down, bracing himself on strong, corded arms. She shouldn't be staring at his ass, but God help her, it was tight, firm, chiseled to perfection, with two little divots denting either side of his tail bone.

Why was he built so beautifully? Not only that, how did he know how to touch a woman with such flawless mastery? His skill was so over-the-top he could coax multiples from a quadriplegic and use that American twang to charm the panties off a deaf woman.

It didn't make sense. None of it added up.

He bought trafficked humans, for Christ's sake. Was that how he'd learned the art of seduction? He must've heard the pained, helpless cries of dozens of slaves.

Abruptly, he shut off the water and prowled toward her. He'd showered without bothering with soap? Even more curious, his dick was now flaccid.

He wasn't as endowed as Tomas—no one was—but his size was impressive, nonetheless. Thick and veiny with a plump head, his manhood hung against heavy balls, the root surrounded by a sparse nest of copper hair.

She didn't want any of that anywhere near her.

When he reached her, she flinched and blamed her jumpiness on her pounding headache and blinding exhaustion.

He collected the ice packs and lifted her from the settee. Goosebumps prickled his flesh, and cold water dripped from his body to hers. *Ice* water.

"You took a cold shower?" She hugged her chest, an awkward position in the cradle of his arms.

"Remember…" He turned toward the door, his voice low at her ear. "Outside this room, they're watching and listening."

Her brows pulled together as he carried her out of the bathroom.

Everything he'd just done to her had been in private. Had that been deliberate? Except… Wait. The door stood open. It had been closed until he'd nodded at Tomas to open it. Right before he'd forced her to orgasm.

They can't hear us in here?

Only when you scream.

Boy, had she screamed. She must've sounded as if John were beating her, and he'd encouraged the noise. Almost as if he'd orchestrated it. But for what purpose?

He carried her into the bedroom, both of them nude. Whoever monitored the cameras would've heard her shrieks and assumed he fucked her in the bathroom. Hell, he'd even taken care of his erection.

But why go through all the trouble when he could've just raped her?

Something was rotten in the state of Denmark.

What, exactly, she didn't know, but this man wasn't who he claimed to be.

If he thought he had her fooled, he was an idiot.

ELEVEN

"There's another steak." Luke set aside her finished plate, bone-tired yet too wired to close his eyes. "You need the calories."

"I can't eat another bite." She slumped against the pillows on his bed, her lashes fluttering closed. "Hand me the tequila."

"You've had enough." He'd allowed her a few sips to take the edge off the pain. "You need water."

"Shut up and let me sleep."

Amusement tugged at his lips. She'd been awake and holding a conversation for hours with that concussion. It was probably safe for her to rest. She needed it.

In the next day or so, her face would be black and blue. For now, the ice had reduced the swelling enough that he could almost make out her features.

Christ, she was magnificent. Rough-hewn but at the same time delicately formed. With shimmering raven hair and flashing brown eyes, she was captivating beyond what he'd imagined a cartel slave could be. Or any woman, for that matter.

No wonder Hector's sons were so possessive of her. *Were.* Not any longer. She belonged to him this week, and during that time, no one would fucking touch her.

Sitting beside her hip, he adjusted the sheet over his nude lower half. Without a doubt, Vera had tuned in from the monitoring room, listening to the screams from his bathroom. She'd shown too much animosity toward this girl to not be glued to the cameras.

If his efforts to make Vera jealous and cozy up against him didn't pan out, he had a backup plan with the little fighter. Being imprisoned here for almost three years, Gina knew things about the compound. Hell, she'd seen what lay outside the wall.

She cracked open an eye, then the other, giving him a full-blown glare, frosty and vibrant with malice. "Who are you?"

"A man who doesn't deserve that look."

The evening could've gone much worse for her, and she knew it.

Delaying the need to cause her more pain was the best he could do tonight. Tomorrow would be a different story.

Tomorrow, he would learn everything she knew, even if he had to fuck it out of her.

What made that more depraved was that he looked forward to it. To capture her tiny waist in the grip of his hands and impale her on his cock… He couldn't wait. Heat snaked through his groin at the thought of claiming her.

He wanted to do it *now.*

With her long black curls spread out over the pillow, she conjured images of a dark angel. The bedsheets tangled around sleek, enchanting hips, leaving the rest of her bare like a sacrificial offering for his gaze. Small firm breasts, flat belly, bronze legs, so smooth and enticing… She had a body that wouldn't quit. Strong, divine, untamed beauty.

The urge to slide his fingers up and caress the reddened skin around her eyes and cheekbones was hard to resist. But she would fight the affection. With the cameras in full view, he didn't want to have to discipline her, which he would do to maintain his cover.

As it was, this girl was already onto him.

The moment she'd realized he wasn't fucking her tonight, her hatred had twisted into bewilderment. Fatigue played a part in her confusion, but he'd felt a shift in her.

She wanted to trust him.

If only he could do the same. He'd tried to test her loyalty, asking if he should send her back to Hector's sons. Her *don't care* response wasn't assuring. Until he knew with certainty she wouldn't stab him in the back, he couldn't tell her who he was. Blowing his cover was the quickest way to ruin the mission.

Despite all that, he loved her explosive temper and quarrelsome nature. She wasn't afraid to throw a bare-knuckled punch or get in his face and run off her mouth.

A mouth that had forgotten how to soften in a smile.

He wanted to force his tongue between her clenched teeth and duel it out.

He wanted to kiss her.

Even after consuming more whiskey and half of a steak, he still tasted her on his lips. He couldn't recall ever contemplating the flavor of a woman's body before. Perhaps because no one had ever tasted so forbidden, like honeyed sin and fiery rebellion.

Shutting the door on those thoughts, he turned on the television, switched off the lights, and slid into bed beside her. After a few adjustments, they lay beneath the covers, face to face, eyes locked.

Tomas had already retired for the evening, confirming that the devices in the ceiling had night vision. But the sounds from the TV should drown out a whispered conversation.

A late-night talk show flickered on the screen. The soundtrack of studio laughter detached itself from the weighty silence between him and Gina.

He wished he knew her real name. He wanted to know everything about her—where she came from, how she ended up here, her schooling, job history, hobbies, family, boyfriends, all of it.

She regarded him with similar interest, her dark eyes pooling with dazed curiosity, lips swollen, and forehead creased as if fighting the lethargy taking hold.

"You can't fall asleep?" he asked.

"Not lying beside a rapist."

"Deal with it."

"Yeah." Her jaw stiffened. "It's what I do."

"Do any La Rocha members force you to spend the night in their beds?"

"Never."

"This is the first time you've slept beside someone since you've been here?"

"I'm not sleeping." She squinted. "So that first hasn't happened."

"You going to stay awake for a week?"

The slits of her eyes become impossibly narrower.

"Tell me, Gina. Where do you wish to be right now?"

"A thousand miles away."

"Only a thousand?" He kept his voice soft, tucking their privacy inside a whisper.

"More like eight-hundred miles."

"That's specific. Given your accent, your home is in Mexico. Exactly eight-hundred miles from here?"

"Where is here?"

"You tell me."

"You writing a book?"

Irritatingly gorgeous pain in the ass.

"We can talk." He reached beneath the covers and tweaked her soft, warm nipple. "Or we can fuck."

As expected, instant hostility fired in her eyes, and she slapped his hand away.

She'd endured his level of douchery from countless men since she'd been here. Three years was a long time, fighting for survival night after night in a cartel compound. The fact that she was still breathing meant she'd learned not to show the slightest weakness.

He appreciated her strength and stood behind it one hundred percent. But to finish this job, he would have to break through that stubborn armor.

A foot of silence separated them. Might as well have been eight-hundred miles.

With a quick reach of his arm, he caught her around the waist and yanked her flush against him. Chest to chest, skin on skin, he felt every inch of her nudity along every inch of his.

Her gaze held, widening only slightly as he hardened against her thigh.

"Ignore it." He pulled the sheet up to their faces and whispered against her lips. "Tell me the location of this place."

Now she stiffened, and her breathing shortened.

"I don't—"

"Don't lie to me."

"I'm not. I swear, I don't know." She looked off-kilter and desperate—this woman who fearlessly stared down cartel gangsters.

She was telling the truth.

"What about Vera?" he breathed against her mouth. "Does she know?"

"Ask her yourself."

He was hard. She was hours past passing out, and they were both gloriously naked. So flipping her onto her back and pressing his erection against her cunt required no effort. She struggled, her movements clumsy, and he waited her out, letting her breathing escalate.

She didn't have to like him. By the end of the week, he'd make sure she didn't.

At last, she stopped resisting and sank into the mattress. "Maybe."

"Yes or no." He kicked his hips, threatening her entrance with the head of his cock.

"Yeah, motherfucker." She bared her teeth, a startling white contrast to her dark complexion. "She knows."

That was the confirmation he needed. If Vera gave him the coordinates, he would leave. Let them put a hood over his head and escort him out. Then he would return with an army.

He slid off her hot body and adjusted them on their sides, settling into the same position as before. "Is anyone looking for you?"

Surprise popped into her eyes, and she jerked away as though she'd been burned.

He dragged her back. "Family?"

"I have one person. One person left in my family, and I won't let you near her."

His interest wasn't in her family. He just needed to know her stakes in this, that she had something to fight for. A life she missed. Someone she loved. If she valued this person over the cartel, maybe he could trust her. Unless the cartel was using her family member to threaten her.

Shifting her lower beneath the covers, he whispered under the veil, "Is this person safe from La Rocha?"

In the dark, her inhale shuddered, and a sheen of distress wet her eyes. "No."

Fuck. "Where is she?" He could've kept his whisper flat, but his anger got away from him.

She heard it, blinking rapidly, and seemed uncertain how to respond.

He needed to explain away his concern, but this girl was too smart. Too perceptive. And maybe, seeing someone pissed in her defense was exactly the kind of thing that would penetrate her shields.

So he remained quiet, watching, waiting to see what she would do next.

It took a year and a day before she reached for him. Tentative fingers crept over his jaw and pulled back when she felt the rigidness there. He tried to relax, loosening the tension in his face.

Inching closer, she touched him again. His neck this time, her warm hand sliding to the hairline on his nape. Her eyes didn't waver from his until she set her mouth against his cheek and breathed in and out, deeply, slowly.

She was testing him. Or testing herself. How long could she hold him like this before he flipped her over and fucked her? If he didn't do what she expected, could she trust him enough to finish the conversation?

Maybe she wasn't thinking any of this. She could be lying to him, manipulating him. Working for the cartel. His intuition disagreed, but he couldn't do this job on gut instinct and emotion. There was too much at stake.

Her fingers twitched against his nape, almost caressing as if seeking the contact. Then she leaned back just enough to search his eyes. Her lips parted to speak, but her voice hid in her throat.

"Tell me." He kept his expression unreadable and his gaze attentive.

"La Rocha…" She swallowed, her voice barely audible. "They took my mother. She's a successful actress. Well-known and well-connected."

"Who is she? Give me her name."

She clamped a hand over his mouth, eyes wide and head shaking side to side. "Don't. Not that. I'll shed every drop of blood in my body before I tell you." She glanced up around the fold of covers, her gaze on the ceiling. "They might kill me anyway."

Not on his watch.

He touched her chin, drawing her face back under the sheets. Then he guided her hand to his neck. "Is your mother connected to someone dangerous?"

"Lots of someones." Her lashes lowered, and her fingers fell away. "I think I can sleep now."

He missed the warmth of her touch instantly. When she rolled and gave him her back, he missed the feel of her body against his. But he allowed her some space to get comfortable.

Shutting off the TV, he blanketed them in a dark hush and waited.

Soon her breathing slowed into the even rhythm of slumber.

Slowly, careful not to wake her, he curled around her tiny frame, with her back to his front and his arm locked around her like an anchor.

Her chest rose and fell with a shuddering inhale before returning to a soporific tempo. She felt so fragile in his embrace, so sweet and sexy. He couldn't stop himself from kissing the bare top of a graceful shoulder.

Breathing in the scent of her skin, he ordered his mind to shut off. But he couldn't sleep.

Minutes blurred into hours, and he lay entwined with a stolen girl while thinking about another one.

Blonde hair. Glassy eyes. Strangling beneath his hand. Squirming. Dying. Unable to gasp. Everything inside him wrangled and twisted anew.

From this night forward, a nameless dead girl would be the only thought he took with him into the hinterland of sleep. She would forever haunt his dreams, breed his nightmares, and admonish him of the decision he'd made.

He would never forget.

TWELVE

She'd been watching him sleep for an hour. Long enough for the first light of dawn to form a glaring halo behind the curtains. His arm lay heavily around her, holding her against his hard chest. It felt horrible.

Horribly safe.

No, not safe. His strange behavior and little mercies were an illusion. A trap. This man had an agenda, one that didn't include protecting her. Certainly not from himself.

With her face inches from his, she must've turned toward him during the night. *Toward* him. Why would she do that? Even unconscious, she knew better.

Why the fuck was she still in bed with him?

At any point, she could've lifted his arm and crept away. For a vigilant, calculating predator, he slept like the dead.

His hair, thick and tousled, glimmered differently in the morning. Metallic lowlights of ruby and brown threaded with strands of copper, creating a tapestry of red hues.

Not a single tattoo on his smooth fair skin, a body hardened to steel, and cold sharp eyes of emerald intelligence, which hadn't cracked open yet.

Blondish-red fuzz roughened his chest and forearms, just a little. Just enough to remind her of his masculinity.

She didn't need the reminder.

Last night was seared forever in her memory. The suction of his mouth between her legs. The deep rumble of his American accent in her ear. The taste of his whiskey breath that still lingered on her lips.

I need to get out of here.

Holding in her next inhale, she made her escape. Out from beneath his arm, down to the floor, she crouched low, waiting.

He didn't stir.

Her muscles protested every movement, stiff and sore, but remarkably better than last night. She scrunched her face, testing other injuries. No swelling that she could tell. No hunger pangs, either. That was a novelty.

His luggage lay open behind her. From the large case, she carefully removed a button-up shirt. No reason to snoop through his belongings. The cartel would've already searched it and removed anything useful.

Backing away on tiptoes, she closed the buttons on the shirt and slipped into the main room. The door to the other bedroom stood open, giving her a view of Tomas' bed.

The sheets lay crumpled on the empty mattress. No sounds came from the bathroom. The bodyguard wasn't here. *Perfect.*

She hurried on silent feet toward the exit. By the

time she gripped the door handle, her heart had clawed its way to her throat.

I'm not running.

That would be against his rules. She just needed… What? Clothes. Coffee. A morning walk. *Space.*

With her defense prepared, she swung open the door and gasped.

Brown hair, crooked nose, steroid-induced torso, and eyes as black as night. Hateful eyes, burning with manic rage.

"Alejandro." She sucked down her panic and faced him with her chin raised. "What are you doing here?"

He'd been gone for several weeks, which meant he'd just delivered a new batch of trafficked girls. And not only to this property. The youngest La Rocha brother sold slaves all over California and elsewhere.

"Imagine my disappointment," he said in scathing Spanish, "when I arrived this morning to discover that *my* whore was whoring for someone else."

"Marco allowed—"

"I don't give a fuck!" His hand shot toward her neck.

She ducked, slammed against the door in her attempt to escape, and tried to flee into the breezeway. He reached for her again, and she threw herself forward, knowing there was no way she'd make it past him.

Except he didn't stop her.

Glancing back was a mistake. She should've kept running. Eyes forward. Always straight ahead. But stupidity swung her gaze around and slowed her steps.

A broad muscled back swallowed her view.

Freckles she hadn't noticed before on the bulging ridges of shoulders. Corded neck, red hair, and a fist that reached back and captured her wrist in an unbending grip.

"You must be John Smith." A sneer edged Alejandro's broken English.

"And you must be Miguel." John's head dipped down and back up, taking in the man's massive size. "Or are you the youngest brother?"

"I'm Alejandro, *vato*, and she belongs to *me*."

"I see. Well, then…" John ruthlessly dragged her forward, making her trip. "Take her. Since you're not interested in my business, I'll leave this morning. You can speak to my assistant about refunding my down payment, as well as the obscene amount of money he wired last night for the time I *won't* be spending with my purchase."

He pushed her toward Alejandro, washing his hands of her. She didn't know whether to sigh in relief or punch his balls into his throat.

"You paid for her?" Alejandro jerked his head back. "For a used-up whore?"

"I paid six digits for a week with her."

Her stomach sank. She knew the buyers dropped serious cash on the virgin girls fresh off the truck. But six digits in exchange for *her*? It was preposterous. Why would he do that? He didn't even fuck her last night.

Alejandro glanced at the workout shorts that John had shoved on. Then his gaze traveled over the stolen shirt she wore. He was a possessive son of a bitch, and it showed in the hard brackets around his scowl. His nostrils widened, and he gripped his nape. Then a decision settled on his face.

The cartel valued money far and above their

women. Her fate was sealed.

"I misunderstood." He shoved his hands in his pockets and backed away. "We honor our deals, *esé*." His Adam's apple bounced, the flat line of his lips barely concealing his displeasure. "Stay. She's yours for the week."

"You hear that, darling?" John grabbed her by the hair and yanked her back against him. "Unless, of course, you'd rather go with Alejandro? Your choice."

What the ever-loving fuck? After all that posturing with Marco last night, he was changing his tune? Talk about whiplash.

Maybe it was a test, but she wouldn't fall for it. Whomever she chose, the other man would find a way to make her pay for his embarrassment.

"What's behind door three?" She jerked at the hair in his fist, unable to free herself.

"I'll show you." John hauled her back into the room. Then he faced the doorway, blocking her view. "Will there be anything else?"

"There's a private dinner in my quarters tonight." Alejandro cleared his voice, his English thick with resentment. "I expect you to be there. Bring the whore."

Fuck no! She didn't want anything to do with that.

With a nod, John shut the door in the cartel *jefe's* face. Then he slowly turned toward her and lobbed a glare so frightening it sent prickles from her nape to her toes.

"You're feeling better." His voice was cold. Terribly so.

She shook her head and retreated around the couch.

"You're recovered enough to run." He prowled

after her, eyes locked.

"I wasn't running, *idiota.* I needed clothes and coffee and—"

"Shut the fuck up." His words didn't match the oh-so calm delivery, which made him even more fearsome. He paused at the side table and removed something from the drawer, concealing it in the palm of his huge hand. "Your disobedience will not go unpunished."

"El burro sabe más que tú. Do you hear yourself?" She shook violently, and that just made her madder. And *louder.* "I bet you were the school bully. The guy who shoved around the smaller kids because your dad took his fists to you? You were hiding your own bruises, weren't you? And the only control you had in your life was beating the shit out of those who weighed less than you."

She was angry and scared and talking out of her ass, but the instant his face paled, she knew she'd touched a tender nerve.

"I warned you." He followed her through the sitting area, his gait too casual for the fists flexing at his sides. "Every foolish action will result in another girl taking your punishment."

"No! This is between you and me, goddammit!"

He paused, tipped his head. "Then you better run."

Her pulse exploded as she spun and bolted toward the door. His footsteps pounded after her, flooding her system with adrenaline. She passed a chair and yanked it behind her. Same with a small table. A glass lamp crashed to the floor, followed by a masculine curse.

She made it halfway to the door when it opened.

Tomas stepped in, holding a tray of food and a bag of clothes.

Fucking hell. She swerved, aiming for the bedrooms, but John was too close, breathing down her neck. He swiped at her, his fingers snagging the back of the shirt. She whirled, stomped a heel on his foot, and drove a fist into his gut.

He grunted, and she dropped to the floor, scrambling around his legs to evade the long reach of his arms. All those muscles made him strong, but they also slowed him down.

She could've outrun him if she had somewhere to go. Tomas blocked the exit, and there was no other way out. Not that leaving this room was an option beneath the gravity of John's threat. He'd told her to run because he clearly enjoyed the chase. She was playing right into his games, but what else could she do? Just stand there and let him punish her? Not a chance.

So she sprinted around furniture and tossed vases and decorative knickknacks at him, recklessly trashing the place. He caught her several times, but she hit, kicked, and bit her way out of his clutches.

Part of her suspected he was giving her those little victories. The other part just didn't care. She wasn't going down without a fight.

And *down* was exactly how it went as he tackled her to the floor. The full force of his weight crashed onto her back and knocked the air from her lungs. They landed in a sweaty pile—his bare chest, her kicking legs, their arms slick and wrestling.

She panted uncontrollably and attacked with elbows to his ribs. He chased her hands, trying to restrain them. She threw back her head, aiming to break his face. He dodged, grabbed her throat, and sank his teeth into her neck.

Her screams rang out loud enough to reach far beyond the walls, but no one would come to her aid. She was on her own, crushed beneath two-hundred-pounds of roguish male hunger. Her pleas and objections weren't just ignored. They were *laughed* at.

Yeah, he was laughing and groaning through labored breaths. And fully aroused. His erection jabbed her naked backside, with the shirt tangled around her waist.

"You're a sinful goddamn turn on, Gina. Can't remember the last time I needed to be inside a woman this badly." He lifted a hand to his mouth and tore open a square packet with his teeth.

A condom. That was what he'd removed from the drawer.

"No, no, no! Fuck you, cocksucker! Fuck you!" She bucked beneath him, breaths wheezing and heart rate in overdrive. "Wait! Just wait. Okay, I'm sorry. I won't run again. Don't do this!"

"Too late for repentance, baby." Lust thickened his voice as he raised his hips and rolled on the rubber. "Time for that punishment."

She didn't stop thrashing, didn't for a second make it easy for him. But he was bigger, stronger, built with the right equipment and the cruel agility to take a woman from behind.

In one thrust, he stabbed past her opening, driving hard and spearing her to the very hilt of himself.

Tears hit her eyes as a strangled groan sounded in his throat. He rocked against her, picking up speed, digging deeper, violating, ravaging, and grunting in her ear. She wanted to die.

He fucked into her over and over like an animal, opening her legs wider with the spread of his powerful thighs. His hands were on her everywhere, grappling, stroking, and mauling while at the same time holding her immobile.

The condom must've been lubricated, because the initial burn dissolved into slippery wet strokes. He was thrusting savagely, jerking out, slamming in, and building a rhythm that made her writhe in agony.

It didn't hurt, and she hated him for that. She hated that he fit inside her just right and that he moved his body so sensually and obsessively, suggesting he was fully engaged in this, physically and emotionally.

This wasn't like the three-minute ruts she endured from the brothers. He fucked her with passion and filled her with fire, penetrating her body with his entire being, forcing her to feel him beneath her skin, taking over every cell, and delving deep into her core.

She gasped and clawed at the floor, frantic to escape the overbearing onslaught of his fervor. Gaining a few inches, she saw Tomas watching from the door before she was dragged back beneath John and utterly devoured.

That was the only way to describe it. His lips locked onto her nape, tasting and consuming, his tongue laving at her damp hairline, only deepening the fevered kisses on her neck, then her temple, her cheek, the corner of her mouth.

Her senses swam, her breathing unmanageable. She tried to struggle, but he only buried himself deeper, stretching her, stuffing her, nailing her to the floor, and rendering her even more helpless.

"Goddamn, you feel unreal." He surged harder, his fingers wedged beneath her chest, tormenting her breasts. "Fucking incredible."

He attacked the shirt, the material ripping and pulling in a flurry of urgent movements, buttons breaking, and her arms forced from sleeves. Her whole body jostled with the frantic piston of his hips and the tugs on the fabric, causing her bare nipples to scrape against the coarse rug beneath her.

She tried to push up, to crawl away, but her arms gave out from under her.

"All that straining and fighting makes your pussy clench." He lurched back with a sudden outward pull, only to ram back in, stretching her wider around the slick steel of his cock. "Christ, you're tight. Hot. Wet. I want to feel you bareback."

"I hope your dick rots off."

"Give me that fucking mouth." His arm banded around her chest, holding her tight as he gripped her chin and fused their lips.

She used her teeth, her hands, the last of her strength, but she couldn't stop his tongue from melding with hers. His mouth ground with maddening pressure, his fist balled in her hair, and he took. Lord have mercy, he took, deep and long and ravenously, while shoving his cock, plunging mercilessly, and groaning with poisonous pleasure.

He was heat and virility, fury and stamina, plundering and claiming with a skill that destroyed everything she knew about sex. No one had ever fucked her so vehemently. Every touch, kiss, and thrust was an effusive blaze, flowing out, over, and through her.

Answering heat simmered her blood. Her insides burned and tightened. Nerve endings sizzled, and her soul shook. *She* was shook. Mentally unhinged. Damned to eternal hell.

She wanted him to punish her. She needed him to beat her, hurt her, smack her back into reality. Anything but this. What he was doing to her, making her crave it… It was sick.

She was sick.

Faster and faster he moved inside her, sparking pleasure she didn't want. Their gasps mingled and mixed into one. A moan escaped her mouth, and he faltered above her, recovered, and began to rock almost reverently into her, the cadence strangely slowed, languorously thickened, and weighted with the dragging pull of his lips against hers.

His hands strayed her hips, gripping tightly as he caught a telltale rhythm. His invasion seemed to swell, growing impossibly thicker and harder in that last painful moment, his legs trembling, and chest heaving as he chased his release.

"Oh, fuck. Oh, fuck…" He came, driving deep and pounding into her with a growling roar.

As he ground into a slow halt, jerking and catching his breath, a wet sheen blurred her eyes. She felt dirty. Twisted. Used.

He twitched, and her inner muscles spasmed around him in response.

Shame. That was chief of her emotions and the worst feeling of all.

Without a word, he pushed off her, flung the condom at the trashcan, and yanked up the shorts he still wore.

"See that she gets dressed and hydrates," he said to Tomas. "We leave in five minutes to work out."

He ambled toward the bedroom, leaving her with a hollow, pulsing ache for something she couldn't possibly want. Her lips were raw. Her breasts tingled with heaviness. Her pussy throbbed with soreness, and her chest cleaved for want of air.

She'd been violated more times than she could count since arriving at the compound. But not once had she ever felt so hot and needy and fucked-up afterward. What the hell had he done to her?

Anger spiked, coursing through her veins. She jumped to her feet, eying the demon who strolled away without a single glance back at the woman he'd just raped.

She didn't think. She just ran. Past Tomas, toward the bedroom, she headed off the monster before he turned the corner. With a hard kick to the back of his knee, she caught him by surprise. He lost his balance, gripped the door jamb, and when he spun, she was ready.

Her fist collided with his granite jawline, sending a jolt of pain up her arm. She swung again, faking the hit, while driving a knee into his groin.

He doubled over and wrapped his arms around her like iron bands, slamming her against the wall as he stumbled. Those were the only strikes she got before he subdued her with a hand on her throat and his body planked along the front of hers.

"Do you want a postcoital cuddle? Is that it?" He wet his lips, his fingers tightening against her tender airway.

"I don't want a coital anything from you."

"You sure about that?" With his free hand, he reached between her legs and fingered her wetness. "Ah. You want a release."

She gulped, dragging in precious drops of air and furiously shaking her head. But the tears that sprung were telling.

This need… The awful, involuntary longing he'd woken beneath her skin had teeth. She didn't know how to fight this new enemy inside her. She didn't even understand it. But she needed to. She couldn't straighten out her head until she figured out the mystery between them.

He watched her closely, his face an inch away. The hand on her throat loosened, melting into fingers that stroked and beguiled.

"Say what you're thinking," he murmured.

"You…" *Kiss differently. Fuck differently.* "You hurt me differently. Not like the others."

Nothing changed in his hard expression. No surprise. No annoyance.

"You want to know why." He did something with his finger between her legs, making her entire body bow off the wall and press into his. "Why does my touch bring more pleasure than pain? Why do I kiss with the patience of a man who worships women, not owns them?" He leaned in and slid his nose along hers, his whisper kissing her lips. "The truth is so disturbing you wouldn't believe me if I told you. Let it go."

He released her and stepped back.

Rubbing her throat, she glared at him, more confused and uncomfortable than ever before.

"You want to come, Gina, even as your brain abhors the idea. That's your punishment, one that will plague your pretty little mind and pussy all day. Get dressed."

With that, he stalked into the bedroom, dismissing her.

THIRTEEN

By *work out*, he actually did mean jogging.

The man had some irritating stamina, but she was no slouch, either. Dressed in the tank-top, spandex shorts, and running shoes that Tomas had found for her—*God only knew whose closet he'd raided*—she pounded her feet along the trail.

Sweat dampened her brow. Sunshine warmed her skin, and the light breakfast she'd eaten sat contently in her stomach.

She was glad to be outside, breathing in the open air. The exercise kept her focused on rebuilding her strength rather than falling apart. She even appreciated the view of the two shirtless psychopaths jogging along either side of her. It was better than being confined in a room with them.

Before yesterday, she'd considered herself fairly perceptive when it came to men. She anticipated their intentions, skill sets, and limitations with a high degree of accuracy.

But not this one.

John confounded her at every turn. Even now, as he veered off the cobblestone trail and sprinted across the lawn, she couldn't guess what he was doing.

The grass was cut short, but a few minutes into the detour, the ground became uneven, the terrain unused and unkempt. When her pace slowed, he shot an aggressive look over his shoulder.

If only he would trip and impale himself on something sharp.

"There are dozens of running trails." She panted, pumping her legs twice as hard to keep up with his long gait. "Do you know where you're going?"

A grunt was all he gave her.

Nasty redheaded gorilla.

As he and Tomas led her farther away from the outdoor luxuries of the estate, she remained a few clips behind them, growing suspicious.

She knew every corner of this property, every building, pathway, camera, and blade of grass. A two-mile, unclimbable stone wall enclosed the compound, every inch of it monitored either by technology or armed guards.

Except one section. One shaded, overlooked nook. And there, behind a maze of cobwebs and dead trees was a way out.

Yesterday, she was caught far away from that area, thank God. She'd attacked a guard near a different section of the wall in an attempt to knock him out and take his clothes, weapons, and earpiece before making her escape. Unfortunately, she hadn't counted on the second guard who had sneaked up behind her.

Up ahead, Tomas angled closer to John and said something too low for her ears. Then he gave a subtle nod to the left, spoke again, and jogged off.

The camera. There was only one in this area, hidden in a tree, and he'd just pointed it out.

So this was a scouting expedition disguised as a run?

John made his way to a small grove beyond the range of that camera. The property spanned multiple acres, and he plopped down in one of the few places that wasn't monitored by the cartel.

Her heart hammered against her ribs. Was he a spy? Some kind of operative in the military? Whatever it was, she didn't want any part of it.

"Come here." He met her gaze from across the field, his tone brooking no argument.

Tomas was nowhere in sight. Not that he would come to her defense, but she didn't want to be alone with this man.

He didn't repeat himself and didn't need to. His look spoke louder than words.

Seconds ticked by. The stare-off extended past stubborn and dipped into dangerous territory. If she didn't obey him, he would physically force her, and she would lose. Again.

Shoving her feet forward, she trudged toward him and paused a few paces away. "What?"

"Sit with me."

"No."

He lunged, and though she was ready for it, he pounced lower than she expected. She didn't see his leg shoot out until it collided with her ankles, knocking her on her ass. With a yelp, she scrabbled away only to be overpowered once again by his sheer size and strength.

Lying on her back in the overgrown grass, she gazed up at him and didn't move. Wriggling beneath his weight would only turn him on, and she still felt the tenderness of the last violation.

Maybe he would hurt her anyway, but his demeanor didn't suggest cruel intentions. He held the back of her head in a firm palm and drank in her features, the brilliant green of his eyes making an unhurried exploration.

Leaning closer, he slid a thumb along her jaw, nudged it down, and forced her lips open. She gulped, and he pressed closer, breathing in her gasp. The way he stared so deeply into her eyes, he looked like he wanted to kiss her, like he wanted to peel her open and climb inside.

"Do you know why I chose you?" The question rumbled from deep in his chest.

"I was the only woman still alive in the room?"

"Alive." He licked his lips, tasting the word. "Exactly. You're so alive you glow with fire. Not only when you fight, but when you watch and listen."

"I'm a side-effect of men's cruelty." She didn't appreciate him analyzing her as if he knew her. "What do you want?"

"Only to talk."

"Talk?" She narrowed her eyes. "Like we did in your room this morning?"

"Since there are no cameras here, we can interact like normal people." He rolled off her and pulled her to her side to face him. "Tell me something. Anything."

"What do you mean?" She was still stuck on the camera comment. "Did you fucking *rape* me because you knew they were watching?"

With a sigh, he stretched out on his back and bent an arm behind his head. "Tell me something about yourself. Or about the world. Pick a topic."

"What's your interest in the cameras?"

"Another topic."

"Fine. When you're not raping women, what do you do for a living?"

"I invest in something important. Next topic."

"Is your job legal? Do you work for the government?"

"No to both of those questions, and that's the last answer you'll get from me on that."

"How many innocent lives have you taken?"

He remained silent.

Disappointment pinched in her chest.

So he was a criminal, which revealed nothing. Every man who walked through here lived on the wrong side of the law. He could be an assassin or an enemy spy. Or maybe he was just another well-funded, paranoid asshole, looking for a new sex slave.

"I'm giving you the chance to speak freely about anything you want." He gazed up at the tree canopy, his handsome face speckled in drops of sunlight. "If you don't pick a topic, I will, and it'll involve you telling me who you are and how you came here. You'll fight me, and we both know how that will end."

He looked at her, and she turned away, feeling extra stabby. She wanted to claw his eyes out.

"You have every right to despise me," he said. "When it comes to taking what I want from you, I'm no different than Hector's sons. But have they ever taken the time to have a conversation with you? Do they know you at all?"

No. Not even a little. They came, and they went. Wham-bam-fuck-you-ma'am. Omar kept her around as long as she won fights. Alejandro was possessive, but he was like that with all his women. The other two didn't even look at her after they fucked her.

That went both ways. She wanted nothing to do with them. But she did miss the simple act of sharing a conversation with someone. She had no one to talk to here. No one who gave a shit what she thought.

She shifted to her back, mirroring his position beside her. Despite the shade from the trees, the air felt unusually hot for autumn, clinging to her skin and making her sweat. Damn global warming.

"Greenland has melted beyond saving." She threw the random thought into the humid breeze.

"Ah." He caught it with a smile in his voice. "The tipping point debate."

"If you look at the science, there's no debate. The ice sheet has lost so much mass over the last two decades that even if global warming ended yesterday, the arctic island won't recover."

He turned slowly, stretching and shaping his body around hers without touching. "What are we going to do about it?"

"We, the human race? Nothing. There isn't enough intelligence or concern on this planet to fix it. Future generations will have to use advancements in technology to adapt to the changing environment."

"How?"

"They'll modify their DNA. It's the only way they'll be able to inhabit a world our species isn't designed for."

"Designed? You believe in a higher power? Intelligent design?"

Oh, she had plenty of opinions on that. Her mouth ran away from her, and for the next few minutes, she stood on a soapbox and outlined everything she speculated on the subject. By the time she realized she was rambling, she couldn't take it back. She'd engaged him in a conversation, doing precisely what he wanted.

The thing was… He *listened.* Actually kept his arguments to himself so that he could hear hers. Was this some kind of ploy to engineer personal information from her?

Except she hadn't revealed anything confidential. He seemed genuinely interested in what she had to say.

Was she being naive?

Lifting on an elbow, he regarded her intently. "You've given this a lot of thought."

Without access to a phone, Internet, or friends, all she had was time to sit around and think about shit.

She met his eyes, breaths defensively taut. "You want to argue my points? Bring it on."

"Nope. I'm not an expert on climate change or God."

"Then where is your expertise? What do you know?"

"I can offer some factoids on testosterone." He bent his head toward hers, making her heart skip. "I've read a lot on the subject."

She didn't like where this was headed. Anything related to men and their bodies was dangerous territory. But she sucked it up and gave him her ear.

"A man's testosterone peaks at puberty." He brushed a wayward lock of hair from her face. "It declines immediately after then plateaus as he ages. Unless he gains weight. Fat pushes testosterone levels into a downward spiral. But you know what doesn't?"

"No." She didn't want to know. Not with that heated look in his eyes.

"Sex. Studies have shown that a man's testosterone increases the morning after intimacy. More so in unmated males, those who are actively *hunting.*

Their testosterone boosts exponentially—we're talking upwards of three-hundred-percent—the morning after sexual activity. Interestingly, masturbation doesn't yield the same results, which suggests there's a socio element to hormone production."

Fascinating. Also, disturbing. Especially with him angled so close to her.

He engaged in sex last night. Not intercourse, but oral sex. Did it count if he didn't come? Was his testosterone in the red zone when he woke?

"Is that why you raped me this morning?"

"Despite what you think, I'm in full control of my baser needs. Case in point…" He dipped his head, hovering his face an inch from her heaving chest. "I want to cover these raised nipples with my tongue and tease them into hard peaks through the shirt. When the fabric becomes too damp and itchy, I want to strip it away and feel you against my lips—your soft skin, the pounding of your heart, the vibration of your moans. What would you do…?" He paused. Breathed in. On an exhale, his voice shifted from seductive to pensive. "For a…?

Uncertain, she flattened her back against the ground and curled her fingers in the grass. "For what?"

"For a Klondike bar?"

She stared up at him and blinked. "Sorry?"

"It's a square of ice cream with chocolate—"

"I know what it is." She gritted her teeth. "Are you making fun of me?"

"Depends on your answer."

"God, you're so…" *Unpredictable. Gorgeous. Perplexing*. She sniffed, trying to hold onto her annoyance. "Strange."

"What would you do for one? Would you lick

that tree?" He nodded at the barky, moss-covered trunk a few feet away.

"I don't know. Maybe?" She couldn't remember the last time she tasted ice cream.

"Would you finish our jog without clothes on?"

"No." *Not willingly.*

"Would you sing?"

"That would be awful for everyone." She made a face. "But I can rap."

"Right now."

"What?" She sat up, forcing him to lean back.

"Rap me a song, and I'll get you a Klondike. Hell, I'll get you a whole box."

"Three."

"Three boxes?"

"The variety packs. All different flavors."

He rolled his lips to hide a smile. "You drive a hard bargain."

"Do we have a deal?"

"Absolutely."

This rich boy wouldn't know a good rap song if it smacked him in his white ass. So she opted for something satirical with a little cheese and a lot of groove.

Closing her eyes, she loosened her shoulders, rocked her head, and hummed the opening rhythm of "Welcome to Chili's" by *Yung Gravy.*

Only the intro was in Spanish, which she sang embarrassingly off-tune. But when she jumped into the rap, she was fire, popping the *P's*, rolling the *R's*, and hitting every word with a kick in her hips.

After a few lines, she leaped to her feet, catching the beat with her whole body. He rose in her periphery, and she turned away, focusing on the lyrics.

Until his masculine heat covered her back. Bold hands glided over her shoulders, down her arms, moving with her. *He* moved with her.

She shivered and rapped out the next verse. By the time she reached the chorus, his voice was in her ear, saying the words with her, nailing the beat perfectly.

Holy shit, he knew this song? Why was she surprised? It was popular in America. But still…

She turned, facing him without losing the tempo. But she was no longer dancing, her body restrained in the intensity of his stare. He faltered over some of the words but knew the rest. They didn't bounce or sway, didn't blink or break eye contact for a single second.

The moment held them in a peculiar other world where a woman and her rapist rapped in a trance.

When had he drifted closer? Was she leaning into him? No, they weren't touching. But she felt him all over, against her skin, in her song, humming through her blood.

When had they stopped singing?

The canopy rustled above them. She couldn't think.

A locust buzzed in the grass. She couldn't look away.

His fingers floated through her hair. She couldn't breathe.

He touched her face, the bruised skin around her eyes, her cheek, her lips.

Push him away.

Her hands landed on his bare chest. Solid bedrock encased in hot skin. Beautifully built. Flawless definition. Carved and sanded with divine precision.

His palm cupped her jaw. So gentle. So goddamn

nice.

Get rid of him.

Her head tipped, slanting into the touch as if compelled by a magnet.

Jesus, his eyes were right there, shining vividly. His mouth slightly parted and waiting.

This was too heavy. Too *cozy*. This… Feeling? It was gravity. Chemistry. Deranged attraction. Why couldn't she fight it?

"Baby," he murmured against her mouth. "There's something I need to tell you."

Dazed, she couldn't feel her tongue. "Mm?

"There's a snake behind you."

"No, he's…" Her chest filled with air. "He's in front of me."

"I'm serious."

"What kind of snake?"

"Black and white with red rings. Three feet long."

"Oh. That's a king—" Her feet left the ground as he swung her up and away. "Wait!"

He spun toward the creature, crouching to attack it as she yelled, "It's a kingsnake! Nonvenomous! Don't kill it!"

"What?" He lunged, catching the squirming body. "I want to help it. Look."

She darted toward him, craning her neck, and gasped.

The poor thing was tangled in a piece of plastic netting, with the webbing cinching it so tightly it couldn't move properly.

"Here." He trapped it against the ground, controlling the whip of its head. "Hold the tail."

She didn't hesitate, and within seconds he managed to break the plastic enough for the snake to work itself free.

He pocketed the trash and watched the animal slither away while she watched him, baffled and conflicted.

"Why did you do that?" Her mind churned to reconcile everything she knew about men with the one standing before her. "What are you trying to prove? That you're not cruel? That you're different from the others?"

His gaze cut to her, his eyes blazing with so much anger it snipped her breath. "There are plenty of snakes that deserve to die. Dozens that are eating, fucking, and indulging in evil right inside those walls." He stabbed a finger in the direction of the estate. "Despite what you saw last night in the basement, I'm not in the business of taking innocent lives."

"But you're still a snake." She shook her head, fighting the impulse to step back. "You're a bad guy."

"I hear the question in your voice." He prowled forward, edging into her space.

"No question." She thrust up her chin. "I was there this morning, remember? Pinned beneath your brutality with my face shoved into the floor."

"Yes, but you're also realizing there's more to me than that moment."

"Like the fact that you're working against the cartel? That you're hiding some traitorous shit that I want nothing to do with? Will you kill me if I discover your secrets? The cartel certainly will if they think I'm involved."

A muscle feathered across his shirtless chest, his expression twitching with contemplation. "I'll tell you my secrets."

Her mouth parted.

"*If*," he said, "you tell me yours."

"Get real."

"Start with your education. You were born and raised in Mexico, but your English is perfect."

If she made up a story about that, he would read her like a lie detector. So all she gave him was a blank stare.

He met it with one of his own, and here they were again, locked in a silent battle of wills.

Could this guy be any more frustrating? Or intimidating? Or good-looking? Let's face it. She'd never been more captivated by a human being, let alone a human with a dick.

And mesmerizing green eyes.

And sculpted lips.

The tension between them passed, and those lips became an open-mouthed sigh. "We're done here."

Turning on his heel, he jogged back toward the estate. He paced his speed to keep her at his side, but instead of heading back to his quarters, he led her to the gym.

She welcomed that idea, hoping to avoid his bed as long as possible.

Strolling into the weight room, he snapped his fingers at the two guests on the weight machines. "Get out."

"Excuse me?" The younger of the two puffed out his chest.

"I didn't stutter."

John had more muscle and strength than both of those men combined. But it was his warlike posture and menacing scowl that sent them hurrying out of the room.

"You're not making any friends." She rubbed her

neck, looking around at the commercial machines and free weights. This was the longest she'd ever been in this building.

"I'm not here to make friends." He glanced at the camera in the ceiling and ambled toward a rack of kettlebells. "Follow me."

"You know, not everything has to be an authoritarian command. You could ask out of common decency."

He extended a finger toward the floor beside him and waited.

"Right." She grumbled a few choice words under her breath and dragged her feet to where he wanted her. "Now what?"

"You know how to hit, but you'll land harder punches if you strengthen the muscles here."

He jabbed his thumbs into her shoulders. Then he proceeded to show her how to build those muscles.

She questioned his motivation just as she questioned everything about him. But she needed to be patient. She'd only just met him last night. Less than twenty-four hours ago.

It's going to be a long week.

Once she got the hang of the repetitions, he left her to it and moved toward the heavier iron on the other side of the room.

For the next hour, they worked out in silence. She transitioned to the machines while he tossed around some deadly weight. His physique glistened with sweat, swelling and flexing obscenely.

The barbell loved him, and he seemed to love the punishment it put on his upper body. His chest, shoulders, and triceps contracted with every heave and pull. His lips curled back from his teeth, his grunts and pained breaths making it impossible to ignore his presence.

He was an erotic destination, a trip she had no business taking with her eyes. But the impulse couldn't be denied. She looked long and often, and he caught her every time, because he was looking, too.

Plenty of men had stared at her, here and *before.* But not the way he did. Not at his level of predatory intensity.

He reminded her of a big, sleek cat, with an air of smugness and danger that came from being well-fed yet always hunting. And why wouldn't he look at her like she was his next meal? He'd bought himself a week with her to do whatever he pleased outside the reach of the law. He didn't need to ask her permission, for anything, and he wouldn't.

But you're also realizing there's more to me than that moment.

Maybe.

Maybe that was what scared her the most.

FOURTEEN

Standing at the vanity in his bathroom, Luke scraped a razor across his jaw and watched his little warrior in the mirror. The view was no less than stunning, and his blood simmered with appreciation.

Beneath the spray of the shower, she rinsed the soap from her hair, smoothing the long coils into a black velvet curtain. Water sluiced down her tawny body, running sensual rivulets around toned curves and muscle.

Her gaze found his in the mirror, and swear to God, that look had a punch, hitting hard enough to make his balls shrivel. Her dark eyes blazed with righteous censure and judgment. But there was desire as well, no matter how hard she fought to hold it at bay.

More than anything, he wanted to see that desire win out.

It was dangerous to hope for such a thing. He only had one week with her, and during that time, his focus needed to be on Vera Gomez.

Dinner with Alejandro was approaching, and he

counted on Vera being there. The sexual chemistry between Gina and him was so potent it wouldn't go unnoticed. Not by Vera nor Alejandro nor anyone else present tonight.

He would flaunt it, not hide it. Let them obsess over his relationship with the fighter. Better that than on the real reason he was here.

Even Tomas detected the energy ricocheting between him and the woman in the shower. His friend leaned against the wall beside the vanity, wearing a scowl full of opinions.

"Shut your fucking mouth." Luke tossed the razor aside and rinsed his face.

"I didn't say anything, you twat."

Gina turned off the faucet, snagged a towel, and strode toward the doorway as if she couldn't get away fast enough.

"Your dress is on the bed," Luke called after her. "Don't do anything stupid."

With a middle-finger salute, she disappeared around the corner.

Tomas stared after her with smoldering interest in his unmasked expression. A jolt of aggression shot up Luke's spine, and he slammed a hand down on the vanity.

"That woman is fucking beautiful." Tomas blinked and finally dragged his eyes away from the doorway.

"That's the last time you'll notice."

Tomas huffed a disbelieving laugh. "Have you lost your goddamn mind?"

A sharp inhale stretched Luke's nostrils, and he pushed away from the sink.

"Oh, shit." Trailing after him, Tomas whispered

harshly, "She's getting to you."

"Don't be a moron. I've known her less than a day."

"It only takes a look, man. You're fucked."

Luke whirled and shoved a finger in that smug mug. "Back the fuck off."

"Save it." Tomas leaned in, putting their faces an inch apart. "I'm the last person you want to fight."

That much was true. Tomas would mop the floor with his ass.

"I've got your back." His friend stood taller, using his height to drive home his point. "Even when it means protecting you from your own mistakes."

"What mistakes are those, Tommy?" He lowered his growl to barely a whisper. "Raping an innocent girl?"

"Next time, it may not be rape. Then what? How will she react when you have to fuck another girl who doesn't like you?"

"That's insulting on so many levels."

"Get the sand out of your vagina." With a scoff, Tomas raked a hand through the flop of his brown hair. "Focus on your target."

"I am."

"Good."

"Fine."

They glared at each other for a hot minute before Luke blew out a breath.

"I'm not doubting you." Tomas clapped him on the shoulder. "To be honest, you're managing this so well I feel useless here."

"You've done plenty."

In twenty-four hours, Tomas had gathered more intel on La Rocha than in all the years their team had been tracking the cartel. He knew the location of the monitoring room, every camera on the property, as well as the names and positions of every man who came and went through the gates.

"Did you find the girl who was in the limo with us yesterday?" Luke asked quietly at his ear.

She hadn't been wearing a hood during the drive. If they found her, Luke might be able to coax crucial information from her.

"Yes." Tomas' face turned white.

"What? What is it?"

"The girl in the basement… The one on the hook—"

"No." His stomach turned, and his chest burned with bile. "That wasn't her. It couldn't be."

"I'm one-hundred-percent certain. But we couldn't have known. Her face was…"

Beaten to a pulp. Unrecognizable. But he should've looked closer. Should've questioned.

"Fuck!" He spun away and slammed his foot into a trashcan, sending it screeching across the floor.

"Pull your shit together." Tomas grabbed Luke's neck and yanked him close, bringing their foreheads together. "Move on. Right now. With me?"

"Yeah." He drew in a breath and released it. Then another. "I'm with you."

Footsteps approached, and Gina poked her head in. "Lover's quarrel?"

Luke shook off the sick feeling in his gut and turned to face her. "Let me see you."

Her fingers tightened on the door jamb, her body out of view. But he glimpsed the edge of a sexy strap on her shoulder.

Stubbornness hardened her expression, her eyes

shifting with indecision. Then she set her jaw, straightened, and stepped into the doorway.

The air rushed from his lungs, parting his lips and caving in his chest.

Tomas gave him a squeeze on the shoulder and left the room. Terrible idea. Luke couldn't be trusted with this intoxicating creature.

She stood before him, dripping temptation and sin in a gown of black silk. Fresh face, damp curls, and spiked heels that seemed to extend the length of her bronzy, athletic legs.

He tried to gather his breath, his voice, but all he could do was stare.

Christ almighty, she was an exquisite, heart-stopping, goddamn knockout. The dress hugged her tiny tits, nipped in at the waist, and flared around her toned thighs. Understated yet elegant. Striking. Just like her.

"This is rather tame for dinner with the cartel." She fingered the hem of the skirt, eyebrows drawn in confusion. "I assumed you'd put me in pleather and chains or something equally distasteful."

"I told Tomas to find a plain dress. I'm sure he tried, but…" The longer he soaked in her immaculate beauty, the tighter his suit pants became. "Nothing could ever look plain on you."

"Why? I mean, why do you want me to look plain? They love their whores to dress—"

"You're not a whore, and while you're with me, you will not dress like one."

Her eyes widened.

He snatched his necktie from the chair and moved to the mirror to wrangle the thing into place. After a few lousy attempts to make a knot, he yanked it free, grunting with frustration.

He was a mechanic, not a pompous high roller. How was he supposed to continue this ruse when he couldn't even knot a tie? Tomas would have to show him again, but not without teasing him excessively for it.

As he turned to call for his friend, a small hand landed on his chest.

"Allow me." Brown eyes stared up at him from the face of a goddess.

He raised his chin, giving her access. "You know how to do this?"

"I thought everyone knew how." She looped the ends, watching him with suspicion. "Especially rich businessmen."

"I never said I was a businessman."

"That's right." With swift movements, she made a tug here, an adjustment there, and stepped back. "You invest in important things. Criminal things that don't require a suit, apparently."

"My offer stands." He rested a knuckle beneath her chin, lifting it. "I'll tell you my secrets."

She turned her head away, rejecting his touch along with his offer.

Probably for the best. What he needed from her was the location of the breach in the wall or whatever she'd seen beyond it. But even that might not be enough to determine the coordinates of this place.

None of it was worth blowing his cover. He'd been asking himself all day if he could tell her the truth. The simple fact that he was on the same side as Vera's sister would make Gina turn against him even more than she already was. She hated Vera worse than she hated him.

He couldn't trust her, no matter how badly he wanted to.

"There's makeup and hair stuff in that bag." He nodded at the supplies Tomas had gathered. "It's yours to use."

"I don't wear makeup."

"Good."

She didn't need it. Even with bruised splotches on her face, the woman had more natural radiance than anyone he'd ever met.

"We leave in ten minutes." He ambled out of the room to find his suit jacket and mentally prepare for the evening.

A moment later, the sound of a hairdryer reached his ears. Surely she wasn't blowing out her curls? He loved the way they bounced and spiraled in every direction. He fantasized about them coiling around his cock as he sank into the back of her throat.

Sick fuck.

In the bedroom, he shrugged on the jacket. After their workout, she'd spent the day in the sitting room watching TV while he and Tomas sent cryptic messages to their team.

They only had access to the laptops and cell phones provided by the cartel. But they'd prepared for that and sent all communication to burner phones and other untraceable devices that were monitored by the Freedom Fighters.

Before departing Colombia, they'd memorized a specific list of song lyrics, each verse with a predetermined meaning, a specific message on the status of the mission. Right now, their friends only needed to know they were safe. They found Vera alive and well, and everything was moving as expected.

Within the next couple of days, he hoped to have a different message to send. If they obtained the location, he would send Tomas away with an excuse and remain here until he returned with a full team and a lot of firepower.

A knock sounded on the outside door. He tilted his head, listening as Tomas answered it.

"Good evening." Vera's sultry voice drifted in, followed by the click of her heels. "Where's your handsome *jefe*?"

Luke strolled into the main room with his hands clasped behind him.

She went still, her gaze sweeping him from head to toe and back again. "Well, don't you look absolutely delicious?"

Bending, she lowered a large brown bag to the floor, and her chest nearly spilled from the tight black leather dress.

At least it's not pleather.

"What did you bring me?" He prowled toward her, causing her breaths to accelerate.

"Ice cream." She smiled and flushed. "When I heard you ordered three boxes of Klondike bars, I had to see it for myself."

"See what exactly?"

"A physically fit, gorgeous specimen of a man consume dozens of ice cream bars. I mean, come on." She cocked a hip, blatantly flirting. "How do you eat junk food and still look like that?"

"It's not for me." He angled his chin to speak behind him. "You can stop spying and come out."

An annoyed huff sounded in the bathroom, and a moment later, Gina strode into the room.

She'd left her hair curly, and those silky, raven

spirals sprung around her arms and chest as she navigated the sky-rise heels with more poise and grace than he would've thought possible.

His eyes tracked her, his insides heating and tightening anew. Tomas was right. She was getting to him, under his skin, in his head, and fucking with his heart rate.

He never had trouble shutting off sexual attraction. But this went beyond shallow interest.

For the first time in his life, he wanted more from a woman than a night of pleasure.

He wanted more with *this* woman.

"Vera," he said. "Give her the ice cream."

He could retrieve the bag himself but wanted to study the interactions between the two women.

As expected, Vera clenched her jaw. Then she slowly lowered and gripped the bag, her eyes locked on him.

"I can't eat that right now." Gina approached his side and curled a hand around his elbow.

An unsolicited touch? This was new, and damn him, but he felt her grip through his entire body.

He slid his other hand over hers, and Vera homed in on the connection, scowling her displeasure from beneath beetled brows.

With his eyes on her, he focused his other senses on Gina, marking the stiffness in her posture, the slight tremble in her fingers, and the overall nervousness wafting from her pores. He suspected it had little to do with Vera and everything to do with Alejandro's dinner.

If she wasn't dreading the next few hours, she should've been.

"Put the dessert in the freezer." He flicked a

finger toward the kitchen, dismissing Vera like a common servant.

She hesitated, her face pinched like she would argue. Then she pushed back her shoulders and obeyed.

Turning toward Gina, he twined his fingers through the soft curls on her shoulder. "Are you ready?"

"Fuck no."

"Good girl. Stay on your toes. But know this..." He bent in and grazed his lips along her cheek. "No one will touch you but me."

"Is that supposed to ease my fragile little rabbit heart?"

"There's nothing fragile about you, and I'm counting on that tonight." He straightened and pivoted toward Vera. "Will you be joining us this evening?"

"Yes, I'm headed there now. We can walk together." She sauntered to the door and looked back at him expectantly.

He emptied his expression, hiding any response she might've sparked in him, which was very little. All criminal behavior aside, there was something off-putting about her.

Tula hadn't shown him any recent photos, but the digital images he'd seen of teenage Vera had alluded to the gorgeous woman she was today. He couldn't find a single flaw in her appearance.

It was her personality. The smarmy way she ogled him, the constant hair-flicking and lip-licking, the overly servile responses to his demands—she rubbed him the wrong way.

Sliding his hand around Gina's, he felt a sudden jerk, her reflex to pull away. Then her fingers curled around his, slick with sweat and nerves.

He was right there with her, anxious to end the evening before it had even begun.

With a nod at Tomas, he followed his friend out the door.

FIFTEEN

"Your hair is the sexiest shade of red I've ever seen." Vera inched closer on the couch, bending over Luke's sprawled leg.

"Mm." His tongue took a stroll through his mouth, casting off the sour taste of her flattery.

She'd openly watched him across the table all through dinner. After dessert, it hadn't taken her long to seek him out in Alejandro's den.

Ten minutes into their private conversation, he knew he would have her beneath him by night's end.

Would…

Definitely should.

He should fuck her into delirium, drug her with orgasms, and win her over once and for all.

With a sharp pang in his gut, his gaze gravitated to the dark-haired beauty sitting alone on the far side of the den. He'd kept Gina in his periphery from the moment they'd arrived but hadn't spoken a word to her.

Her eyes shone with alertness, her posture cautiously still. The purple markings that splotched her face lent a tough edge to her feminine appearance. But it wasn't just the bruises that made her unapproachable. Her entire aura screamed, *Fuck off.*

She and Tomas had that in common.

Luke didn't want her here, for her own protection and his peace of mind. But Alejandro had instructed otherwise, and the reason for that wouldn't make itself known until the entertainment began.

Given the tautness in her shoulders, she knew what was coming.

"She belongs to my brothers." Vera slid a fingernail beneath Luke's jaw, attempting to turn his attention back to her.

"Not this week, she doesn't." He gave Vera his eyes. "Tell me why you hate her."

"Tell me why you want her."

"She's available, and that availability allows me to do anything I desire to her tight little body."

As she mulled that over, her eyes dilated, and the rise and fall of her chest slowly sped up.

"If *I* were available…" She trailed her nail down his neck and hooked it beneath the tie. "What would you do to me?"

"Your answer first." He captured her wrist, holding it immobile. "Why do you hate her?"

"She makes my brothers stupid."

"Explain."

"The whore is a distraction." At the clench of his fingers around her arm, she narrowed her eyes. "That's exactly what I'm talking about. You all turn into cavemen the way they fight over her."

"I'm not fighting."

"Semantics. I can't help but wonder if she can cast spells with her pussy. Every man who falls in doesn't come out with his brain intact."

"That's a pretty powerful trick." He smiled, unable to deny the claim.

"It's sorcery. My brothers need to get the fuck over her."

Jealousy. That was the real answer to his question. Vera was insanely, viciously jealous of the attention that Hector's sons gave to Gina. If he had to guess, Vera was in love with at least one of them.

"You know…" He released her wrist. "The best way to get over a woman is to send her home with another man."

"You mean, send her home with *you?*" Her spine went ramrod straight. "You actually want to keep her?"

"Perhaps." He stretched his arms along the back of the couch, reclining with his legs spread and his gaze locked on Gina. "There's something quite enchanting about her."

There was something, all right. She made him feel restless and possessive, like an alien predator trapped in his skin.

Tomas stood like a sentinel behind her, allowing Luke the opportunity to work on Vera. But his focus was shit. Every brain cell seemed to be on a single track, one that had nothing to do with the operation and everything to do with protecting his fighter.

Marco and Alejandro were the only other two men present tonight. Evidently, Omar didn't attend family dinners, and Miguel was still out of town on *business.* A few scantily dressed cantina girls milled about the room, collecting empty glasses and taking orders.

The brothers didn't give the girls the time of day. Nor did they seem the least bit concerned with him cozying up on the couch with Vera.

No, they only had eyes for Gina.

If either man touched her, the night would be over. He'd made that announcement the moment they arrived for dinner.

"They'll never let you keep her." Vera sniffed. "They'll kill her before they let her leave the property."

"They call her a whore, but you and I both know that's bullshit. Who is she?"

"Don't know." She shrugged.

"Don't know or won't say?"

"Poor pathetic man." Vera shook her head. "You're bewitched by a woman who despises you."

"Is that right? Have you watched us together on the cameras? Sleeping? Working out? *Fucking?*" He wrapped the last word in gravel and heat, marking the raising goosebumps along her arms. "Ask your question again."

Her lashes fluttered, and two pink blooms rose to her cheeks. "If I was available, what would you do?"

"Let's go for a drive tomorrow."

"A drive? How would—?"

"I'll borrow one of Marco's hypercars."

"He would never—"

"I can be very persuasive." *Not that persuasive.* But he had another plan. Angling toward her, he gave her the full force of his gaze—the look that *always* got him laid. "I want to get out of here for a few hours. Just you and me. We'll drive somewhere nearby." He drifted closer, letting her feel his breath against her neck. "Then I'll show you what I can do to you."

"We don't need to leave." She was leaning, floating into him, caught in his snare. "I have my own room."

"So do I." He parted his lips around her earlobe, barely touching, but it was enough to melt her next breath.

"Mine doesn't have cameras."

His rush of victory was instantly strangled by a fist of guilt. He felt Gina's eyes on him before he looked in her direction.

Their gazes clashed and tangled, yelling soundlessly and swinging invisible punches. Disgust steamed from the cracks in her expression, her hands flexing into white-knuckled weapons on her lap.

Did she not like seeing him with another woman? Or just this woman?

If only he could tell her this was a job, that he was serving a greater cause.

But that was the problem. He wasn't here to pursue romantic interests. Gina was collateral. A means to an end. He didn't owe her an explanation. She'd put herself in the cartel's grasp, and not once had he promised to get her out.

This wasn't about her.

Returning his attention to Vera, he embraced the vow he'd made to his team and their newest member, Tula Gomez.

He was holding Tula's sister in his arms. She was alive and growing pliable by the second. Bedding her was the quickest and surest way to get inside her—in her head, in her trust—to locate the key to finishing this mission.

Molding his lips around her earlobe, he suckled it like a clit. The technique lay in the pressure of his tongue, the precise amount of suction and friction, and the low, vibrating hum in the back of his throat. He did it exactly as he'd been taught by Van and Liv, the mechanics executed with an unrivaled skill that was so effective her head fell back, and her breathing careened out of control.

He felt nothing.

Lost to his tongue, she moaned, gasped, and arched her back as her hands grappled for a landing place. Frantic fingers grazed his flaccid cock, and he swatted them away, repulsed and suddenly, irrationally angry.

Old hang-ups rose to the surface. He'd been trained to lick and suck, pleasure and serve. All for a master who had bought him and ultimately died at the hands of his friends. But he'd never felt more like a whore than he did right now.

He didn't want this woman. His *heart* wanted someone else.

Since when did his heart have a say in sex? It was inconceivable, yet the damn thing hammered at him, demanding he change course and find another way.

He slowed the roll of his tongue, hating the taste of her skin, the scent of her hair, and the sounds of her gasps. Easing back, he grimaced inwardly at the sight of her body splayed in lust.

With her legs parted as far as the dress allowed, her hand moved between her thighs, stroking her greedy cunt. Eyes bedazzled, tits heaving over the bodice, she was ripe and ready.

From just a kiss on her ear.

So goddamn easy.

He could fuck her right here. She would fall apart on his cock and beg for more, guaranteeing him access to her room, her bed, and the thoughts in her head. He wouldn't even need to resort to orgasm denial. The way she was looking at him now—eyes hooded and thighs trembling—she would sing her secrets in just a few thrusts.

His move.

Voices murmured around him. Ice clinked in glasses. Soft, classical Spanish music thrummed from hidden speakers, and somewhere deep in his soul, his sense of loyalty won. Loyalty to his friends, his family, and their mission.

He slid a hand along Vera's inner thigh, the skin damp and hot, quivering beneath his touch. Slipping his other hand beneath her head, he threaded his fingers through her hair. Coarse hair. Straight. Too short and all wrong.

Focus, asshole.

He leaned toward her face, and she lifted her mouth, offering, silently pleading for a kiss. He wouldn't fuck her here. Not in front of Gina. She was too much of a distraction. Even now, he felt her gaze pounding blow after blow against his back.

Maybe he imagined it, hoping for it like a desperate douchebag.

Clearing his mind, he focused on the plump, red-stained mouth before him, the lips he could conquer and ruin for all others. He'd made women come from just a kiss, and with her fingers vigorously working between her legs, she was already climbing, panting. A puddle of lust and need in his hands.

A breath away from her mouth, he paused, wrestling with the inescapable urge to steal a glimpse behind him. He had to know if she was watching.

If she cared.

Tilting his neck, his gaze unerringly latched onto her waiting eyes. Punishing eyes, flaring with all the violence and scorn of a damaging storm. Despite the distance, the rage in her barely contained breaths blazed a fire around him, burning him alive.

Alejandro leaned over her chair, speaking in Spanish, trying to get her attention. But her gaze remained on Luke, blistering his skin and manipulating the flow of his blood.

He fucking adored her for that. In the space of one look, she roused the darkest, most twisted parts of his nature, stirring awake uncontrollable desires and stretching them beneath his skin.

His balls tightened. His cock swelled, and he had to reach and make a crude adjustment. The feelings she unleashed in him were unwieldy. Monstrous. Impossible to tame. And the dangerous surge only intensified when Alejandro got in her face.

Luke seethed, fighting the vicious explosion inside him. Pulling his hand from Vera's thigh, he veered his mouth past her lips and spoke in her ear. "I'll give you some time to think about this."

It was the best he could do without completely destroying his progress with her.

Pushing off the couch, he crossed the room in a few unstoppable strides and grabbed Gina's arm. With a hard tug, he had her off the chair and out of Alejandro's reach.

"Is there a problem?" he asked the stocky muscle head.

"No hay problema." The man glared daggers. "But I find it odd this…she…" His English broke up as he searched for the right words.

"She watches you." Marco strolled forward with a hand in his pocket and an arm around a scowling Vera. "Why is this?" He nodded at Gina. "This man-hater stares at you with venom, sure. But something else lurks between her eyes and yours. I want to know what it is."

Marco wasn't an idiot. None of them were. They didn't run the largest, meanest, most dangerous cartel in Mexico on luck. They knew what they were doing, and the biggest part of that was understanding their enemies.

"I give her things." Luke tightened his grip on Gina's arm as she angrily tried to jerk away.

"Things?" Marco rubbed his jaw. "What *things?*"

He met Vera's eyes and shaped the word like a kiss. "Orgasms."

Her gaze dipped to his mouth, darkening with hunger.

Marco threw his head back and laughed. "This, I don't believe. The whore is incapable of pleasure."

"Perhaps you're incapable of giving it."

It was the wrong thing to say.

Sudden, heavy silence clotted the room, the atmosphere too strained to breathe.

Well, fuck. He'd just thrown down the gauntlet, challenging the cartel in their own house.

SIXTEEN

"Prove it." Marco's command fell like thunder through the room. "Show me this power you claim to have over women."

Burn in hell.

Luke had a mind to tell the motherfucker how he felt about being ordered around. But doing so would end with his body rotting in whatever hole the cartel deemed deep enough.

Carefully, he released Gina's arm, and carefully, he clasped his hands behind him. "What did you have in mind?"

"This isn't necessary." Vera tensed.

"Yes, it is." Marco paced beside her. "You watched the monitors this morning. The whore fought him, rather pathetically. She did *not* come."

"Since you were spying on me," Luke said, "you know she tried to sneak out before Alejandro came by. You also know that I brought her to the point of begging and denied her release. It's called *punishment*."

Marco and Vera shared a look. Yeah, they'd seen

the whole damn show. He'd counted on it.

"You seem to know your way around a woman's body, Mr. Smith." Vera touched her throat, toying with a wisp of hair. "But how many of your untamed whores reciprocate?" She flicked a hand at Gina and laughed mockingly. "This one would never put her mouth on you. Not without biting off your dick."

"Exactamente." Marco studied him with a pensive mien.

"You're wrong." Luke knew how to control the human jaw and feed in his cock without so much as a scratch.

Alejandro gulped back a swig of tequila and lowered into a nearby chair. He was the brother to keep an eye on. The quiet ones were usually shifty and underhanded, the ones who stabbed their victims during consoling hugs and hid the bodies under their beds.

"I'm curious." Marco paused behind Vera and slid his hands around her waist. "If given the choice, whose face would you fuck? My beautiful sister's?" He reached up and caressed Vera's cleavage, prompting her lashes to lower submissively. "Or the bruised face of a whore?"

His gorgeous fighter. Hands down. No question.

But this wasn't about his personal preference. The cartel loved their games. Every play had a price, and the wrong move would be costly.

What did Marco want out of this? To see if Luke was too cowardly to tempt Gina's teeth? Or if he was stupid enough to take the risk? Maybe this had nothing to do with him? Could it be a test of Vera's loyalty? Or Gina's?

The biggest mindfuck of all was the way Marco

continued to fondle Vera's tits after referring to her as his sister.

Luke shuddered. "How are you related? Same mother? Father?"

Neither option made sense. Tula Gomez shared a father with Marco and a mother with Vera. Vera's father was unknown.

"It's not important." Marco punctuated the point by palming one of her heavy breasts and kissing her neck. "You have a great mouth, don't you, *mi reina*?" His eyes lifted to Luke while he nibbled. "Hot, wet suction. No one gives head like my sister."

Alejandro watched from the chair, his heated expression vacillating somewhere between disgust and lust.

Incest aside, Luke wanted to leave the lovebirds to it and haul Gina out of there. The fastest way out was the path of least resistance, and Marco wanted a show.

Vera would offer no resistance. Luke only needed to snap his fingers, and she would be on his cock like a fly on honey.

He sensed her staring and reluctantly met her eyes. What he saw there was blatant desire, but beneath the thirst lay a shining gleam of vulnerability.

What were her stakes in this? Yesterday, she wanted nothing to do with him. Now, seeing him with Gina, she was playing right into his plan. But what if her role here wasn't so black and white? Everyone was playing a game. For some, it was a game of survival.

"Make a decision." Marco smoothed a hand down Vera's arm. "Whose throat will you fuck, John Smith?"

"I thought you didn't share your sister."

"I make the rules and change them as I please."

"You know what I think?" Luke rested a hand on Gina's lower back. "You're setting me up."

She went rigid, and he flattened his palm, waiting for her to feel him, to *listen* to his touch.

"Setting you up how?" Marco's face turned to marble.

"You tell me." He was stalling.

Moving his thumb, he stroked her spine. Tapped. Stroked again. Only Tomas stood behind them. Cameras were there, but to anyone monitoring them, it would just look like nervous fidgeting.

Make a move, Gina.

He circled his thumb, applying pressure, releasing, and tapping again. Sending her a message.

This is your choice.

He could force her to suck his cock. Or he could make her watch him face-fuck her archenemy. If she didn't give him some sort of signal, he would choose her. Her mouth. Her body. He wanted her heart.

The sickest part of him hoped it would come to that. He wanted to shove himself so deep in her throat that she felt him in her chest. He wanted to lose control in her body, torment her with passion, and wreck her as thoroughly as she was wrecking him.

On the heels of those thoughts, he felt the mission unraveling in his hands. For the life of him, he couldn't choose Vera. Or his friends. Or their cause. Not this time.

"I'm only interested," Marco said, "in seeing which mouth you intend to take."

Luke increased the rhythm of his thumb, silently urging Gina to make a decision. "Maybe I want both. At the same time."

Both women bristled.

"No-no-no." Marco wagged a finger, grinning. "That is not the deal."

"All right." He dropped his hand from Gina's back. "I made my decision."

At the edge of his vision, she flexed her hands into fists and stared at her feet. His neck stiffened as she drew in a breath. Then she turned toward him and slowly moved her arm.

The moment her fingers touched his cock, his pulse burst into a gallop. Blood rushed to his groin, and he swelled, hardened, *throbbed.*

His desire for her was visceral, but it wasn't just based in lust. The most benign things set it off. Like the sound of her *Rs* rolling on her tongue. The intoxicating taste in the air when she yelled in his face. The way her scent carried through his nose and hit his brain with comforting familiarity.

And the feel of her hand curling around his erection through the suit pants.

Her touch wasn't benign at all. It was detrimental to his job. He wanted this tiny little warrior with a ferocity that felt foreign. Inexplicable. Completely out of his depth.

He gripped her wrist, dislodging her fingers from his leaking dick. But he didn't let go. Shifting around, he spotted a nearby couch and dragged her there.

"You're choosing *her*?" Vera boiled, her voice an octave above horrified.

"Yes."

And she chose me.

Why? He had no idea. Maybe it was to one-up Vera. Or maybe she planned on castrating him with her teeth.

With a furious pivot of heels, Vera spun toward

the door.

"You will watch." Marco caught her hand and pulled her into a chair.

Luke lowered onto the couch and pointed at the cushion beside him. "Kneel."

Gina looked shell-shocked, uncertain, as if she was only now coming to terms with her decision. But she owned it profoundly, exquisitely, with each knee she set on the couch.

"You should know…" Marco reclined in the chair beside Vera, sitting directly across from him. "When she bites your dick, I'm not calling the doctor."

"Noted." He deepened his sprawl on the couch, stretching out his arms and getting comfortable. Then he let his head fall back like a man in control of his universe. "Pull me out."

Her eyes flashed. "Are you going to give me step-by-step instructions?"

"Do I need to?"

"Shut the fuck up, and you'll find out."

That's my girl.

"She's going to bite the dick!" Marco roared with laughter and clapped his hands.

Vera scowled, and across the room, Alejandro remained in his chair with a cantina girl perched on his lap.

Tomas' steady gaze stayed with Luke. A silent, bolstering presence. No one knew him like those among his kindred. United in strife, he and Tomas had been forced to perform sexual acts for an audience during their time in captivity. This was nothing new.

But it felt new as Gina unzipped his fly and wrestled his pants to his thighs. It felt so goddamn significant he was shaking. Not noticeably, but she felt it. With her hand on his bare hip and his cock jutting toward her mouth, she raised her eyes to his.

Compassion. It glowed in her gaze and socked him straight in the chest. This woman… She was the living reality of the only dream he'd ever dared to want for himself, the most precious, indestructible, viciously beautiful creature in and out of any fantasy.

She was an impossible possibility in the flesh.

"You're so fucking beautiful." He wanted to give her so much more than trite words. But not here. With the cartel watching, he could only be John Smith. "Suck me."

"Don't coach me, asshat."

"Don't test my patience, sugar."

A glimmer lit her eyes. Her jaw opened slightly. Slowly, her head lowered, and he watched, breathless and overtaken, as this fierce woman lay her claim on his cock.

Soft lips. Hot tongue. Oh, God. Oh, sweet holy fuck. She sucked him straight to the back of her throat.

His toes curled, and his hips shot off the couch, thrusting, plunging, digging deep, so fucking deep before he caught himself and pulled back.

Down boy.

He wasn't going to last. No way in hell. She felt too fucking unreal.

"Unbelievable." A string of Spanish spewed past Marco's lips.

That was the last distraction Luke registered before everything faded. The room, their audience, nothing existed but the overwhelming stimulation of her mouth moving on his cock.

Her tongue traced veins and ridges. Her hands explored, caressing his abdomen, hips, thighs. By the time she reached his balls, he was panting, grunting, fighting the demands of an impending release.

Christ, he was going to come. Or black out. Fuck, he would die from the pure agony of it.

Not yet. Holy fucking hell, not yet.

He didn't want it to end. But her mouth was relentless, sucking the sensitive glans beneath his head, tasting the endless flow of pre-come, swallowing him deeply, and coaxing him to shoot his load.

With throaty groans, he couldn't stop the movement of his hips. His hands flew to her head, and he crushed her face to his groin, rocking, stabbing, cutting her air. He had to have her, kiss her, fuck her, and touch her everywhere. God almighty, he'd never needed anything or anyone like he needed this. *Her.*

Mindlessly, he fucked her throat, and she took every inch, gripping his thighs, gagging, choking, and sucking even harder.

Let her breathe, idiot.

Releasing her, he reached beneath her dress, between her legs. His fingers found her panties, ripped them away, and sought her wet center. Soaking. So silky and warm. Her arousal gushed over his knuckles, and her pussy sucked his probing touch into its hot, welcoming recesses.

She writhed, gyrating her hips and moaning around his cock. He thrust a finger into her again, added two, three, rimming her opening and massaging the sensitive muscle inside. She cried out, grinding against his hand, her breaths faltering, eyes squeezing shut as she rode the pleasure like a hellion.

Dragging her tongue along his length, she flicked and teased without mercy. His head spun at the unpredictable rhythm, his body hard, every muscle flexed, his entire world caught in her spell.

Over and over, she sucked the tip into the back of her throat, closing her lips around him, sealing him in delicious warmth. It took every ounce of concentration to remember the fingers he still held inside her. What a distracting little succubus.

Two could play at this game.

He moved his hand between her legs, seeking her clit with his thumb, rolling it, adding pressure until she cried out and pulled her mouth off his cock.

"Oh, you're in trouble now." She flashed her teeth, gripped his hip and thigh, and sucked him hard and deep into her throat.

His vision blurred. The world spun, and he shut his eyes against the onslaught.

"Jesus. Goddamn. Fuck, fuck, fuck!" He flung out his free hand and gripped the back of the couch, desperately anchoring himself in some semblance of control.

She was ready to come, dripping all over his fingers. If he didn't send her over now, she would win. She'd milk him for all he was worth before he had a chance to have her here, on the couch, wild and rabid and absolute.

Circling his thumb around her clit, he fingered her sheath with hard strokes, harder, until he thought she would tumble into his lap. Trembling on the cusp of ecstasy, she fought it valiantly. And lost.

The hot clasp of her body squeezed, constricting his fingers through violent spasms. She tore her mouth off his dick and screamed, her head tilting back and mouth wide in stunned oblivion.

Her release shuddered through her, and her hoarse cries dissolved into moans. As she gulped for air, he yanked a condom from his pocket and rolled it on.

Glazed eyes found his, satisfied but not sated. His heart pounded. The tumultuous sounds of their breaths caught fire, and they launched at the same time.

Chests colliding, arms grappling, they came together in a tangle of limbs and sexual heat. There was no pause. No hesitation. Her legs wrapped around his hips. Their lips met in a frenzy, and their bodies took over.

She rose above him. He adjusted the angle, and *Ahhh, fuuuuck!* He sank into her hot, drenching glory. Tight and swollen, she urged him deeper, wriggling, slamming down her hips, and hardening him beyond human endurance.

Sweaty and breathless, he started moving, thrusting, and fucking her mouth with his tongue. She grabbed his necktie, lifted along his length, and lowered, dipping him inside her oh-so-slowly.

He couldn't take it. With his hands on her waist, he took the reins. Then he took her fully, setting the tempo, widening her thighs, and pumping into heaven, his body a piston of pent-up urgency and hunger.

She clawed at his neck, his shoulders, holding onto him as if wrestling for every inch of closeness. Their lips smashed and bruised, teeth clashing, tongues hitting and sliding, too frantic and reckless to execute a real kiss.

But it was more than real. It was what every kiss should be. Untrained. Unhinged. Just pure raw fire.

He drove his hips harder, hitting the spot inside her that would send her into rapture. She clenched her thighs around him, pulling herself closer, moaning helpless sounds of want.

Yeah, she was close, her gasps becoming

shallower, her cunt growing slicker. He fucked her steadily, completely, knowing no man—not even the two in the room—had ever possessed her the way he owned her now. In this, she was his alone.

At the edge of his awareness, he heard arguing. A glass crashed. A door slammed, taking Vera's angry voice with it.

Reality crept in.

He felt things for this woman, feelings too new to analyze. Maybe he was crazy, but it wasn't one-sided. She felt something, too.

By no means could the cartel get a whiff of it. Not until he had a plan. As much as Luke wanted to carry Gina out in tender embrace, he couldn't. The cartel needed to believe what they witnessed tonight was just a moment. Just sex. Nothing more. And he needed her cooperation to pull it off.

She slipped her hands along his arms, holding tight as he trailed his lips across her cheek, into her hair, peppering slow feverish kisses.

At her ear, he tasted her sweet skin and whispered, "You hate me. The instant you come, show them *exactly* how much. Then leave. Go to my room. Tomas will make sure you arrive safely."

She leaned back and searched his eyes. Their hips came together, grinding in a fusion of conflict and intimacy. He watched her closely, looking for a sign that she understood.

But she was already lost, drowning in the grip of pleasure. *Jesus fuck,* she was coming, straining against his hold, her body shaking, her voice whispering in Spanish over and over.

The splendor of her surrender was his undoing. He increased his strokes, the intensity beyond anything he'd ever experienced as he clutched her neck and roared, releasing himself in hard, violent jets. He came and came on the verge of passing out.

Until a hand crashed across his face, shooting blinding pain through his jaw.

He blinked, panting, and she punched him again.

"I hate you." She shoved off his cock, jumped from his lap, and straightened her dress in a raging fit. "What do you think just happened? That I wanted it? Fuck no! That was coercion. Rape. You sick, unholy bastard!"

"That's what they all say." He tossed her a grin and rubbed his jaw. "Try not to come so hard next time."

A livid flush spread up her neck. She flexed her hands, pivoted, and raced out of the room.

He didn't have to signal Tomas. His friend was already moving, hot on her heels.

She did it. Exactly what he'd told her, she pulled it off. Pride filled his chest. Whether she liked it or not, she was on his team now.

She was *his.*

Vera, Alejandro, and all the girls had vacated the room, leaving him alone with the cartel capo.

Nervousness set in, but he didn't let it show.

"Women." With a sigh, he removed the condom and stashed it, along with her discarded panties, in his pocket. Then he straightened his clothes and zipped up.

"You can't live with them, so just fuck them and kill them. *Si?*" With a chuckle, Marco stood and set a drink in Luke's hand. "Congratulations, my friend. Now tell me how you did it."

SEVENTEEN

She sat in John's bathtub, hugging her knees to her chest as unanswered questions pounded in her head.

When the water cooled, she let it out and refilled it again. With each passing minute, her hands turned pruney, her heart numb.

After leaving Alejandro's quarters an hour ago, she'd headed straight here. Not because John had commanded it. But because she needed to talk to him, to find out what was real and what was an act.

He'd put his hands and mouth all over that hateful bitch. Was he with her now? Kissing her? Thrusting between her legs?

Gah! She yanked at her hair. Why did she care who he was with?

More importantly, why had she willingly swallowed his cock and fucked his damn brains out? What made him so different than the others?

I give her things.

Orgasms.

Yeah, he doled those out like party favors.

If it was only that, she could work with it. She'd already accepted her attraction and given into the lust. How could she not? The sex was…

Her thighs squeezed together. Her nipples hardened, and a fluttery sensation lit up her belly.

Yeah, he knew how to fuck. And kiss. And touch all the right places. He was turning her into an addict.

Point for him.

It would be no hardship to spend the rest of the week in bed with him. As dangerous as he was, he'd given her more blissful moments in twenty-four hours than she'd experienced in the past three years.

But this wasn't just sex. There was a rare, deep-reaching, unstoppable force blooming between them. A magnetism that jacked up her blood pressure and consumed her mind. A supernatural connection that she'd never shared with any other person.

She desperately wanted to believe in that connection, trust it, and fight for it. Damn her, but she felt outrageously possessive of it. The thought of another woman touching him sent her into a homicidal rage.

That was why she'd gone down on him after dinner. Watching anyone else do it would've gutted her. Which was maddening. She didn't even know him.

What was his name? Where did he grow up? How did he earn a living? What were his crimes?

What did he want with her?

She secretly harbored wishes about him. Recklessly whimsical hopes. The kind that only came true in fairy tales. Because there were no white knights in *Casa de La Rocha.* He couldn't rescue her. Not even if he tried.

Sinking into the water, she let her face float just

above the surface and stared at the hole in the ceiling.

This morning, he'd said La Rocha hadn't replaced the camera because he made them believe he was discussing confidential business details in here with Tomas and threatened to take down the cartel if they invaded his privacy.

He would be gone soon anyway. After they squeezed all the money they could get out of him, he would leave.

What would happen to her? Would they keep her alive? Continue to use her as bait? Or put her in another fight, one she didn't have a chance at winning?

She needed to get out of this bathtub.

Rising to her knees, her gaze landed on the doorway, and her breath abandoned her.

John stood on the threshold, his tie hanging loose around his neck. Red hair tousled from raking fingers, suit jacket dangling from a finger, he looked tired and pensive.

She rested her hands on the edge of the tub, holding his gaze. With his chin dipped downward, he watched her from beneath dark brows. Just watching. Breathing. After too many inhales and exhales, he stepped in and shut the door.

"My parents were drug addicts. When they were sober, they beat me. When they weren't…" He toed off his shoes and removed the tie. "They forgot they had bills and…a child."

She closed her eyes, instantly regretting the mean things she'd said about his father leaving bruises. "I'm sorry."

"Don't be. You were right about that." He unbuttoned his shirt and dropped it. "But you were wrong about me bullying kids in school." His lips quirked. "I only bully women who know how to bully right back."

A smile tickled her lips and faded quickly. "What happened? With your parents?"

"Dead. Overdosed." He ambled to the tub and stripped the rest of his clothes. "I ran away before that happened. Finished my last year of high school while living on the streets."

"How did you do it?" She touched her chin to her shoulder, meeting his eyes. "I mean, you're clearly successful and wealthy. How?"

"A single, horrifying, unfortunate event." He stepped in, sliding into the water behind her.

She stared at his legs, so hard and powerful as they wedged in around her, dwarfing her body. "An unfortunate event led to…a fortune?"

"A fortune in things that matter." His arms glided around her waist, pulling her back to his chest. "I'll tell you about it some other time."

"You're leaving in a few days."

"Not without you."

She melted. Every muscle, sinew, and bone dissolved before she could stifle the reaction. No matter what he promised, she couldn't leave. Was he an idiot? Or maybe he thought she was.

Pushing herself upright, she refused to let any man, including this one, make her feel weak and manipulated.

He held onto her hips, and she yanked at his hands. When he finally released her, she spun away, splashing water over the edge.

The tub wasn't big enough for the two of them, but she wasn't leaving it until she had answers.

"Where have you been for the past hour?" She

inched back against the opposite end, facing him.

"With Marco. Instructing him on how to bring a woman to orgasm."

"What?" Her jaw dropped. "Why?"

"He wanted to know my technique." He pulled her feet onto his lap beneath the water and stroked a hand along her ankle. "Giving him a few pointers seemed less painful than pissing him off."

"Did you…?" Her face flamed. She really didn't want to ask this, but she needed to know. "Did you demonstrate on someone?"

"No." His voice lacked insistence or any emotion. He didn't seem to care if she believed him or not.

"Marco doesn't do things without causing discomfort or pain to someone else. He was probably fucking with you."

"I don't disagree."

"And you associate with him. What does that say about you?" She yanked her legs away from his touch.

"Why are we discussing him when there's something else weighing heavier on your mind? You're not one to hold back, Gina. Let's hear it."

"All right. Why am I here when you were all over *her* tonight?"

"If I wanted Vera in my bed, she would be here right now." He studied her carefully, his arms draped over the back of the tub, his presence overbearing, unnervingly still. After a long, watchful moment, he released a breath. "I need something from her."

"The location of the compound." Her pulse increased. "You think you can fuck it out of her."

"I know I can."

Irrational pain swelled behind her breastbone and seeped into her voice. "If she gives it to you, what happens next?"

"You're jealous." He lunged forward and touched a finger to her mouth, silencing her objection. "I'm giving you the truth, even when it hurts." His hand trailed along her jaw, flaming her skin. "I'm jealous, too. I feel this constant, unreasonable impulse to piss a circle around you, to throat punch anyone who looks at you, including Tomas…" He laughed and dragged a hand down his face. "That's definitely a first for me."

She liked the sound of that. Too much. Sucking in a tight breath, she turned her head away. "Answer my question."

"I've answered enough for now. Trust goes both ways. I give a little. You give a little. Eventually, we meet in the middle." He glanced at the closed door and leaned in, bracing his elbows on bent knees. "I know that confiding in me means risking not just your life but your mother's life, as well. I'll help you the best that I can, but you have to help *me*."

He extended a hand to her, and she stared at it with a lump in her throat.

From what she'd surmised, his role as a slave buyer was a cover-up for something far more insidious. She knew crucial things about the organization and the compound that could help him, whether he was gathering intel or planning a hit.

But if he killed Marco and started a war, what would happen to her and the only person she cared about?

What would happen if he left and she never saw him again?

She could die either way. But if she helped him… If she could bring herself to trust him, he might be her only way out.

Reaching out a hand, she clasped his strong fingers. Their gazes held as he pulled her toward his chest. She slid over his hard physique, setting a palm on his flat hipbone, corrugated abs, sculpted pecs, until she found a gripping spot in the warm juncture between his neck and shoulder.

With her lower body floating in the cradle of his thighs, she rested on his chest and pressed her cheek against the whiskered hardness of his.

"Three years ago," she whispered, "I made the worst decision of my life."

EIGHTEEN

She reached back through time, aching so brutally with loss she couldn't breathe. With her mouth against John's cheek and his heat beneath her body, she welcomed his stillness, the intensity in which he waited and *listened.* His attentiveness bolstered her.

"There are things I don't recall, like how I arrived here or the first few days I spent in the basement." Her whisper went as taut as the coils knotting in her belly. "But I remember the day Miguel La Rocha walked into the *taqueria* where I worked and offered me the world."

He tensed beneath her. "Did you know who he was?"

"No idea. He gave me a fake name and a warm, irresistible smile. He's the most charming of the brothers. The best looking. He wears expensive suits and has this captivating, alluring demeanor about him, you know? Yeah, of course, you know. You're very much like him in that way."

"I've never met him, but I assure you, I'm nothing like him."

"Well, he knows how to charm the pants off a woman." With a sigh, she set her chin on his shoulder and closed her eyes. "By the time he asked me to dinner, I was ready to run off with him."

His jaw hardened against her face. When she sensed the judgment forming on his lips, she cut him off.

"Imagine living in a country ridden with cartel wars and poverty. Jobs are hard to come by. There's never enough food or medicine. Education is a pipe dream. As a woman, my value is insignificant at best. I was beaten by boyfriends. Abused by employers. My father fled before I was even born. I only had to look at my mother and her mother before her to understand that the life I was born into was the only one I would get. No matter how hard I worked. No matter how many beatings I endured. My existence would continue another forty years with no improvement. And that would be it."

"Then one day," he said, running a gentle hand along her back, "a dashing, wealthy man with a silver tongue walked into your life."

"Yeah. He singled me out from all the other girls, made me feel special, and treated me to the most expensive dinner I've ever had. He dated me for *weeks.* The lying, cold-blooded son of a bitch made me believe he was falling in love with me. Little did I know, his father had sent him after me. I didn't even suspect that he had cartel affiliations. That's why Miguel is so good at his job. Ever elusive and sophisticated, he lures girls in and wins their trust."

"Why were you targeted by his father?"

Her gaze darted through the bathroom as a crawling sensation prickled her scalp. Could she trust his word that there were no devices in here? What if the cartel was listening right now? She hadn't over-shared yet, but answering his question would end as gruesomely as the girl on the meat hook.

Sensing her tension, he glided his fingers through her hair. "Give me what you can for now."

She breathed in slowly, relishing the clean, masculine scent of his neck. "Miguel offered to help me escape to the United States, promising I would become a free, legal citizen and make more than enough money to pay off my debts. That was the pivotal, most important thing he could've offered me. I have years of debt, accrued through desperate means." Her chest squeezed. "I owe a lot of money to some shady collectors for reasons I'm not ready to talk about."

"Don't be embarrassed."

"I'm not." Sudden anger spiked through her, and she leaned back, causing water to lap around their chests. "I have regrets, but not about that. My debts were necessary. I did what I had to do and will never ever feel ashamed about it."

"Good girl." His touch on her cheek wasn't pitying or shaming. It was supportive. "The water's cooling."

He opened the drain and stood, taking her with him. Out of the tub, he led her to the settee, where he dried them both off and snagged two robes. Once they were wrapped in terrycloth, he lowered onto the seat beside her.

She hadn't finished her story, but he didn't press. He simply sat beside her, quiet and patient.

How much could she tell him? Not all of it. But if she gave him some insight into how the cartel trafficked girls, it might help him stop the operation. *If* that was his aim. She hoped.

It was more hope than she'd had in years, and that scared the shit out of her.

"Miguel offered me an installment plan." She hugged her waist, hating how naive she'd been. "All I had to do was sign a contract that promised to pay back the money I borrowed by working for his connections at a restaurant or factory. The going rate was thirty-thousand dollars. It sounded too good to be true. But hey, everyone gets rich in America, right? So I signed, ignoring the clause that said my family would be responsible for my debt if I couldn't pay."

"You didn't know what would happen."

"I should've known. There were so many warning signs. I ignored them all and paid for phony identification documents, adding to the debt I was already trying not to freak out about. Then I let him put me into a car with a strange man, who drove me to a strange city in California."

"What did you tell your family?"

"I didn't. I left Mexico thinking I would call once I was settled." Her chest constricted against the stabbing guilt. "I was taken to a place that was neither a restaurant nor a factory. There, in a filthy backroom packed with dozens of girls just like me, I was handed off to Miguel's *connection*, who told me I would be a prostitute. I would be charged room and board while I paid off the thirty-thousand dollars I owed them. Just like that, I went from being in debt to being in more trouble than I could've ever imagined."

He gripped her hand on her lap and bowed his head. At the edge of her vision, she watched his jaw grind and flex.

"I protested." She sat taller, recalling the painful

memories. "God, I fought. I don't even know how many times I tried to cut and run. I even enlisted the other girls to rally with me. But every effort I made ended in agony. He beat me, starved me, kept me awake for days on end until I was too disoriented and weak to lift my head. That's when I caught a glimpse of my future."

"You knew you'd been trafficked."

"I was starting to suspect that. I mean, I understood all along that what they were doing wasn't legal, but part of me still believed I was in control of my situation. I remember lying in that backroom—eyes swollen shut, ribs cracked, my stomach twisted with hunger—and that's when I finally came to terms with how grim my predicament was. I'd unknowingly sold myself to La Rocha Cartel and became an illegal immigrant, without a cent to my name. I didn't know where I was, had no access to a phone, and no options because no one allowed me to go anywhere alone."

He scooped her into his arms and held her tight across his lap. It was a big lap, warm and protective, reinforced by rock-hard thighs and a sense of security that shouldn't have made sense.

After Miguel, she'd sworn she would never be fooled by a man again. But her relationship with Miguel had never been *this*. He'd bought her expensive food, wooed her with pretty words, and fucked her without fireworks. Not even a spark.

He'd never held her, never embraced her without throwing her against the closest surface and rutting atop her.

Angling her head, she sought John's vibrant gaze. Sweet Lord, he was so close, regarding her as if nothing else existed in the world. She nuzzled so deeply against his chest she felt the rhythm of his heart in her soul, dancing with hers. Endlessly, he held her, his mouth nearly upon her lips, chasing her breaths with unspoken questions.

"I was out of options," she whispered. "What was I supposed to do?"

"You survive by doing what you're told." Green eyes glared down at her.

"Fuck that." She glared right back. "I will *always* fight. And I did, earning more punishments. More beatings. More days without food. But you know what? Every infraction ensured that he couldn't whore me out. Since I refused to be a prostitute, I was completely useless to him. So Miguel was called in. He drugged me, and a week later, I woke in the basement of *Casa de La Rocha,* only to become his personal whore. Then he gave me to his brothers."

He tucked her head beneath his jaw and caressed her hair. His fingers swam with strong, powerful strokes, every touch made to comfort a woman as if he'd been born and bred to it.

For long minutes, he just cradled her, arms locked around her back, controlling her breaths with the confident, steady rhythm of his chest. She shouldn't want him like this or find pleasure in his affection or feel so full of him.

Sleek with muscle beneath the terrycloth, his thighs shored up hers, supporting her like the arm tight around her back. An arm roped with cords of strength. The scent of raw masculinity, soft copper hair, flawlessly fair complexion, speckles of random freckles… How could she not admire his physical attributes?

The carved cut of his features lent him a rugged look, whether he wore a suit, gym shorts, or nothing at all. A unique mix of polish and roguishness, he was insanely gorgeous by any measure.

Oh, how she wanted to spend some time with his sinful mouth. Without an audience. With no agendas. She wanted to kiss him for no other reason than to savor his taste and delight in the tingles he delivered.

Dammit, get a grip.

She wiped a hand across her lips, but it didn't erase the hot, virile feel of him, the potency of his skin, the answering electricity in her blood. Every drip of remembered pleasure drew her deeper into his trap.

It was no use. He was too tempting, and she was too interested. So she let herself indulge, just for a moment.

Running a palm up his chest over the robe, she slid her fingers between the lapels to brush the sparse hair on his pecs. His breaths grew shallow, but he let her explore, bending down to kiss her head. Then he leaned back and watched.

Her hand roved lower, to his abdomen, to his waist, as lean and strong as a pillar, chiseled with sexy ridges and indentations. She spread open the robe to roam along the thin trail of hair, defined hipbones, and the proud, semi-hard length of his response to her touch.

"What's your real name?" he murmured.

She closed her eyes and pulled her hand away. "I can't."

"Hector La Rocha knew it. That's why he sent Miguel to take you." His American accent turned growly. "Why is the secrecy of your name so important?"

"What's your real name?" She moved to crawl off his lap.

He caught her waist and wrenched her back, wrapping her legs around his hips to straddle him.

"I'll give you mine…" He gripped her jaw and brushed his lips against hers. "When you give me yours."

"I want to tell you." Her heart hammered as she cupped his powerful jaw, his beautiful, sculpted face. "I'm scared. I'm…" She cast her gaze around the room, knowing if she gave him this information, it wouldn't happen here. "Hector was murdered in prison and—"

A strange, unguarded look swept across his features, there and gone too quickly to analyze. "What does his murder have to do with you?"

"His sons are looking for his killer. They believe the assassin belongs to a cartel in Colombia. Rest…ari…something."

"Restrepo," he whispered, his face paling. "The Restrepo Cartel."

"Oh, my God." She scrambled off his lap. "You're one of them? You work for a rival cartel?"

"No, I work for myself. Tell me what you know." He rose and grabbed her robe. "This is fucking important."

Adrenaline poured through her veins, and she spun, stripping free from the terrycloth in his grip and racing toward the door, naked.

"This is the first time I've heard any mention of Hector's death since I've been here." He prowled after her, all long legs and stony determination. "You're going to tell me everything."

"I swear I don't know anything about Hector."

He caught her at the door, slamming his hand against it and preventing it from opening. "How does his death involve you?"

"They're using me as bait."

"For Hector's killer?"

"Yes."

"Why?"

"I. Don't. Know." She yanked on the door handle, frantic to get on the other side, where there were cameras, where he wouldn't interrogate her and force her to talk. "Let me out."

"Do you know who killed Hector La Rocha?"

"No one knows. It could've been an inside job by one of the inmates. Probably an attack by the González cartel or one of the enemy gangs in the prison. I grew up in that city, and everyone wanted him dead."

He zoomed in on that last part like a laser beam. "You grew up in Ciudad Hueca?"

Her stomach dropped. She'd said too much. "It's a big city. Lots of people have lived there."

"More specifically, you and Vera Gomez." He bent at the waist, putting his face in hers. "What is your relationship with her?"

Heavy iron seemed to clog her ears, her blood running rabidly through her system, chilling her insides with fear. A cold sweat formed on her skin. Her lungs struggled for air as a vicious quiver overtook her body. She shook so violently she rattled the door at her back.

"I can't…" She gulped for breath, unable to maintain a whisper. "Please, you don't know what you're asking."

The steely intimidation in his expression faded, replaced with a storm of turmoil and something else.

"It's okay." He hooked his arm around her and pulled her against him, pressing his lips to her head. "Shh. Easy. Breathe with me."

She couldn't stop trembling, wrestling with the

need to tell him everything. It was right there, all of it, twisting up her tongue. But she fought it. She had to. It wasn't just her life she was risking.

Maybe tomorrow. With a clear head and full night's sleep, maybe she could find a way to tell him who she was.

He read the decision in her eyes and released a slow breath. "Go to bed. I'll be in later."

The instant he opened the door, she fled to his room like a coward.

NINETEEN

An hour later, she rolled to her side in a bed of Klondike wrappers and groaned. She shouldn't have eaten that last ice cream bar. Or the six bars before it. But for a while, the delicious chocolate had kept her mind off the man making plans in the other room.

When he'd followed her out of the bathroom, he'd made a beeline to Tomas. After some very cozy whispering, they turned their attentions to their phones, their fingers furiously tapping out messages to whomever they were working with.

The Restrepo Cartel?

John didn't look like a Colombian cartel gangster, and he'd denied the accusation that he worked *for* them. But he knew the cartel. The mere mention of them had put him on immediate guard. In a blink, he'd gone from patient and affectionate to demanding and all business.

For a few minutes, she'd spied on him and Tomas from the bedroom, unable to hear their hushed conversation. When her snooping got the best of her, she stormed in and tried to join the discussion. The fuckers clammed up, moved to the bathroom, and locked the damn door.

They didn't trust her, and why should they? If she knew their plan, she could run straight to Marco with it.

What she'd witnessed the night she met them made sense now. The bromance hug they'd shared in the bathroom, the camera removed from the ceiling, the feeling that they weren't who they claimed to be… Whatever reason they were here, they were in it together, and it was all related to Hector's killer.

If they'd come to finish off Hector's sons, she sure as hell wouldn't stand in their way. At the same time, she didn't want to become an unintended casualty of war. Maybe John wouldn't throw her on a grenade to save his mission. But if forced to choose between his goal and hers, he wouldn't pick her. He didn't even know her.

She couldn't trust him. Not with her life or that of the one person she'd spent three years protecting.

With a heavy heart, she cleaned up the ice cream wrappers and waited for him to come out.

And waited.

And waited.

Eventually, she fell into a restless sleep.

The next morning, she opened her eyes to an empty room. The mattress lay untouched beside her. He never came to bed?

Her heart plunged to her stomach.

You're leaving in a few days.

Not without you.

His luggage was still here, his clothes draped over the chair.

"John?" She leaned up on an elbow, listening.

Silence.

Sighing, she threw back the soft coverlet, warm and bright with the kiss of sunshine, and went to investigate.

A full breakfast greeted her in the main room, eggs and high-fat pork still steaming beneath the dome covers. She forced herself to eat, needing the calories, but her nerves prevented her from tasting it.

Where was he? Was he already executing some reckless plan against La Rocha? Why hadn't he woken her? What if he got himself killed?

Cold dread slithered up her spine.

"You're deranged and paranoid," she whispered under her breath. "He's just working out."

She showered and got ready for the day. By mid-morning, he hadn't returned.

She went for a walk.

Keeping to the low-traffic areas, she followed winding paths through the gardens and ventured away from the main buildings.

All was quiet here in the morning, opening her ears to the sounds of chirping birds and busy bees. If she closed her eyes, she could almost imagine she was in a peaceful place, surrounded by nature and harmony. And freedom.

She'd forgotten what freedom felt like. To exist without someone watching. To run without someone chasing. To make decisions without painful corrections lashed upon her body.

It had been so long she didn't know how to wish for such an ideal.

Lost in thought, she wandered until her feet carried her to the garage on the far side of the property. The door creaked as she opened it, the aroma of metal and engine oil tickling her nose. A comforting scent. Her sanctuary.

A camera hung high in the corner, tracking her movements until she veered around a large shelving unit and climbed into the back of an old Dodge Dart. The rusted thing might've been a rock-star muscle car in the sixties, but the only purpose it served now was a place to hide beyond the reach of the camera.

The paint was so worn and dusty only a few bits of blue shone through. The long backseat, however, made a comfy bed. She crawled in and curled up on the blanket she'd placed here forever ago.

From beneath the seat, she removed a small journal and flipped through the pages, reading her handwriting, savoring the words. Memory after memory filled her vision. Only good memories. The best ones from her childhood. She'd written them all down when she first arrived and added to them over the years. On her worst days, she read them, relived them, and rediscovered her smile.

But she hadn't come today to recharge with happy thoughts. She was here to think, weigh her options, and make a decision.

The last time she trusted a man, she got schooled. Miguel had promised her a dream and delivered a nightmare.

John had made no such promises, save for one.

He'd said he wouldn't leave without her.

It was a promise he couldn't keep. La Rocha would never let her go. Not for any sum of money. Not even at gunpoint. Well, maybe if it was a lot of guns. Like a whole army.

If John was connected to the Colombian cartel, he had the means to gather a militia. But he didn't know *where* to send them.

It all came down to the location of the compound.

She couldn't help him with that, but she could tell him what she saw on the other side of the wall. Maybe it was nothing.

What if it was everything?

The thought slingshot her heart into the garage rafters. She jackknifed up, shoving the journal beneath the seat on her way out of the car.

She wouldn't be naive, but being stubborn was just as bad. She could help him figure out the location without giving him her name. If his plan went south, or worse, if he betrayed her, her family would still have anonymity.

Decision made, she turned toward the door. But before she stepped into view of it, it creaked open.

She froze, her senses amplified as a single set of footsteps crunched across the dirt floor.

Heart thudding in her ears, she rounded the shelving unit and came face to face with Miguel La Rocha.

"Ven aquí, mi pequeño zorro." He smoothed a hand down his tie, his Spanish a silken caress. "Are you hiding from me?"

"No. But had I known you were back, then yes, you bet your ugly ass I would've hidden somewhere you couldn't find me." She sidestepped, veering toward the door.

"Careful." Graceful and deadly, he moved with her, blocking her escape. "I'm not in the mood today."

"You're never in the mood, *pachuco*."

His lip curled with distaste. "Watch your mouth, or I'll find a better use for it."

A sting of fear knifed through her. "You didn't

come here for a blowjob."

He would never force her to do that particular act. He knew better. But there were worse ways to hurt her.

"No." He stalked toward her, dressed in a black suit, shiny shoes, and hair slicked back like he'd just stepped out of a salon. *"Quiero tu coño."*

"Nope. No sex." She eyed the door with longing as her insides tumbled through shards of ice. "Marco sold me to one of the guests."

"Ah, *si.* He *loaned* you to John Smith. You still belong to us."

She flexed her hands. If she didn't make a break for it, Miguel would rape her. His intent smoldered in his eyes and filled her stomach with lead.

"Mr. Smith doesn't share." She inched toward the exit, her pulse careening into the red. "I don't want to get in the middle of that, so I'll just go find him and let you—"

"I saw him." His mouth spread into a grin—the one she despised, for it promised a world of hurt. "I didn't get an opportunity to talk to him. Not with his tongue shoved down my sister's throat and his hands up her dress. They could hardly remain upright as they stumbled and groped like animals into her room."

No.

No, John wouldn't do that.

Except he'd told her that was precisely what he would do.

Agony like nothing she'd ever felt seared through her chest and wrenched a horrible sound from her throat. She rubbed a hand over her mouth, trying to conceal the shameful reaction. She didn't have feelings for that man. She couldn't. She fucking *wouldn't.*

But her damn heart took a detour around logic and self-preservation and attacked her with everything it had. She couldn't breathe against the onslaught. It hurt too badly—the pounding, caving, internal pressure. She gripped her throat, her chest, and raced for the door.

"What's wrong?" Miguel was on her in a flash, an arm locked around her waist and a fist in her hair. Then he slammed her back against the wall. "You like this John Smith?"

He drew a featherlight finger down her temple, tracing the creases of her fractured expression, his gaze sharp and observant, seeing too much.

"You know how I feel about your sister." She gnashed her teeth, bucking uselessly in his grip. "You also know how competitive I am with her. If she's moving in on my turf, I'm going to fucking defend it!"

"Oh, sí, lo sé." He flipped his hand over, brushing the backs of his fingers across her cheek, making her shudder. "You were possessive of me once."

"Until I saw the size of your dick." She held up her pinkie finger and wriggled it. *Delusional pervert.*

His expression clouded over, and the cords of his neck strained beneath his collar. She knew the strike was coming before he reared back his hand.

Hard knuckles collided with her jaw, and she deliberately fell to the dirt floor. Pain ricocheted through her face, bringing tears to her eyes. But it was better than the alternative.

Miguel abused her either through sex or violence. Never both at the same time. She'd baited him and taken the hit because she couldn't endure his rutting. Not after John.

John, who was currently fucking that bitch.

Her insides bled venom, and her vision tunneled in blinding rage. She had to go to him. She needed to see for herself.

Not once had she thought he would choose her over his mission. But had every touch, every look, every intimate whisper they'd shared been just a task for him? A means to gather information? Had he felt even a fraction of the beautiful chaos she felt when they were together?

Or was she just a stupid girl who continued to let herself be fooled by assholes?

"Are you finished?" She tipped her head up at Asshole *Numero Uno.* "Or do you want to hit me a few more times while I'm down?"

He scoffed and shook out his hand. "Not worth my time."

That much was true. He could beat or fuck anyone he wanted. He didn't care about her or his sister or any other woman in this god-forbidden place. He was motivated by money, plain and simple.

As he glowered down at her, she thought he might kick her for good measure. But instead, he adjusted his tie, brushed off his suit, and strolled out the door.

It shut behind him, and she let out a stream of shaky air. Then she ran back to the old car, where she kept a few medical supplies just for these encounters and cleaned the blood from her face.

Everything hurt. Not from the punch of Miguel's hand, but from his words. From the images they evoked.

John with another woman.

She wanted his kisses to herself. She wanted his affection, his honesty, his story, good or bad. She wanted a shot with him because he was the first man in her life that made her feel significant.

She didn't need anyone to validate her worth, but it was really something to spend time with someone who treated her like an equal.

He'd bought her, and not once had he made her feel like a whore.

Maybe he was just really good at deception.

Stowing the medical supplies, she made her way to the estate. She knew where to find him, her steady strides carrying her to a part of the compound she'd avoided since arriving.

When she reached the breezeway to those lavish private quarters, she stopped. Glared at the door. And waited.

If John was in there, he wasn't having goddamn tea. If he wasn't in there, he was resourceful enough to find her.

Minutes passed. Hours. Years. She waited long enough to lower to the floor and take the weight off her feet. Then she waited some more.

At last, the door handle jiggled. The door opened, and she rose, standing twenty paces away with a vise around her chest.

The first thing she saw was red hair. He stepped into the breezeway, and her heart shattered upon the floor.

Head down, tie loose around his neck, the collar crooked and unbuttoned, he tucked in his shirttails and closed the door behind him.

Paralyzed, she couldn't move. No matter how badly her legs burned to run, no matter how hot the pain stabbed behind her eyes, she ached to see the look on his face.

He sensed her instantly, his head snapping up and gaze glowing, stark and bright. "Gina."

"That's not my name." She directed her focus at the door behind him, refusing to cry. "Did you get what you came for?"

His jaw set, and his presence grew dark. Menacing. "Go to my room. I'll be there in a moment."

He might as well have hit her, in her stomach, her chest, her face.

"Sure, John." She curled her lips into the shape of a smile and hoped he couldn't see them quivering. "Whatever you say."

His eyes turned to hard slits. Yeah, he hadn't missed the livid sarcasm staining her voice.

The next thing he said was lost beneath the hollow drum in her head as she pivoted and strode away. The moment she turned the corner, she flew. As fast as her legs could pump, she sprinted away, away, away.

Then she heard him. The fall of his footsteps, racing, chasing, gaining speed.

She ran harder.

TWENTY

Bitter tears stuck in her throat like sand, and the dirt path blurred beneath the speed of her feet. Given John's longer strides, he would catch her quickly. She needed to reach the grove before that happened.

Because she was unraveling. Splintering apart by the second. She'd reached her breaking point and needed to be out of camera range when she self-destructed.

This was why she never subscribed to hope. There was always disappointment, and this time, it hurt beyond reason, crippling her with every punishing step.

When she'd learned of Miguel's betrayal three years ago, it had crushed her. But that despair wasn't in the same realm as what she felt now. As she sprinted harder, faster, she tried to process and compartmentalize her thoughts.

Her brain, however, wasn't working right. Grief watered down reasoning. Panic drowned out logic. She swam in anguish, unable to surface for air.

If only John would suffer the same betrayal.

Heartbreak. Loss of love and faith. He deserved nothing more than to spend the rest of his days alone, miserable, and forgotten.

When she reached the field, she sensed him slowing behind her. He knew where she was going, their confrontation inevitable. She girded herself for it.

In the grove, safe from the cameras and shaded by the canopy of trees, she skidded to a stop and spun to face him.

"What happened to your face?" He stalked toward her, eyes blazing with temper. "Who the fuck hit you?"

"Doesn't matter." She blinked back tears. "No one can hurt me as deeply as you have."

"I want a name!" he roared so viciously it rattled her nerves. "Answer me!"

Her mouth opened, vocal cords and tongue working and failing to produce discernible sound. When she found her voice at last, it broke with a sob. "Miguel is back."

"He's a dead man." He charged closer.

She stumbled away, enlarging the space between them. "How could you fuck her?"

"I didn't." He pounced.

She dodged. "Liar! I saw you!"

Back and forth, they went. Lunging and darting, they circled each other through trees. He chased, and she evaded, nimble and furious. Then he caught her. Tangling her up in his muscled arms, he pinned her against the trunk of a large oak.

She grasped at breath and engaged her entire body in a frantic burst to break loose. Squirming and writhing and thrashing about, she snarled her wrath and spat noises of defiance.

"Shh." He remained calm, pressing a forearm against her throat, his strong, agile physique coiling about her like a kingsnake constricting a wriggling mouse. "It's all right."

"No! It's not all right! It's not fine!" Tears fell too hot and fast to stifle, further enraging her. "Nothing in my life is all right!"

She escaped from his hold only to be snatched again by a hand as unbending as stone. He hauled her back so forcibly her trapped limb felt as if it pulled from the socket.

Gathering her wrists, he held her against his chest, his mouth a severe slash. "My name is Luke Sanch."

"I don't give a fuck! It's too late." She bucked, her vision smearing with tears. "Let me go!"

"You *will* hear this." He shook her until her head tipped back and her watery gaze snapped to his. "I lived on the streets in Texas until I was nineteen. Until I was abducted, snatched off the park bench where I slept, by a small-town sex trafficker." He lowered his face to hers. "He raped me in his attic for eight weeks. Whipped me every day until I learned how to *enjoy* giving head and getting fucked in the ass. Then he sold me to a monster for six figures."

Good God. Her heart surged and spilled over in waves of denial. "You're lying."

"His name is Van Quiso. I was his fourth captive. Tomas, number three, escaped before I arrived. The day I was delivered to the man who'd bought me, Tomas—along with Van's other escapees—showed up, shot my buyer, and took me in. That was eight years ago."

"You had sex with a man? *You?*" She laughed upon a slapping breeze, her pulse stammering and mind whirling in flux. "How can I possibly believe anything you say?"

"Listen. *Hear* me. Then decide." He released her and ran a hand over the top of his head as though it might arrange the order of his thoughts.

"You have five minutes." She folded her arms across her chest.

"I'll see your defensive posture and raise you fifteen minutes."

"Eight."

"Ten. It's a complicated story." A rough finger crooked beneath her chin, forcing her head to turn so he could examine her swollen jaw. "Then I have a man to kill."

"Just spit it out." She knocked his hand away.

A crease appeared between his copper brows. He dragged a palm down his face, over his mouth, and stared off in the distance. Then he started talking.

He told her about a woman named Liv Reed, who gave birth to Van's baby in captivity. Van's father stole the child to control Liv. She became Van's accomplice. A captive-turned-captor. From there, the tale spun into the far-fetched land of make-believe, packed full of courageously gruesome misadventures about how Van's nine slaves escaped *then* befriended their captors. Afterward, they all banded together with the Colombian cartel to take down other sex traffickers.

Freedom fighters, he called them. As part of this vigilante group, he said they infiltrated the darkest corners of the world and fought evil-doers outside the boundaries of the law.

Seriously.

His story had no merit. Nothing he said sounded sane or credible in the slightest. What kind of fool did he take her for?

He was a liar and criminal. She'd encountered enough of them, so full of their own poison they couldn't fathom how a woman could resist drinking the Kool-Aid and falling in line.

"This isn't Gotham City, Batman." Her head pounded. "I live in reality."

"Open your mind." He stepped into her space and, for a moment, the sliver of air between them seemed to lengthen, over-stretched and fragile, like a strand of hair pulled too taut.

She felt vulnerable beneath the masterful demand of his stare, his breath, the way he controlled her time and space. His proximity did terrible things to her heart and the temperature of her skin. Like a hallucinogenic, he altered her senses. A temporary high.

"Your ten minutes expired ten minutes ago." She stepped back.

"Listen to me, goddammit!"

"I *am* listening. You sound like a lunatic."

"You think I'm making this shit up? For what purpose?" He angrily threw his hands in the air. "I'm risking everything—my life, Tomas' life, our mission, the freedom of every woman here—to tell you the truth."

"Then you're a fucking moron."

"Jesus Christ!" He grabbed at his hair and pulled, growling through clenched teeth. "You are so…"

"What?" She fed on his seething rage and flung it right back, screaming, "What am I?"

"Frustrating beyond words. Stubborn as a mule. The most irritating, hardheaded, quarrelsome creature I've ever met."

"Why are you here, Luke?"

He went still, eyes locked on hers, the anger draining from his posture. "I knew the reason… I thought I knew. Until now." He blinked, and his eyebrows furrowed. "It seems every path I've taken, every decision I've made, all of it was meant to lead me here just so I could hear my name pronounced on your tongue."

Her lungs tightened, requiring a gulp. And another.

He drifted closer and touched her cheek. "Say it again."

She wet her lips, slipping, spiraling, losing her soul to four letters. "Luke."

"What are you doing to me?" He sought her with his hands, fingers gliding, fisting in her hair.

"Luke—"

"I didn't fuck her." He brought their foreheads together, his gaze digging deep. "I didn't touch her or kiss her or do anything I wouldn't want another man doing to you." His voice cracked against her lips. "Believe me. I need you to do that more than anything else. I need you *with* me. Please."

It was his plea that penetrated the ice in her chest. His mouth latched onto hers, seizing, heating as if attempting to thaw the blood in her veins.

She resisted for the space of a breath, then surrendered, opening upon a cry, her hands closing around his shoulder and neck.

His deep, sweeping strokes simmered with desire and something much deeper. This wasn't a kiss to satisfy a physical need. It was emotional. Poignant. Staggering. Sheer madness.

As she took the warm, firm, skillful lick of his tongue between her lips, she replayed everything he'd said. In his arms, pressed against him, she tasted the truth. She *felt* it. Every conversation, look, and touch they'd shared backed up his claim, driving away all argument and leaving only her belief in him, in his strength and unstinting heart.

This man, his body, his veracity, his gallant devotion to those he loved—he had endured the unthinkable, escaped the same hell she'd been trapped in, only to return so that he could make the world a safer place.

She saw that man the night they met and his agonizing turmoil when he gave a tortured girl a merciful death. He wasn't a killer of innocents. At his core, he was an avenging hunter.

He hadn't come for her specifically, but she believed him now. He wouldn't leave without her. And she wanted it. All of him.

In that defining moment between love and hate, heaven and hell, life and death, she lost her heart, definitively, irrevocably. It was his.

The kiss melted into mingled breaths, the air heavy with unspoken words.

"That man, Van Quiso…" She framed his chiseled face in her hands, absorbing his tragedy. "He raped you for eight weeks? That was your horrifying, unfortunate event?"

"The unfortunate event that led to a fortune." His expression showed no trace of shame. Only a pure appreciation for life. "Because of Van, I have the deepest friendships, a family who loves me, and a vital purpose. In that, I'm the wealthiest man alive."

He was the bravest man. Noble. Dauntless. Beautiful inside and out. She'd known it all along and had refused to accept it.

"This purpose…" She ran her fingers through his hair, unable to resist the urge to touch him. "How can I help?"

"I came here to find Vera Gomez and—"

"Vera?" A chill froze her bones, and her heart slammed against her ribs. "You knew that name before you arrived?"

"Yes. Her half-sister is Hector's daughter. Tula Gomez—"

"What do you know about her?" She staggered backward, pulse racing, emotions leaking, freaking the fuck out. "Where is she?"

"Until a few months ago, she was in prison." He stayed with her, eying her suspiciously. "She's safe now. Protected by my team. What's wrong?"

She clapped her hands over her mouth, strangled by a torrent of rising sobs. Confusion, fear, relief, joy—it all collided in a jumble of face-drenching tears.

"I'm not interested in Vera." He caught her jaw, searing her with cold, angry eyes. "I only sought her out because her sister—"

"Tula is *my* sister." She grabbed his wrist, squeezing ruthlessly. "She's *mine*!"

"What did you say?" He shook his head, his face stark white as he stared at her, surveying her features as if seeing her for the first time. "That's not possible."

"I'm Vera." She closed her eyes, choking on the secret. "I'm Vera Gomez."

TWENTY-ONE

For the first time in nearly three years, Vera felt alive, electrified, and impossibly, wonderfully free. To say her name out loud, to verbally own it… What an empowering goddamn relief.

And petrifying.

She scanned the surrounding grove, her skin crawling with paranoia. The cartel couldn't have heard her. But if they somehow learned that she'd broken the rules, they would kill her and the only family member she had left.

Except Tula was safe?

"You said your mother is a famous actress." John…*Luke* stood unmoving, every muscle flexed to strike, his face an unholy sculpture of retaliation. "Vera's mother is dead."

She flinched. "I had to give you something. You wouldn't leave it alone. So I lied."

Panic paralyzed her, for even in the dark shade of the trees she saw the enraged glint in his eyes, the cruel set of his unforgiving mouth, the animosity in his stance. He was *not* happy about her dishonesty.

Without warning, he grabbed her. Imprisoning her neck in a startling grip, he bent it roughly to the side and pushed away the hair behind her ear.

"Stop!" She shoved at him, unable to free herself. "What are you doing?"

"You can't be Vera." His thumb pressed against the back of her ear, folding it forward. "She has a tattoo. A small black—"

"Petunia. My sister's name is Petula, and when we were little, I called her Petunia." The memory surged fire through her sinuses, searing the backs of her eyes. "Miguel had the flower lasered off when I arrived here. There's a faint scar, like a stretch mark."

She knew the moment he saw it. His breath left him. His grip loosened, and he angled her face toward his.

"You speak English flawlessly." His gaze raked her, flinty with skepticism until it dipped to her lips. He lingered there then slowly returned to her eyes, his own widening with realization. "Tula is a teacher."

"Even before she earned her degree. She taught us both English when we were kids."

"You should've fucking told me."

"I couldn't. The cartel is watching her. When she was released from prison, they sent men to follow her. Marco said they would leave her alone as long as I went along with Silvia's ruse to be me."

"Silvia." He said the name with disdain, his mouth a puckered grimace. "Who is she?"

"She's the half-sister of Omar, Miguel, and Alejandro. The four of them share the same mother. Hector La Rocha's only wife. She died years ago. When Hector met her, he already had two children—Marco and Tula—from two other women. And his wife already had a child."

"Silvia..." He pinched the bridge of his nose. "So she's related by blood to Omar, Miguel, and Alejandro. Marco is her step-brother."

"Yeah, but the five of them grew up together. Raised as full siblings by Hector's wife."

"Add in Tula, and it's the fucking Brady Bunch."

"Where's my sister?"

"Colombia. Hidden and protected with the Restrepo Cartel. With my *friends*. I swear on my life that she's safe."

"I can't believe this." Her mind swam, and old guilt rose to the surface, unleashing a well of tears. "She served time in that brutal prison because of me. *Years*. If I hadn't called her that morning..." Her voice broke as wet trails streamed down her face. "She would've stayed in Arizona. But no, I had to make that damn call, and she dove head-first right into my mess."

"And fell in love." He cupped her face, his accent soft and rumbly. "Twice."

"What?"

"Martin and Ricky, my roommates..."

She remembered the names from his story. "Van's ex-captives."

"Yes. Three years ago, they infiltrated Jaulaso Prison as part of our on-going operation to take down Hector's sex trafficking organization. Tula was with Hector in that prison when they arrived. She went to Mexico because you called her for help. But if you were already enslaved here, how did you make that call?"

"Shortly after I arrived, one of the guards left his phone unattended while using the bathroom. I had seconds to use it and didn't know how law enforcement worked in America or if they would even believe my story and come. I didn't even know where I was. But I knew Tula would know what to do, that she would find the proper authorities and get help. So I called her, whispering frantically, *I'm in trouble. Need you. Come now.* When I lowered the phone to look up the GPS location, Marco was there. He'd been watching me, waiting until I called her, and destroyed the phone before I could tell her I wasn't in Mexico. It was a fucking setup, and stupid me, I fell right into it."

"Vera…"

"It's all my fault. I'm a worthless sister, and I know it. I never intended to involve her. God, I spent years keeping her oblivious to what was going on."

"Let's talk about that." He brushed a lock of hair from her face. "Why were you in trouble and accumulating debt?"

"Our mother…" Her scalp tingled, and though she was whispering, it sounded like a roaring gale in her ears. She searched the spaces between the trees and probed the field beyond.

"Tomas did another sweep of this area today. No one is listening. And he's out there just over that hill right now, guarding. He'll let me know if anyone approaches. Your mother…"

"Died of heart disease."

"I know, and I'm sorry for your loss." He stroked her cheek, her neck, his fingers constantly brushing her skin as if he couldn't stop touching her. "Tula gave us a comprehensive rundown of your background to help us rescue you. Hector tried to convince her that you were working for him, but she never believed that. She was adamant about your innocence."

"I miss her so much. I'm surprised you didn't

recognize me. We look alike." She glanced down at the bones protruding on her frame. "Or, at least, we used to."

"She didn't have recent photos. The teenage girl in the pictures we saw…"

"I've lost a lot of weight."

"You were beautiful then. And now." A heated look came to his eyes, lazy and hooded. Arresting. The transformation drugged her with narcotic desires, turning cravings into a full-blown addiction. "You're so fucking gorgeous. Sometimes, I look at you and think you're an illusion. You can't be real. Then you return the eye contact, and I feel like a teenage boy all over again. A fumbling, fuzzy-headed, walking hard-on."

The foolish, constricting organ in her chest jumped madly at his words, sinking deeper into him.

"Your sister told me that trouble often found you. But she didn't know about your debt." His fingers feathered along her collarbone. "What did your mother have to do with that?"

"Medical bills. So many. She was in and out of the hospital for years before she died. I had no money, no way to pay for her care. Doctors started refusing her, and I just… I couldn't tell Tula. She made it out of Ciudad Hueca, escaped to America through hard work, brains, and *legal* means. If I told her about the bills, she would've forfeited the life she'd worked so hard to achieve. She would've come home. I couldn't let her do that."

"So you lied to her." He held his chin tight to his chest, green eyes sparking beneath thick copper lashes.

"Don't you dare judge me."

"Judge you?" He half-laughed, half-groaned. "I'm insanely turned on. It's all I can do to not throw you on the ground and have my way with you. Your ferocity, selflessness, courage, outrageous beauty… I'm fucking beside myself with admiration. I won't even apologize for it, because you know exactly what you're doing to me."

"No, I…." A pulse burst in her temples, and her mouth went dry. Desire. It tore through her belly, low, deep, and ill-timed. *Focus.* "I want to hear about Martin and Ricky."

"They're two of my closest friends. I told you their histories with Van. They're also bi-sexual, openly now, with Tula. The three of them are in a polyamorous relationship."

"You're kidding." She couldn't imagine it. "My sister… In a threesome?"

"From what I saw just a few days ago, she's happily, ridiculously in love."

"Wow. How do you feel about that?"

"I don't swing that way, despite what I went through in Van's attic. I'm not the sort of man who shares women, not even with my best friend. But if they're happy, I'm happy for them." He leaned in, eyes glowing. "Ask me how I feel about *you*."

Heady warmth spread through her stomach and radiated to her thighs. He was so obscenely handsome and sexy, and that heady warmth gathered into a delicious ache. "How do you feel about me?"

"I'm here to free Vera Gomez by any means possible." He lowered his lips, settling his mouth upon hers, soft, barely touching, yet certain. "The task felt impossible because I didn't want to help the woman who pretended to be you. I wanted to kill her. Still do. Especially now, knowing the part she played in making your life a living hell."

His voice was a deep caress with an edge of vindictive fury as he kissed her face, her neck, nuzzling and touching her everywhere. The yearning he stirred in her was frightening, scrambling her concentration.

"I want the real Vera Gomez. Madly." He started to remove her clothes.

"Luke." Torn between lust and needing answers, she twined her fingers through his hair and dragged his mouth against hers, the flavor of mint clinging to her lips. "I have so many questions, and you make it damn hard to think."

"Multitask." He rubbed his thumb over her nipple through the shirt and slipped his tongue in her mouth. "I'm listening."

"I didn't know Tula's father was Hector until Marco told me." She groaned, letting him kiss her for a long moment, soaring in a decadent fusion of lips and tongues. "My mother took the identities of both our fathers to the grave. I'm still trying to get used to the idea that my sister is La Rocha by blood."

"I can tell you what I know." He lifted her into his arms only to lay her on a soft patch of grass. Then he stretched out on his side against her and toyed with the curly strands of her hair. "When Petula Gomez walked into Hector's prison, her name keyed him off. So he had a paternity test done without her knowledge. He was as surprised by her incarceration as she was. We don't know if her arrest was coincidence or—"

"When I heard about it, I suspected that the Mexican military mistook her for me. There are a lot of dangerous people looking for me in Ciudad Hueca. The more money I owed, the deeper I entangled myself with wanted felons. My sweet sister—"

"She murdered Hector in his prison cell."

"What?"

At her stunned gasp, a smile overtook his face. "She's fierce. Just like you."

As she spluttered a million questions, he gave her a full retelling of how her sister, a Spanish high school teacher, outsmarted and cut down the capo of La Rocha Cartel in prison. His hands roamed her body as he narrated each heroic detail and reassured her about Tula's safety and wellbeing.

His mouth shared the story while his lips vibrated the words along her ribs and the undersides of her breasts, dampening the shirt. By the end, he had her shoes and jeans off, her top and bra pushed to her neck, and her breasts glistening with the moisture from his panting mouth.

With impatient hands, his thumbs caressed the pink peaks. They rose to his touch, hardened for his mouth, and throbbed for his tongue. She arched to bring him closer.

He was so heartbreakingly gorgeous. Everywhere. Sunlight dappled his skin to gilded ivory, his half-lidded eyes rich and gleaming with sensuous hunger. He slipped a hand between her thighs and stroked. She moaned, hot and clenching, even as she tried to focus on the conversation.

"Before now, I didn't know why the cartel was using me to bait Hector's killer." She smoothed a hand across his cheek.

The day's growth of whiskers tickled her fingertips, igniting sparks of delirious anticipation as she recalled the scratchy feel of that roughness along her inner thighs.

"Hector's sons knew all along that Tula was the killer." He slipped his tongue around her nipple and down her flat belly. "If they followed her like you said, they're aware she sided with the Restrepo Cartel."

"You know what that means, right?" Panic rose, and she sat up.

He pushed her back down. "They're expecting us to come for you."

"That's why Silvia stole my identity, Luke! She's waiting for you to seek her out under the belief that she's me. And you did. You went straight to her. What if she knows who you are?" She clutched a handful of red hair and yanked, dislodging his mouth from her hipbone. "What happened in her room today?"

"She doesn't know." He gripped her waist and covered her stomach with kisses.

His scent invaded her nose, clean and woodsy. If testosterone had a fragrance, he was it. Ineffable, potent, *distracting* man.

"Luke, if you don't start talking—"

"I teased her with words." With a sigh, he rested his cheek on her abdomen and met her eyes. "I made her believe I would fuck her if she gave me something. A vulnerable piece of herself. A secret. Anything that would prove she would choose me over the cartel."

"Miguel said you were groping and going at it on your way into her room."

"Miguel said he would pay off your debt and make you a legal citizen in the States."

"Fine. Point made. So what happened? Did she refuse your offer?"

"We went back and forth for over an hour. Lots of talking. Negotiating. Mind games. I really thought I had her."

"Because she wants you."

"Like a bitch in heat."

Her molars crashed together. "Had she told you the location, you would be fucking her right now."

"No." The sharp planes of his face turned to limestone, like a fairy-tale villain carved by a demented artist. But his skin, the blood beneath, and his entire aura were alive and real with a vengeance. "Had she given me what I wanted, I would've wrapped my hands around her throat and snuffed the life from her body."

"Brutal." She blew out a breath.

"Brutally honest. I'm going to end her, Vera. Her *and* her brothers. But first…" He nudged her naked thighs apart, bent, and ran his tongue along her slit. "I'm going to end this agony between us."

TWENTY-TWO

Vera swelled so hard and fast between her legs she went mad with her need for him. *Luke*. The only man who had ever held this much power over her.

He wasn't so cruel to make her beg. Dipping a wicked finger inside her, he sent rivulets of pleasure everywhere. A second digit compelled her hips off the ground, her entire body reaching for more, harder, deeper… Oh God, right there.

Fingers thrusting and lips trailing a line of fire to her clit, he buried his face and smothered her senses with his devilish mastery.

She clamped her legs around his shoulders, the delicious ache intensifying as she drank in the vision of him with new eyes.

This proud, virile, intimidating alpha had been forced to perform sexual acts with another man. But he also knew his way around a woman's body. A skill that could only come from experience.

Jealousy sank in its teeth, but more than that, she felt a kindred connection. He knew what it was like to be a slave. He'd experienced the terrifying loss of freedom. He understood her in a way no one else could.

And she understood him.

He'd raped her, not out of self-serving cruelty, but out of necessity to maintain his ruse. A ruse that followed justice.

"I forgive you." She quivered and heated beneath his attentive touch.

"I don't deserve that." He lifted his face, his expression blanking as he removed his fingers.

"I'm about to change my mind." She bucked her hips. "Don't stop."

In a tailored suit, tie tossed over his shoulder, red hair tousled, and gaze fixed upon her, he stole her breath. Her sanity. Then he smiled, and she lost her dignity.

"Fuck me, Luke." She squeezed her thighs around him. "Right now."

As she pulled on his shoulders, firm muscles rippled beneath her hands. He lowered his grin and kissed her deeply, claiming every inch of her pussy. She stabbed her fingers in his hair, gasping and weakening at the hum of his hungry groans against her sensitive flesh.

He lifted her legs with gentle pressure beneath her thighs, spreading her open and sinking his tongue. Her heart burst into a sprint, flooding thick, languorous sensations along her limbs. Dizzy energy and heat, crackling static and syrup, all of it spiraled through her blood and rocked her to her core. Wave after wave of stimulation slammed through her, centering in the bundle of nerve endings at the apex of her thighs.

His lips ground against her, firm and demanding. Then his fingers penetrated her achy depths, curling, pumping, freeing the last of her tension, and sending her tumbling into oblivion.

Strength left her body as she came, moaning and trembling through the stunning, blissful high. Then she crashed, clutching at the grass beneath her, anchoring herself back to reality.

He lowered her knees and removed his jacket and tie. Unbuttoned his shirt. Gave up halfway and tore open his fly. Removing a condom from his pants pocket, he rolled it on in record time. Only then did she notice his hands shaking.

"Luke." Dazed, she reached for him and opened her legs.

"Christ, you're a vision." His gaze traveled over her nudity as he lowered himself in the cradle of her thighs. "There's no place I'd rather be. I want to spend eternity inside you."

Where her heart had been, there was only him. A thrumming stronghold of love and raw intensity.

"Touch me." He held his hips above hers, his hand wrapped around the root of his cock.

She eagerly did as he asked, her questing fingers finding him hot and rigid, rubber over steel, twitching against the slide of her touch.

"Someday soon…" Hips rocking in her grip, he lowered his mouth to the hollow at the base of her throat and released a vibrating groan. "I'm going to feel you without a condom."

"I'll hold you to that." She teased the thick length of him, her thumb roving over the tip, her fingers squeezing.

"Enough." He grasped her wrist, stopping her. "You make me crazy, woman. So utterly outside of my control I fear I might burst."

She knew the feeling.

Repositioning, he took his time lining up. Gliding the plump head between her folds, he teased and tormented until sweat broke out on her brow.

By the time he pressed against her opening, the world had narrowed to the rapid hammering of her pulse. Then he pushed, sinking, stretching her body, taunting her with every agonizing inch in one unhurried stroke.

Once he was seated, his breath rushed out on a strained grunt, his face so close she could see flecks of gold in his green, dilated eyes.

"You're beautiful," she whispered.

"I was just thinking the same about you."

They were still. Throbbing, tingling, clinging to each other with their arms, their gazes, and the heavy rhythm of their heartbeats.

"It's never felt like this." She stared up at him, searching for the right words. "Like a surreal dream. I'm afraid to blink."

"My thoughts exactly."

"Why is it like this with you?"

"It's *us*. We fit, and not just on a physical plane. It's molecular." He began to move within her, drawing back, pushing forward. Tight, shallow strokes. "Indescribably elemental."

"Our souls match, and I don't think it's accidental. It's as if they were merged together long ago, separated, and are finally *re*connecting."

"Maybe we were born for this exact moment. Deliberately designed to find each other and bind on a level that we can't comprehend."

"Fated. You believe that?" She slid a hand beneath his shirt and touched his chest, the muscle there hard and ridged with definition.

"With you, anything is possible."

A sense of peace washed over her, but with it came a spike of fear. She wound her arms around his neck and pressed herself against him. "This scares me."

"Us? Together?"

"Us, *not* together. I'm terrified to lose this. Everything good in my life is taken away. I can't lose you, Luke."

He didn't make promises he couldn't keep. He knew the risks, the dangers they faced ahead, and seemed hellbent on keeping her in the present. Sheathed in her wet heat, he thrust hard and deep, setting a toe-curling rhythm and effectively ending all thought and conversation.

His tongue swept between her lips, drawing hers to him. The kiss deepened, and he palmed her backside, gripping her possessively while guiding her to meet his strokes, not too soft, not too hard, but so damn hot.

He surrounded her, filled her, moving in and out as if to satisfy a desperate craving to have her in every way, beyond sex, deeper than flesh, to own her once and for all. She needed no encouragement, lifting her hips, bowing her back, and riding the tide of elation.

The temperature rose, in the air, beneath her skin, between their lips. He rubbed his tongue against hers, and she gripped his shoulders, holding him, keeping him near, aching everywhere with a thirst that couldn't be quenched.

"Christ, Vera, you feel sensational." His hands found hers and held them against the grass above her head. "You're my salvation. My heaven. An unbelievable dream."

Strong fingers closed around her smaller ones,

cradling her in the warmth of his palms, thumbs caressing with an intimacy that sent heat roiling through her body.

Her breasts felt heavy with it, her belly shimmering with butterflies. His eyes never left her face, except when he kissed her, which he couldn't seem to do enough. Her lips welcomed the slippery, warm caress of his tongue, and she opened to him, always, delighting in his rumbled grunts and panting groans.

Flattening a palm between her breasts, he slid it to her throat. Rather than fight him, she gifted him with a vibrating moan beneath his hand, followed by her joyous laughter.

He lost his rhythm, his smile blinding as it tripped across his beautiful face. Then he pressed his advantage, tightening those powerful fingers and controlling her airflow. She saw stars, and amid the burst of light, his gasps joined the sounds of her strangling breaths.

The man had a mean streak, but she wasn't scared. Not anymore. Her body danced for him, writhing in a wordless plea for his pain and his pleasure while trusting him to know her limits.

That realization only fueled her hunger. Liquid heat simmered through every extremity, welled in every hot crease, and sparked flames in all her pleasure centers.

Kissing her harder, he drowned her in his heat and dominated her with his tongue. He knew how to kiss so well it turned her brain inside out, his technique fluctuating between the exquisite softness of his licks and the ferocious bites of his teeth. All she could do was hold on and arch against him, thrusting her breasts against the hard press of his chest and whimpering her cries for more.

He sought, and she gave, mindless against the unstoppable pull to fuse everything of theirs into one—breaths, bodies, souls. He dragged her hips tight to his and clutched her ass with a bruising hand, fingers splayed, owning her over and over.

Nothing in his touch hinted at uncertainty. Only conquering demand and desire. She tasted it in his mouth, felt it in the frantic grip of his fingers, and saw it burning the green depths of his eye contact.

God, she was wet. Rivers of arousal ran hotly between her thighs, squelching where he thrust, lubricating when he drew out and rammed in. Each time he left her, she felt a cold, horrifying emptiness. When he pushed back in, he was like gravity between her legs, a pressure so heavy and intense, so agonizingly wonderful that everything inside her clung to him.

"You're squeezing me. Strangling my fucking cock." He embedded himself deeper, a groan breaking from his chest. "Milking me before I'm ready."

"Stop whining." She laughed, shifting her hips and bearing down to torment him further. "Try to keep up."

"Witchy woman."

"Filthy ginger."

"That mouth… You wreck me." He captured her lips, his tongue sweeping in and devouring her next breath.

She could anticipate him now—the tempo of his quickening gasps, the slicking heat of his skin beneath her pressing fingertips, and the building of his thrusts into a rhythm that was entirely his own.

His hand cupped and caressed her breast, making

her all the more grateful that he'd taken the time to remove her clothes. She moaned her body's acceptance with each impassioned kiss, touch, and grind of his hips.

She loved being naked with him, and as the excitement in her blood grew hotter, so did pulsations between her thighs. He was still kissing her, wielding his tongue like an instrument of seduction, licking her deeply, wildly, until she hurt with the need to come.

The hot friction of his cock grew sharper, more centered, and her breath burst forth, giving birth to shooting stabs of pleasure.

It started in the deepest, darkest, most untouchable recesses of her body and spread outward, the unbearable ache peaking and exploding within her.

Her cries were lost to his mouth, her fingers anchoring in hard muscle and knotting in the sweat-dampened hair at the base of his skull. She felt him in her soul, swelling, pulsing, shattering into a million pieces as he surrendered with her.

"Vera, Vera, Vera." He panted and shook, driving his cock into the back of her cunt, spurting, groaning, and digging himself as deeply as he could possibly go. "It's never felt like this. Ever."

They clung to each other long after the tremors dissolved. With his weight on one arm, he held her hand with the other as they lay in a pile of entwined limbs, catching their breaths and floating in their starlit high.

She drifted off to the gentle caress of his lips kissing her face and his fingers tracing the lines of her body.

When she woke, he was sitting up, his attention locked on something behind her.

Approaching footsteps.

As she moved to turn, he caught her shoulder, stopping her from exposing her nude front. "Get dressed."

Her clothes landed near her head.

He rose and stepped over her, his tension palpable. "What's wrong?"

Blindly reaching for her underwear, she stole a glance over her shoulder and locked onto Tomas' golden eyes.

Face pale, posture stiff, he looked like he'd seen a ghost.

"I need to talk to you," he said to Luke, his fingers clenching around the phone he held tight to his stomach. "Privately."

TWENTY-THREE

Unease trickled through Luke as he took note of Tomas' stark expression. "Start talking."

"This requires…" Tomas glanced at Vera while white-knuckling the phone in his hands. "Discretion."

"Speak freely in front of her. We had a breakthrough. Didn't we, Vera?" he called over his shoulder, watching Tomas' eyes bulge.

"Sure, Luke." Her clothing rustled behind him as she dressed. "If by *breakthrough,* you mean we had a come to Jesus, where you underwent the difficult but amazing realization that the reason you're here is for me, and therefore, I'm in charge from this point forward."

"We're still working on her listening skills," he said to Tomas. "Obedience training takes time."

She made a sound of exasperation. "I don't know what fantasy world you live in but—"

"If you don't cover your ass in two-point-five seconds," he said, stabbing a finger toward her naked lower half. "I'll blister it red."

"Fifteen seconds."

"Five." Slightly irritated and overly amused, he turned back to Tomas and nodded at the phone. "Tell me what's going on."

"Okay, just… Hang on." Tomas scrubbed a hand over his head, his gaze fixed on Vera. "I'm still processing. *She* is Vera?"

"Eyes up here while you process." Luke shifted, blocking Tomas' view of her getting dressed.

"I have something to tell you." Growing agitated, Tomas looked away. "But first, you're going to fill me in on what I missed."

Luke spoke quickly, hitting on the critical details about Vera's identity until she interrupted, expanding on his bullet points and overtaking the briefing. She zipped up her jeans and pulled on her shoes as she finished talking.

Tomas looked at Luke for confirmation.

"That about sums it up." His chest swelled as he regarded her, unable to hide the untenable adoration he felt for this woman. "Hector's sons suspect that Tula Gomez is protected by Matias. They're expecting a rescue party to come for Vera."

"So Silvia assumed Vera's identity and is waiting around for the rescuer to reveal himself." Tomas scratched his jaw. "It's smart. I mean, Silvia and Vera look a lot alike."

"That so?" Vera's eyes turned to threatening slits.

"You're prettier." Tomas shrugged.

She flexed her hands, temper fuming through her hot little figure.

"Calm down." Luke hooked an arm around her, pulling her against his chest. "Tomas, has that phone left your possession?"

"Not once since we arrived. The microphone is disabled. Physically disconnected. There's no way the cartel can hear us."

"All right. What's going on?"

"I fucked up." Tomas' expression emptied as he looked at the device in his hand. "In light of Vera being on our side, it makes it a little easier to say this… We need to leave. As soon as possible."

Dread curled in Luke's stomach. "I'm listening."

With a glance at the empty field behind him, Tomas began to pace, dragging a hand through his hair, fidgeting and restless. His uncharacteristic behavior put Luke on edge.

"When I was a boy…" Tomas stopped and stared off at nothing, his eyes clouding over. "I fell in love."

Stunned, Luke jerked his head back. That was the last thing he expected to hear from Tomas Dine. His friend had never brought a woman home for longer than a few hours. In fact, Luke had never heard a romantic word pass Tomas' lips.

"She died." Tomas bent at the waist as if overpowered by sudden, excruciating pain, and his voice took on a harrowing tone, making Luke's blood run cold. "She fucking died."

Vera reached for Luke's hand, her silence as heavy and bewildered as his.

"I was three years older than her." Tomas straightened, composing himself. "Her parents forbade her to see me. So I created an email account for her, wrote the address and password on a piece of paper, and gave it to her at school. She never had a chance to use it. That night, she and her entire family died in a car accident."

A hot ember formed in Luke's throat, and he

swallowed, grasping for words.

"I'm so sorry, Tomas." Vera stepped forward.

Tomas held up a hand, warding her off. "I started emailing her. I just…couldn't let go. I know she wasn't receiving the messages, but I needed to talk to her. Fuck, I needed her. She was my best friend. My girl. My whole fucking world. So I wrote to her through email. For years."

"The email account…" Luke cleared his voice, uncertain why Tomas chose this moment to tell him this. "It eventually exceeded its size limit, right?"

"Every few months, I cleaned it out. I had the password, and other than spam, I'm the only one who ever sends messages to it." He held the phone up and stared in a daze at the screen. "Every time I go in to wipe the history, I intend to delete the account. But I can't. The messages I'm writing are dangerous and stupid, but I can't stop. I couldn't…"

His spine tingled. "Dangerous how?"

"I've told her everything over the years. Every time a miserable goddamn thing happens in my life, I write it in an email to her. Every tragedy, every victory… Every *secret*."

"What secrets?" Luke stopped breathing, seeing the writing on the walls.

"*Our* secrets." Tomas met his eyes, his face bloodless. "I told her about Van and everything before and after."

"Like a journal." Vera touched her throat. "You write to her as if composing your thoughts in a diary."

"Diaries are forbidden in our business." Luke couldn't stop the ire from leaking into his voice. "No incriminating evidence. You know the rules, Tomas."

"Yeah. I fucking know, Luke." Tomas bared his

teeth. "I always email her from a fake account and also… She. Is. *Dead!*"

"Do you use your real name in the signature? When you end each message?"

"Just *Tommy.*"

"What about locations, events, missions? Other names, like Matias? Mine? Did you include any of that in your love notes?"

"Yes."

"Goddammit!" Luke seethed.

"The night before we came here, I sent an email from a new untraceable account, stating it was my last message. I intended to delete her account the moment we returned. I was finally prepared to move on."

"What happened?"

Tomas handed over the phone and paced away, gripping the back of his neck.

Luke woke the device, and an email app filled the screen. It showed the inbox of Tomas' fake account, which had one single message. A correspondence with *Tommysgirl.*

Oh, fuck, Tomas. What have you done?

He opened the email and read the initial message. It confirmed that Tomas had composed a short, incisive goodbye to *Tommysgirl.*

Knowing the cartel monitored every transmission, Luke was relieved to see nothing in the text that could condemn their operation.

"Did you log in to the *Tommysgirl* account from this device?" Luke asked.

"No, I'm not a fucking moron."

But there was a problem, and it stared back like a ghost from the grave.

Someone had responded to Tomas' goodbye

email.

His pulse exploded as he opened it.

Tommy,

Please, don't stop messaging me. I've been reading your emails for ten years, anticipating and living each and every one. I'm sorry I never responded, but I didn't know what to say. At first, I felt terrible for logging into this account. I found the login information in the pocket of a coat that I bought at a thrift store.

I shouldn't have logged in, but investigation is my job. After your first few messages, I knew the account belonged to someone you lost. A girl you loved.

You grieved so painfully in every email you wrote I couldn't ignore it. You loved her deeply, and I felt it deeply. I'll be honest, I envied her. To be on the receiving end of such devotion… I wanted to be her.

But I remained silent. I listened and looked for signs of self-danger in your words.

Then your messages stopped. For ten weeks, I thought I lost you.

Until you wrote again.

You changed. After everything that happened to you during those weeks, you became so cold and angry. You needed an ear, someone to hear your story and watch over you. I was here for you, even when you thought you were alone.

Over the years, I felt your continuous evolution and adaptation to the dangers around you.

I know you better than you know yourself. I've heard every feeling and thought you sent. You needed this outlet. A place to share your thoughts without judgment or consequence. And through it all, I realized I needed it, too.

Please, don't end this. I know you don't know me. But I need to see you. I've been sitting on your emails for so long, worrying about your safety and telling no one.

I'm still worried.

I'm on the good side of the law, Tommy, and I sense you spiraling. You're trying to do the right thing, but you've gone too far.

Meet me in one week. I know you have the means to fly home. Your childhood house is still abandoned. I'll be there at sunset on Saturday.

Come alone.

"Fucking fantastic." Luke passed the phone to Vera, his nerves strung like a live wire. "Assuming she's a *she,* does she know where you are now? That you're here on a mission that involves the Mexican cartel?"

"Some of it, yes. I wrote about gearing up for this operation." Tomas set his hands on his hips, his posture challenging and angry. "I'll handle it."

"Yeah, you'll fucking handle it." He strode toward his friend and lowered his voice. "She knows who we are, what we do, and every crime we've committed."

"She's also delusional."

"Whether you like it or not," Vera mumbled, her eyes on the email, "you've been talking to this woman for ten years. She knows your entire life story, and it sounds like she just wants to help. Like she cares about you."

"She's in law enforcement," Luke said.

"Doesn't mean shit." A vein bulged in Tomas' forehead. "She's probably a small-town cop. I grew up in the Chihuahuan Desert in Texas. She must be a local there. It's the only way she would've ended up with my girl's coat."

"She probably printed every message you sent.

She could send those transcripts to someone who can destroy us."

"I said I'll handle it." Tomas gritted his teeth.

"La Rocha will see the email she sent, if they haven't already."

"There's nothing damning here." Vera gave the phone back to Tomas, her brow furrowing. "She was careful in her wording. She knows exactly what she's doing."

"It could be a trap," Luke said.

"I'll find her before Saturday and follow her." Rage boiled through Tomas' voice, turning his neck crimson. "I'll figure out who she is and what she wants before she ever sees me. *If* she sees me."

"You're taking this personally."

"Damn right, I'm taking it personally. She invaded my fucking privacy for ten years!" Tomas rubbed his hands down his face and reined in his temper. "I'll be careful."

He studied Tomas for a moment, gaging his friend's emotional state. Tomas was the calm one in the group. The level-headed, stern-faced, untouchable guy who handled his problems on his own and avoided drama like the plague. He would deal with this as quietly as possible.

"All right." Luke blew out a breath. "I'll arrange an escort with La Rocha to get you out of here."

"You're coming with me."

"No, I'm not. I planned this out before you showed me the email." He glanced at Vera, bracing for her fury. "I'm going to make an offer to buy Vera, an offer the cartel can't refuse, and you're going to take her with you."

"No!" Tomas and Vera shouted in unison.

"They won't let me go." Vera raged, shoving him in the chest. "Even if they agree, I won't. I'm not leaving without you."

"They will, and you don't have a vote in this."

"You son of a bitch." She spat a rapid-fire barrage of Spanish before switching back to English. "I will fight you and—"

He clapped a hand over her mouth and hauled her against him. "Shut up and listen." He looked at Tomas. "There's a massive wall surrounding this compound. How many properties in California are built like this one?"

"A lot," Tomas said. "Paranoid rich folks, hiding their dirty deeds from outsiders."

"But you've spent the last few days studying the layout, memorizing every detail. Once you're outside these walls, you're going to pass along those specs to the team. They can survey maps and fly a chopper over the region. You'll find your way back."

Vera squirmed and bucked in his hold until he released her.

"Great." She spun away, panting through labored breaths. "You can both leave and return with your army."

"I'm not going anywhere until every single person who hurt you is dead."

"Oh, for fuck's sake."

"What happens, Vera, if all three of us leave and never find our way back here?"

Her stubborn chin tipped down, her eyes blazing with rancor. "The girls remain enslaved, and the bad guys win."

"I won't let that happen. What did you see on the other side of the wall?"

"I'm not agreeing to this."

"Answer the question."

"A junkyard." Her nostrils flared with indignation. "The compound is bordered on one side by a massive graveyard for old cars."

A grin pulled at his lips as he turned to Tomas. "How many properties in California are surrounded by a stone wall and a junkyard?"

"Probably not more than one." Tomas' mouth twitched, unleashing a matching smile.

"Excellent. I'll arrange your immediate departure and negotiate a purchase price for my mouthy new sex slave."

"You can go right to hell, Luke!" Tears welled in her eyes, and her hands balled into infuriated fists. "I won't let you do this. They'll kill you. No. You know what? Fuck that. *I* will kill you."

She could despise him and curse him to hell. He would still win.

Sending her far away from this place was priority number one, even if he had to shackle and gag her to see it done.

TWENTY-FOUR

Luke had to shackle and gag her.

By nightfall, Vera still wouldn't see reason. She threatened to scream his secrets from the rooftops if he forced her to leave without him. She would never blow his cover, but he didn't put it past her to race off and hide somewhere on the property.

He didn't have time for that. So he bound her with rope and silenced her with a strip of cloth. Then he ordered Tomas to carry her to the waiting limo. The sight of her thrashing and heaving with every fierce breath in her body gutted him at a depth that couldn't be mended.

He was hurting her in his attempt to save her. Taking away her right to choose. Removing her free will. It was the worst possible thing he could do to her.

Except risking her life.

From where he stood, ensuring she lived superseded all ethical and moral obligations.

Maybe his decision was selfish, but at that moment, watching Tomas wrestle her into the back of the limo, he realized he would never survive her death. He couldn't even consider the possibility.

He remained on the sidewalk, stomach knotted, lungs collapsing, fighting like hell to maintain his ruse as a wealthy, suit-wearing, heartless slave owner.

His face felt like marble, his numb hands clasped loosely behind him. He was a stone-cold monster, who had just purchased a trafficked girl.

His first and last.

The negotiations with Hector's four sons had dragged out for two hours in Marco's lavish office. Over tequila and cigars, Luke cajoled, and the brothers strung him along with no real commitment to his offer.

His top price was one million. Six-hundred thousand of that was his own money. Van had given each of his ex-slaves that amount. It was the only money Luke had to his name.

Before he left Colombia, Martin and Ricky had offered their portions, as well. They desperately wanted Vera to be returned to Tula. Tomas had also thrown his share into the pot.

In total, Luke had two-point-five million to bargain with. But he'd had no intention of draining his friends' bank accounts.

He was a fool.

Marco haggled with him for two hours. Marco's brothers wanted no more part of the negotiations. Selling Vera meant surrendering their bait for their father's killer. Of course, they didn't know that Luke was privy to Vera's true identity.

It had been several months since Hector died. Vera believed they were losing patience, and it wouldn't be long before they killed her. She was a liability. A flight risk. Too smart for her own good.

In the end, Luke bought her freedom for three million dollars. A bid the cartel hadn't been able to refuse.

If they suspected he had something to do with their father's murder, he was the one they wanted anyway. Not Vera.

To seal the deal, he announced that he would be staying on the property for the remainder of the week with the possibility of purchasing a second girl.

Dollar signs glowed in four pairs of gluttonous eyes.

Another three-million-dollar purchase? He didn't have that kind of money. But they didn't know that.

When he'd left Marco's office, he'd sent a message to one of the burner phones that Matias Restrepo carried. The cartel *jefe* agreed to cover the half-million that Luke was short for the purchase of Vera.

It was a huge ask. Camila's husband had already invested a hefty chunk of change into this operation. If Luke succeeded in taking down La Rocha, maybe he could liquidate La Rocha's assets and recoup the investment. But there was no guarantee.

There was no guarantee he would ever see his friends again.

From within the limo, Tomas signaled him to approach. With a calming breath, he moved on lead feet and bent into the open doorway.

Shackled to one of the long benches, Vera sank her teeth into the gag and glared at him with pure venom in her eyes. A wet sheen shimmered along her lashes and welled in the corners.

He felt sick to his stomach.

Straps crisscrossed her torso, restraining her to the seat. She still fought, bucking and snarling, her chest rising and falling with the furor of her breaths as a livid flush reddened her cheeks.

She was pissed. But more than that, she was terrified. *For him.*

Tomas perched beside her, donning a stoic expression. Across from them sat their escort. Probably the same man who had accompanied them here a few days ago.

"She doesn't look happy to be your new toy." The man chuckled.

"Are any of them happy at first?" Luke forced a smile with predatory teeth. "Give me a minute with her."

With a nod, the man slid out of the limo, and Tomas followed.

He shifted back to Vera and cupped her face. "I know you're angry."

Muffled screams clotted the air, her eyes shouting viciously over the gag.

"Shh." He kissed the curve of her neck, the hollow between her collarbones, and the rough fabric over her mouth. "I'm yours. From now until the termination of my soul, I belong to you and you alone."

Tears stole along her cheeks and dampened the gag. He leaned in and caught the streams with his thumbs, then his lips. Suddenly, viscerally aware of the pounding of his heart against her breasts, the feel of her soft curls against his neck, he wrenched her legs open and knelt between them.

Without a moment's hesitation, their bodies sought, instantly gravitating together with the torment of their impending separation. He pressed his lips to her face, her heart, and everywhere, claiming her with each kiss, each ragged breath drawn as one. When the violence of her grief grew too great, he touched her with worshiping hands, caressing her skin and clasping her body to his.

She began to tremble, crying out in muzzled, wordless misery, then again when he pulled away.

Tremors of anger rocked him, ignited by the salty taste of her tears on his tongue and the primal, instinctual impulse to never let her out of his sight.

But above all, he needed her safe.

Behind him, Tomas cleared his throat. Then a black hood was pressed into his hand.

"Don't give Tommy any trouble." He slipped the material over her head and held it against her brow. "I'll see you soon."

She whimpered, a desperate edge of anguish that locked up his lungs. He might never see her again. He trusted Tomas to keep her safe, but Luke would be on his own. He might not make it out of here alive, and she knew it.

It was why she had to be shackled. His little fighter would've never willingly left him.

I love her.

The realization rose from deep inside him and fired through his bloodstream. He would tell her when they reunited. He would see her again if only to give her the three words he'd never given anyone else.

He held her gaze a moment longer, kissed her lips around the gag, and lowered the hood.

She didn't cry. Didn't kick or growl. Instead, she composed herself, sitting calmly in utter blackness as he backed away.

So much strength in this woman. He was completely and irrevocably besotted.

Passing Tomas on the way out of the limo, he

gave his friend a squeeze on the arm. Then he turned and ambled toward the entryway, unable to breathe.

There, he watched the cartel escort climb in. He didn't move as the limo pulled away. He didn't take a breath until they vanished around the bend. He couldn't help it. His precious, beautiful future was in that car, and she was on her way to safety.

The most important part of the operation had been accomplished. She would be reunited with her sister by tomorrow morning.

Now he had to finish this.

As he made his way back to his room, his mind circled around the plan he and Tomas had devised after the meeting with Marco. He couldn't sit around and wait for backup. His team could take weeks to locate him and mobilize an attack.

They might never find him.

He needed to learn the exact coordinates of the compound and get the fuck out of here. Then he would return with his team.

Now that he knew who Silvia was, he wouldn't waste his time seducing information from her.

He needed her key card.

Tomas had given him the layout of the property, including the location of the monitoring room. Despite Vera's seething reluctance, she helped by telling him how to find the breach in the wall. Then she told him about the armory.

Beyond the largest pool, nestled deep in the garden, stood a small concrete building. She claimed it housed enough weaponry and ammunition to take down the entire cartel. It was also monitored by multiple cameras and could only be accessed with the top cartel members' key cards. Silvia was among that membership.

Loading up with guns and crawling through the hole in the wall was a life-or-death option only. If he broke into the armory, they would know. He could only resort to that if his identity was discovered.

Hell, it might come down to exactly that because his plan was shoddy as hell.

He intended to steal a cartel member's street clothes and cover his hair with a hat and bandanna. Disguised as a thug, he would use Silvia's key card to enter the monitoring room and steal a peek at the monitors that showed the surrounding area. With any luck, no one would question him before he turned heel and left.

He had about a five-percent chance of success, and that was optimistic.

First, he had to spend some time with Silvia.

A few hours later, he ordered an old fashioned with rye whiskey and found a quiet corner on a vacant veranda. Sprawled in a comfortable chair, he waited.

She didn't make him wait long.

Pausing in the doorway, Silvia wore a red body-clinging dress and matching lipstick. Black hair, black eyes, she looked like Satan's mistress. He hid his repulsion and pretended not to notice her.

She approached his chair, placing one strappy heel before the other. Heel to toe, heel to toe, she really put a lot into that walk. Always trying too hard. This time, it was a waste of effort.

"Good evening, handsome." She lowered into the seat beside him.

He sipped his drink, brushed imaginary lint off his suit jacket. Then he gave her his attention. "Good evening."

At the edge of his periphery, her key card hung from the front of her dress by a claw clasp. The same clasp that attached his plastic card to his pants pocket.

The cards looked identical. A swap should be effortless.

She leaned in, giving him an eyeful of plumped-up cleavage. Heavy mascara lined her lashes, hooding a gaze that darkened with hesitant hunger. She wasn't certain of his interest. Hell, he'd teased her enough over the past couple of days to leave her hot and bothered and unsure about everything.

"Why didn't you leave with your new purchase?" She trailed a finger along his arm.

"I have unfinished business here." He raked his gaze down her body and lowered his voice into a suggestive caress. "Something I want."

"If that's true, why did you spend three million dollars on another woman?"

"Because I can."

"But why *her?*"

"The one I want said she couldn't be bought." He traced a finger along the curve of her jaw.

Her breath caught. "For that much money, my brothers would've made an exception."

"Good to know." He bit his lower lip in a way that women seemed to love. "I might make another offer, but I always sample expensive things before I invest in them."

"Is that right?" She purred, an actual feline sound in the back of her throat, and rubbed her face against his touch like a contented cat.

He wanted to backhand her, which, even for him, exceeded his tolerance of violence. He adored women and treated them as such.

But not this one.

This one, he ached to kill.

Stifling those urges, he reclined in the chair and sprawled his legs in a blatant invitation for her to join him.

She did instantly, crawling over his lap and straddling his hips. Then she touched him, her hands wandering and exploring his body unfettered. He allowed it, biting back bile and guilt.

He'd told Vera he belonged to her, and he meant every word. But Silvia's key card was hanging against his chest, so close, right fucking there.

"You're so goddamn sexy." She slid her palms over his shoulders. "So big and strong and beautifully formed."

As she groped his muscles and nuzzled his neck, she went on and on about his physical appearance. He barely attended, his focus on his goal, waiting for the right moment.

When her breaths sped up and her eyes clouded over with lust, he knew she was lost in her aching need, thoroughly distracted by her greedy desires.

Without warning, he yanked her tight, bodies flush. In the span of her startled yelp, he unclipped the card from her dress. Her hands flew to his face, her hips abhorrently grinding as he switched the cards and secured his to the same spot on her bodice. Her card went into his pocket under the guise of his knuckles teasing her inner thigh.

She bent in for a kiss.

He captured a hunk of her hair, stopping her an inch away. "I do the kissing, not the other way around."

Her ruby lips bowed downward into a moue of frustration.

The easy part was done. Now he needed to untangle her from his body before she put her hands on his cock.

He wasn't hard, not even a little. The very thought of her touching him stirred nausea in his stomach.

Too late.

Her fingers slipped past his guard and caught him between the legs. He didn't move, didn't twitch, for fear he would knock her across the room.

"You're not into this." Her grimace deepened as she squeezed his limp dick. "Almost as if you're not into *me*."

"I've been *very* straightforward about what I'm into." He removed her hand and chose his words carefully. "While you match my physical specifications perfectly, you fail to meet other expectations."

"You like a fight."

"Always."

"You want me to struggle and cry while you dominate me." Her throat bobbed. "You want to rape me."

No. He didn't want anything to do with her. "Yes. Brutally."

"I see." Her eyes flared, and the skin on her neck pulled taut. She wasn't into that. Not at all. "How would that work if you bought me? Would you rape me *and her* at the same time? Or would you assign us days of the week and alternate between us?"

"I would do whatever the fuck I wanted because I would own you."

"The day you arrived, you said you would buy my freedom, and when I walked out of here, I would be free."

"I'm revising my offer." He cupped her throat and applied pressure. "You require a leash."

That did it. She shoved off his lap and straightened her dress, her nostrils pulsing with indignation. She brushed a hand over the key card, checking its presence.

Standing taller, a spark of cruelty lit her gaze. "Have you heard from your bodyguard?"

Alarm spiked through him. He started to reach for his phone and changed his mind. Tomas wasn't supposed to make contact until he put Vera on Restrepo's plane and began his drive to Texas to deal with the email issue. That would've taken hours.

Except it had been hours.

He swallowed down his rising panic. "I'm not expecting a call."

With a smirk, she curled a lock of hair around her finger and angled her face to the camera in the ceiling. "Turn his service back on."

What the fuck? They'd cut the signal on his phone?

All the blood in his body drained to his feet. His skin prickled, and his stomach bottomed out as he removed the phone from his pocket. His hand shook as he turned it on and flipped through the screens. No missed calls. No texts. She was fucking with him.

Before he could release a relieved sigh, the phone started buzzing, blowing up with incoming texts as the service came back on line.

The first message had been sent three hours ago, and when he absorbed the words, his heart stopped.

Unknown: Your tie is crooked.

It was a code phrase, designed to convey that something had gone terribly wrong. Only Tomas knew that code.

More texts followed, timed several minutes apart.

Unknown: The escort took her.

Unknown: Kicked me out of the limo on an abandoned road and drove off with her.

Unknown: Hello?

Unknown: Answer the phone.

Unknown: I'm sorry. I couldn't stop them. I was forced out of the limo at gunpoint.

Unknown: I don't know where they took her.

Unknown: Are you getting this?

Unknown: Where are you?

Unknown: I'm tossing this phone. Will be in touch.

Pain detonated in his chest, lungs, and throat. The roar of his heartbeat thrashed in his head, and terror paralyzed him, making it impossible to think.

The cartel had Vera.

She wasn't safe.

They knew. They fucking knew he'd been playing them in an effort to rescue her. They were going to hang them both from meat hooks.

Silvia watched his reaction, studying him too closely, way too hard. He kept his expression in check, and in the next breath, he flipped a switch.

The calculating side of him took control, squashing all fear, wrath, and love. He extinguished every ounce of emotion and let the coldness creep in, numbing his limbs and deadening his heart. He blinked, drew a steady breath, and focused on the facts.

If his cover was blown, they would've killed

Tomas. And Vera, too. Unless they kept her alive to use her as a hostage to question him.

Why would they question him if they knew he was the rescuer they'd been waiting for? Why had Silvia tried to fuck him just a moment ago?

There was no way the cartel knew he was part of a vigilante group or that their lives were targeted by such a group. The brothers simply wanted to retaliate against Tula Gomez, their father's killer, and whomever she'd sent to save her sister.

If they truly knew Luke's identity, he would've already been tortured and cut into pieces.

This was another game. A test. Maybe they suspected that he'd been sent for Vera, but they weren't convinced enough to risk his backlash if they were wrong.

From their viewpoint, holding Vera as a hostage was forgivable. She was just a whore. Killing Luke's assistant, however, was just plain bad for business.

So they let Tomas go, effectively removing Luke's bodyguard from the property with no way to return.

The cartel didn't know that during the hours that Tomas had been texting Luke, he would've found another phone—would've stolen one from a random stranger if necessary—and contacted their team.

The Freedom Fighters would've learned at least an hour or two ago that Luke was in trouble. They just had to find him.

But they had intel now. They had everything Tomas would've passed along.

Luke turned his attention to Silvia, taking his time to speak.

"Why?" Slowly, casually, he rose from the chair and pocketed the phone. "I paid for her. You received the money. Alejandro assured me that you honor your deals."

"It's just a technicality. A hiccup in the deal. I'm sure we can work it out."

"Explain the *hiccup*."

"I'll show you. Follow me." She pivoted and strode away, giving him no choice but to follow.

TWENTY-FIVE

As Silvia led Luke outside, a disarming chill saturated the air. Maybe it was just him. His skin rippled with the prickles of a cold sweat, and the drum of looming doom sounded in his ears.

Unarmed and without backup, he had to keep his wits about him. Maintaining his composure and talking his way out of this were his only lines of defense.

Unless his cover was already blown. In that case, he was a walking corpse.

She escorted him along a trail through the lush garden, her heels carefully maneuvering the cracks in the cobblestones. He considered making a break for it, his flight-or-fight instinct gripping him hard. He could outrun Silvia with ease, but he couldn't escape the cameras and the armed guards.

Even if he could, he would never leave Vera. If she was even here.

The path led to a small pond encircled on all sides by dense trees. The moonless shroud of nightfall cast the water in inky black, the muddy edge occupied by half a dozen man-shaped silhouettes.

Nothing like walking into a waiting throng of armed, distrusting, coldblooded murderers. His anxiety surged into overdrive.

As he approached, he squinted through the darkness, searching for Vera's small frame among them.

Marco, Omar… All four brothers were here, dressed in a range of suits and street clothes. A few others in the cartel accompanied them.

No Vera.

"Where is she?" Luke paused a few feet away and wiped his slick palms on his pants, trying to control his nerves.

"Did you know," Miguel asked, tilting his head, "that the black widow is the deadliest spider in America? At times, the female eats the male after mating, hence her name."

He could've gone without that visual.

Impatience dogged him as he probed the pond and surrounding trees, his temper growing short. "I paid a lot of goddamn money for that girl, and you fucked me over. If this is how you do business, I will—"

"Careful." Miguel's accent sharpened. "A smart man would think twice before making threats against La Rocha."

"Fuck you. Where's my property?" As the insensitive question left his lips, he detected a disturbance at the center of the pond. His pulse lost rhythm, spiraling turbulently, his eyes refusing to adjust in the darkness. "What's out there in the water?"

"The black widow's bite is venomous." Miguel slid a hand down his tie, needlessly straightening it. "But not usually deadly to humans. A single bite doesn't have the potency. But many bites? Dozens attacking at once, especially when threatened? That would be fatal to a small woman. I've seen it with my own eyes." He chuckled. "Nature is not merciful."

Tension breathed down his neck, and vertigo threatened to buckle his legs.

Spiders.

A pond of tenebrous water.

Nothing foreboding about that.

Put Vera in the middle of it, and they couldn't have orchestrated a more sinister nightmare.

If the desired effect was to scare the ever-loving fuck out of him, job well done. His throat felt like smoldering ash, his chest a cavern of dry ice.

But he only showed them the man he wanted them to see—an arrogant prick whose time was invaluable. "Get to the point."

"Omar." Miguel nodded at his brother.

Omar flicked on a portable spotlight. The blinding beam shot across the pond, illuminating two shapes at the center.

An unfamiliar man sat in a kayak with a paddle resting across his lap. A few feet from him, a small dome floated on the surface, wrapped in some sort of metal mesh, like the screening material in windows. It allowed in airflow and light, but little else.

He didn't have to look closer to know what he'd find inside. The contraption was only slightly larger than a human head, and that was what it held.

Vera's head.

With her body submerged to her neck—presumably anchored to the floor of the pond—her eyes squeezed shut against the glare of the spotlight. Her mouth angled above the water, but she couldn't shout or make a sound because her lips were stretched open by a spider gag.

The metal ring sat behind her teeth, holding her jaw in a gaping *O*. A buckle secured it around her head, and four steel legs fanned out from the ring. Those curved legs extended over her chin and cheeks, preventing her from turning the ring in her mouth while forcing her jaw wide open to accept anything into her throat. Like probing fingers. Or a cock.

Or a black widow spider.

His stomach churned. His heartbeat tightened, and his insides ran too hot and too cold as he fought the excessive need to swallow. He couldn't trust himself to speak without a quaking voice.

"She can put her head underwater." Marco stepped to Luke's side, his dark features ever darker in the thickness of night. "Though I don't think she'd enjoy that. Have you ever tried to keep your throat closed while your mouth is held open underwater?"

He'd learned many survival tricks during his time in Van's attic. But nothing related to water play.

"She can't dislodge the mesh hood," Marco said. "It's connected to her life vest. Her hands are bound, and her feet are tied to a cement block, keeping her vertical."

"Why?" He girded his backbone, forcing strength in his tone. "What's the point of this?"

"We don't trust you, John Smith."

"I assure you," Luke scoffed, "after this double-crossing bullshit, the feeling is fucking mutual."

"We haven't double-crossed you. We're merely being cautious. See, we investigated you, as we do with all our guests, and we can't find a single piece of information about you."

"I didn't give you a real name."

"No one does. We use facial recognition software.

You can't hide your face in public these days. Not with all the cameras spying and recording your every move. Except you've done exactly that. It's as if you don't exist, and that makes you…questionable."

Luke had fallen out of the system when he ran away from home. When Van abducted him, no one knew he was missing. No one cared. He was as good as dead. After he escaped, he remained dead. He never used his real name. Never had an encounter with the law. When Cole Hartman joined their team, he erased all of the Freedom Fighters from every hidden corner of the Internet and dark web.

None of them existed.

"This shouldn't surprise you." Luke squared his shoulders, watching Vera hold her shit together at the center of the pond. "If a man has the means to spend three-million dollars on a slave, he should certainly be able to cover his tracks effectively."

"Yes, we've taken that into account. This is why your assistant is still alive. Once you've answered our questions, your property will be returned to you, and your life will resume unmolested."

"I don't owe you a goddamn thing." Fury flushed through his body, hardening his muscles. "Release her."

"Who do you work for?"

"Myself."

"What is your business?"

"None of your fucking business."

"Mr. Smith." Silvia sidled up beside him and stroked his arm. "You can tell us the easy way. Or we can force you the hard way."

"You think I would choose a girl over the critical confidentiality of my business?"

"A girl you paid three mil for?" Silvia narrowed

her eyes. "That's the question, isn't it?"

"You've threatened me, and now it's my turn." He directed his gaze over her head and met Marco's eyes. "You can apologize and escort me and my purchase directly to my plane. Or you can suffer the backlash of my exceptionally powerful and ruthless business partners. I'm connected, Marco, deeply and dangerously, and I will turn every magnate within my far-reaching circle against your cartel. You are fucking with the wrong man."

That much was true. Between Van Quiso, Tiago Badell, and Matias Restrepo, Luke had some brutally violent allies. Add Cole Hartman into the mix, and they were ingloriously, terrifyingly unstoppable. Whether or not he and Vera died tonight, La Rocha would be annihilated. There was no doubt.

Marco stood so still he didn't seem to be breathing. Only his eyes moved, scouring Luke's blank expression. Without looking away, he slowly raised an arm and snapped his fingers.

For an asinine moment, Luke thought he'd won.

Until the man in the kayak tossed a lid off a large container and poured the contents atop the dome on Vera's head.

Luke lost his mind as a cascade of teeming, shiny black bodies glimmered in the spotlight, tumbling down the mesh sides and hitting the water. Vera's face froze in a silent scream and quickly vanished behind a writhing wall of spiders as they raced back up the dome, climbing over one another to safety.

The kayak jostled, rocking wildly beneath the man's sudden and frantic attempt to paddle away. The oar whirled around him as if he were fighting off an invisible monster. Within seconds, he was beached on the shore and running, shouting in Spanish, and slapping at his arms.

"Black widows don't like water." Miguel's amused voice penetrated the panic that lay siege to Luke's mind. "Eventually, they'll find their way into her hair and slip under the net. Once they start biting, the venom will attack her nervous system. With her diaphragm in paralysis, she'll struggle to breathe. Severe abdominal pain will set in, along with tremors in her legs, vomiting, profuse sweating, and swollen eyelids. The number of bites and the depth of the punctures will determine how quickly she dies. That's if she doesn't drown first."

Fear was a vicious, quivering entity inside him. Tunnel vision invaded, and light-headedness crippled him with an overwhelming need to sit down before he fell down. But more than that, he was ruled by the savage, reckless urge to run to her. His legs contracted and burned to go, go, go. Now!

That was what they wanted.

This was the test.

Dozens of eyes watched him from all directions, waiting for him to strip his disguise and rescue the girl.

A slave buyer wouldn't dare dirty his expensive suit to save the life of a whore. But a cartel *sicario* or *teniente* would endure torture and take a bullet before returning to his *jefe* empty-handed. That would be career-ending. Life-ending. The ultimate disgrace.

To survive this, he had to prove to them that he wasn't with an enemy cartel. He was John Smith, shrewd businessman and unfeeling slave owner.

He stood motionless, ice-cold and dead inside, calling their bluff.

Seconds stretched. Spiders swarmed. His lungs

refused air.

The longer he waited, the more deadly Vera's predicament became.

Seeing her smothered beneath a blanket of black widows burned away the lining of his stomach and turned his guts inside out. There was only so much stress a body could bear—hers and his.

With her mouth forced open, her limbs restrained in murky water, and her head enveloped by a hood of venomous spiders, her panic would've exceeded volcanic by now.

Long black hair floated around her, skimming the surface and providing a landing place for clinging legs. Were they swimming beneath the dome? Sinking fangs into her tender skin? Injecting her with venom?

Enough.

Everything inside him switched gears. Tendons turned to steel. Muscles flexed around fortifying joints. Adrenaline spiked, and his mind cleared.

He would die for her.

He didn't remember removing his suit, but by the time he reached the pond's edge, every stitch of clothing was gone except his pants and shoes. He toed off the latter and scooped them up to use as weapons against the spiders. Then he calmly waded into the chilly water.

"What are you doing, Mr. Smith?" Marco asked, not bothering to chase him.

"Retrieving my property." He wouldn't survive their gunfire, but he would do everything in his power to ensure that she escaped.

Beyond the spotlight's beam, he waited until the water rose to his hips before discreetly removing the key card and phone from his pocket. Both went into one shoe, which he kept above the water and shielded from their view.

"Come back here," Marco called in a bored tone. "We *will* shoot you."

"Do it, Marco, and you'll invite an army of enemies you won't win against."

"How will they find us?" Marco laughed.

He met the man's eyes over his shoulder. "How did *I* find you?"

Marco's face went taut. Let him stew on that for a while.

As the water rushed over his shoulders, he kept the insides of the shoes dry, floating them smoothly along the surface.

The swim toward her was the longest half-minute of his life. The spot between his shoulder blades tingled beneath the aim of multiple guns.

They could shoot him at any moment, but he counted on them waiting. He was providing them with a show of human suffering and vain hope. It was the ultimate entertainment. They lived for this shit.

He slowed at the center, scanning the illuminated water for squirming black bodies. Thank fuck for the light—

It clicked off, dousing him in pitch black.

"Turn it back on," he roared, panic setting in.

The laughter of monsters erupted on the shore.

Fuck them. Without the light, he couldn't see the spiders. But it also meant the cartel couldn't see him.

He released the shoes, letting them float. Then he inched toward the bobbing spider-covered dome.

"It's me," he whispered. "I'm going to remove the gag first. Don't make a sound when I do."

He couldn't see her face through the squirming

bodies to know if she was still above water. There were too many, some falling into the black depths around him. He could splash the mesh hood or hit it with a shoe to clear it, but that would just scatter the threat and waste time.

His skin erupted with the sensation of crawling legs, and he spun, shaking himself beneath the surface. His blood pressure exploded, and paranoia set his teeth on edge.

He breathed through it, drew a deep gulp into his lungs, and dove.

His eyes opened to sheer blackness, but he found her legs quickly. Sliding his hands over her jeans, the life vest, and her neck, he reached the surface with questing fingers.

Her skin felt warm and alive, her face still above water. Still breathing.

Hang on, Vera.

There wasn't enough room in the dome for both of them. So he tucked his head downward, kicked his legs to maintain buoyancy, and blindly unbuckled the spider gag.

A sudden, searing prick erupted on his forearm. He screamed, unable to control the reaction, and his lungs expelled precious bubbles of air.

Motherfucking fuck! That hurt!

It was just one bite. God only knew how many she'd suffered already.

His pulse pounded as his fingers located her lips and pried the metal ring from her mouth. Pulling the gag away, he tackled the rope on her hands.

He couldn't hear anything, didn't know if the cartel was yelling for him. He couldn't care. His lungs burned for air, but he needed her out of this rope.

When the knot around her hands finally gave, his chest was on fire. He kicked hard, shooting upward and surfacing only long enough to take a huge breath. Then he dove for her feet.

The rope there took longer, the knot too tight to loosen with fingers. He wasted invaluable seconds trying to untie it from the cement block.

They'd done this before. Everything was too perfectly measured. From the anchor to the life vest, her body was stretched in a vertical line, allowing no wriggle room. The dome was fastened to the vest, which she should be able to unzip and slip—

Her knees bent above his hands, eliminating the taut stretch of her legs. She'd removed the vest.

Soft fingers curled around his, and together they tore at the knot around her ankles.

He wanted to sigh beneath her living, breathing touch. He ached to hold her and whisper kisses across her skin and show her how much he loved her.

The rope fell away.

They reached the surface together to the sounds of Marco shouting from the shore.

"Mr. Smith, bring her here."

"Did you get bitten?" he whispered.

"Just a few times." She cupped his face in the dark, her legs sliding soundlessly against his as she stayed afloat.

She was close enough that he could make out her exquisitely fierce features. *And the movement in her hair.*

Near her temple, a black widow clung with long legs, seemingly tangled in a curly lock.

"Oh, God, there's one in my hair, isn't there?" Her question rode on a hesitant breath.

"Hold still." His chest constricted as he pinched

the hard black body, cringing as he flung it away.

"Thank you."

"I love you."

"Luke—"

He covered her mouth with his hand. "You're dead."

"John Smith!" Marco called again.

"She went underwater, goddammit! If she's dead, I'll be extremely displeased." He whirled, finding the shoe with the phone in it floating nearby. He pushed it toward her while pulling her close and whispering quickly. "This contains a phone and Silvia's key card. My team is on standby in Orange County. Call them. Help them find you. I'm going to create a diversion."

Her eyes turned colder than the Greenland ice sheet, flickering with flames of rage. "You can go to hell."

"On my way. But I need you to do this." He rattled off a phone number, his nerves raging with frantic energy. "Repeat it back to me."

Her jaw set. Then she whispered the numbers. "I'm not leaving you again."

"If we both run, we're both dead. Go."

Her gaze, as sharp as a blade, absorbed everything from the restless men on the shore to the dense trees on the other side. She knew he was right, and she hated him for it.

"You can't fake my death," she said. "They'll search the pond for my body."

"That'll take time and daylight. Avoid the cameras and get to that breach in the wall before sunrise. I know you can do it." He kissed her hard and fast. Then he pushed away and started screaming.

"Ow! Fuck. Get them off of me!" As he splashed

around in the water, he marked her retreat.

She swam beneath the surface, guiding the shoe along the top as she raced to the far shore.

"Get me out of here!" He continued to thrash, moving away from the floating dome of spiders. "I can't find her, you son of a bitch! Get your men in here and fix this!"

The spotlight switched on, blinding his eyes. It pointed away from the direction she'd swam. The cover of trees should hide her exit from the water, but he kept flailing, ensuring all attention remained on him.

No one came to his rescue. They stood around like the heartless fucks that they were and waited for him to drag his ass to the shore. He took his time and made a lot of noise, giving her an extra minute to flee.

"You killed her." He trudged out of the pond and collapsed onto his knees, heaving. "You owe me three million and a lot of goddamn groveling. Take me to my plane."

"I don't think so." Marco prowled forward.

Yeah, he hadn't thought so, either.

As he pushed to stand, he was so focused on *not* looking for Vera on the far shore that he missed the butt of a rifle swinging toward his head. He saw it just as it collided with his skull.

Pain ricocheted. The ground rose up, and the world went black.

TWENTY-SIX

Luke woke without clothes.

The room was austerely gray. Prosaic. No windows. One door. Fluorescent lights. Concrete walls. And a large steel table, which he was bent over. With his feet on the floor, his arms stretched over his head, his hands were shackled with handcuffs—the standard-issue police variety.

It was a cartel interrogation room.

The cuffs connected to a chain that fastened beneath the table. A rod between his ankles forced them apart and secured to something beneath him. He gave the restraints a testing yank. No give.

His skull pounded from the collision with a rifle, and a burning itch flared on his forearm around two red fang marks. But those were the least of his problems.

He wasn't alone.

"Oh, good," he murmured, his voice cracking with dry rot. "The whole family is here."

Ignoring him, Silvia and her four brothers communed beside a wall of shelves filled with fetish equipment and instruments of torture.

He was no stranger to the array of tools that sadists used to correct, fuck, and break a body. Eight years ago, he'd learned how to endure the full spectrum of pain, purgatory and hell, and every torment in between. He'd barely survived those weeks.

I won't survive it again.

That disparaging thought was overshadowed by a more pressing one.

Vera.

Was she still alive? Had she made it through the breach in the wall? What if she'd been bitten too many times to recover?

He shook off his worst fears and fantasized about her sprinting through the junkyard in the cloak of darkness, armed with weapons from the armory, reaching a busy street, and waving down a motorist with a gun.

It was an impossible notion. She'd had three years to escape, and God knew she'd tried.

But maybe this time was different. The cartel was distracted with whatever they were planning for him. And she had Silvia's key, which gave her access to places she hadn't been able to go before. Places she could hide without cameras. But if she'd gone to the armory, she would've been detected. Alarms would've sounded.

What had he missed while he was unconscious? He couldn't have been out for longer than a few minutes. Not long enough for Silvia to leave his side and discover that her key card had been swapped out.

Hopefully.

He wouldn't ask the cartel a single question about Vera. If they told him she was dead, he wouldn't believe them. He couldn't. By the looks of the instruments they were considering, they intended to torture him. Physically. Psychologically. Any manner they pleased.

The silver lining? He didn't see a container of spiders anywhere.

Silvia turned and sashayed toward him. Her red lips curved into a smirk, causing his heart to whack against his ribs like a caged animal. Then he saw the apparatus in her hand.

A metal dildo the size of Tomas' dick strapped to a leather harness. Strap-ons were Liv Reed's specialty, and he'd been on the receiving end of her thrusts more than once. But she'd used phalluses with a squeezable texture. Never metal.

Wordlessly, he watched Silvia lift her red dress and expose her bare cunt. Just as wordlessly, her brothers gathered around, staring boldly at the disturbingly erotic view their sister gave them.

This was an area of kink he had no experience in. She was blood-related to three of these men. They'd all been raised together since childhood. Talk about a mindfuck.

The sounds of quickening breaths coming from them made his blood shudder. Twitchy hands, chilling grins, the stench of anticipation. Then the deep voice of the oldest son, echoing through the room. "Answer our questions, and we'll let you go."

No, they wouldn't.

He lay his cheek on the cold steel table and tried to relax his muscles. Van had trained him how to endure this without injury. The key was in *not* fighting the invasion.

Marco and Silvia stepped out of sight behind him,

making it impossible to remain calm.

"What's your real name?" Miguel approached the table near Luke's head and unzipped the fly of his suit pants.

"I'm not interested in your dick, sisterfucker."

"I'm not interested in yours, either. But I do love to watch my sister fuck."

Feminine hands curled around the muscles of Luke's ass, stroking and fondling and coiling him with anger.

"He's so beautiful." She bent over his back, fingers wandering everywhere, her hair tickling his spine with dread. "Just look at this body. Big and strong and powerful. I want to keep him."

"We'll see." Miguel pulled out his erection and lazily stroked it. "Tell us who you're connected with, John."

Luke squeezed his eyes shut as her hand found his flaccid cock.

Please, don't react. Dear fucking God, don't give her what she wants.

His body would respond to her touch eventually. But he stalled it by casting his mind back to the pond and replaying his horror and fear as spiders teemed over Vera's head. He thought about how close she'd come to dying in that water and the anguish he would've been experiencing now had he been forced to witness that.

"He's not getting hard." Silvia tightened her strokes, her grip too clumsy and aggressive.

It was the wrong hand.

The wrong fucking woman.

Miguel slammed a fist on the table, prompting Luke's eyes to flash open. "Then make him hard."

No, no, no. He couldn't do this to Vera. He couldn't respond to another woman's touch.

A voice in his head whispered, *You're not doing it. It's not your fault. This is rape.*

Didn't matter. As Silvia slipped under the table and drew him into her mouth, he saw red. He roared. He thrashed in the shackles. And he hardened.

Spittles of rage sprayed the steel surface beneath his lips. He choked as she sucked. His balls withered as she groped. His skin peeled away from burning muscles, shrinking with the force of his unholy wrath. And still, his cock did what it was designed to do. It swelled in the suction of wet heat.

Shame threaded through him. Vulnerability and helplessness throttled him on all sides. He'd been here before. Pinned down and degraded beneath Van's cruelty. Only this time was worse.

He belonged to someone else. His body wasn't just betraying him. It was betraying the woman he loved.

Voices barked in a fog around him. Questions. Demands. They fired their inquiries one after the other as a dry finger probed his ass and forced its way inside.

Her fingernail scratched through the unbearable penetration. He tried to relax, but a strange buzz flogged his ears. Heat pricked the backs of his eyes, and his vision blurred.

He checked out, left the room, and went to a place inside his head.

He couldn't be present while Silvia sodomized him, milked him, and repeated the torture. And he couldn't allow himself to succumb to a moment of weakness and expose his vigilante operation, his friends, or anything related to Vera.

He burrowed so effectively inside his mind that he didn't sense the world around him. Until blinding agony seared through his rectum.

A strangled scream burst from deep in his chest. He knew the metal phallus had torn something inside him before she pulled back and rammed into him again.

Cold fire. Scathing pressure. If he'd still had an erection, it was long gone. Bile welled in his throat. He came close to blacking out as his spirit vacated his body and crashed back into his organs so violently that he shook, heaved from an empty stomach, and felt horribly, miserably dead.

And so it began.

Silvia fucked him with a ruthlessness that aroused everyone in the room but him. Omar and Miguel continued to volley their questions, but the pauses in between grew longer as they watched Marco mount their sister and thrust into her from behind, driving the velocity and force of the strap-on.

Then the interrogation was forgotten altogether as they jerked off to the show.

Alejandro was the only one not participating. He stood off to the side, arms clenched across his chest. But he wasn't unaffected. The bulge in his pants confessed his arousal.

It was apparent then why no one else was in the room. How would the cartel members feel about the incestuous orgies that took place among their leaders? No wonder the brothers never answered questions about how they were related to her. This wasn't okay. The most depraved criminals wouldn't find this sibling fuckery amusing or acceptable.

The fact that they were doing it in front of Luke meant they had no intention of letting him live.

Watching them together, however, helped him understand Silvia's motivation. She loved her brothers, sickeningly and unlawfully, and craved their attention. When they brought in Vera, Silvia was no longer the center of their world. She didn't approve of how possessive they became over another woman.

The crazy, jealous bitch moaned behind him, and Marco joined in, shouting in Spanish as he came.

Inside his stepsister.

"I need something to eat." Silvia pulled out and gave Luke's ass a hard slap. "But don't worry, handsome. I'm nowhere near finished with you."

She might be when she found out her key card had been swapped.

Marco escorted her out, using his own key. They came and went in pairs, presumably to freshen up, refuel, and check on the cartel's operations.

Hours passed.

No one mentioned Vera.

Luke didn't speak a word, and they didn't free him from the restraints. After bending in the same position for so long, his muscles and joints ached. The contusion on his head hadn't stopped throbbing, and his ass burned in ways he hadn't experienced in eight years.

He had no plan. No hope, save one.

Vera was alive.

He couldn't accept the alternative. It was the only thought keeping him sane.

Eventually, Silvia returned with Omar, wearing a silk robe and fresh lipstick. She dropped the garment inside the door and strolled toward Luke, completely nude.

He turned his head and looked the other way.

"Oh, handsome. Don't be that way." She climbed atop him, straddling his back and grinding her wet pussy against his spine. Then she angled forward and licked his ear. "I want your gorgeous cock inside me."

His insides curdled, and his breaths caught fire, searing past his nose.

"His dick is thick like yours, Alejandro."

The youngest brother glowered from his post near the door. "Don't—"

"Don't what?" She returned to Luke's ear. "Whenever he fucks me, it makes him so angry. God, I love his angry sex."

Out of the five of them, she was clearly the most psychotic. What kind of deranged shit had to happen to a person to turn them into the grinding, sex-crazed demon on his back? She didn't belong in this world. She might even be too damaged for hell.

The door opened, and Marco stalked in. All five of them were here now, which meant the torture would begin again.

Sweat chilled on his brow, and his ass clenched, unbidden.

Silvia slid off his back and perched a naked butt cheek on the table beside his face. Her hand drifted to his hair, stroking him like a pet.

He seethed, jerking and bucking, unable to stop her. Exhaustion pressed into his bones, and prolonged stress fumbled his thoughts. But no matter what they did to him, he would *not* talk.

"Tell me." She toyed with the hair at his nape. "Do you love her?"

He bit down on his lips.

She lowered off the table and put her face in his. "Do you love Vera Gomez?"

Fuck, fuck, fuck.

He arranged his forehead in an expression of confusion. If he remained silent, would it give too much away? Maybe. So he formed a fitting response. "I despise you with every drop of blood in my body."

Her head jerked back, and her eyes tapered into reptilian slits. "Harsh. But you know that's not what I asked. The woman you paid three million for? Vera Gomez? Was she just a job to you? Or did you love her?"

He didn't like her speaking about Vera in past tense. "I don't know what you're talking about, you demented bitch."

"It's time to remove some of his extremities." Marco strolled forward, holding large steel-bladed pruning shears. He opened the handles and snapped the blades closed, his expression chillingly lethal. "Starting with the one you love most."

"No!" Silvia straightened. "You're not cutting off his dick. That's mine, and I'm keeping it."

"You can keep it in a jar."

If Luke's bladder had anything to expel, he might've pissed down his leg.

"I want to feel him inside me, Marco." She sidled up to her brother and cupped him between the legs. "I want to feel both of you at the same time."

"Fucking insatiable." He smacked her hand away. "Never happy. Look what we built for you." He swung out an arm, indicating the estate. "We give you everything you want, and it's never enough."

"That's not true." She burst into Spanish, throwing around her hands.

Marco yelled back, getting in her face. Miguel and Omar joined in, and the dysfunctional family began to scream over one another.

Luke kept his eyes on the hedge shears in Marco's grip. His blood ran cold at the thought of that thing going near him. And it would, as soon as they stopped arguing.

Think, goddammit.

What could he say to get out of this? What bargain could he make without revealing the existence of his team? Could he fabricate a believable story on the fly?

His ruse as a wealthy slave buyer had taken weeks to prepare, every detail memorized and thought out. If he changed his story now, they would know he was lying. Besides, anything he told them would only delay the inevitable. He couldn't stall them for weeks.

As his captors continued to quarrel about which limb to remove first, the door opened.

They didn't hear it.

His heart pounded at the sight of a gun, connected to an outstretched arm, the body out of view. Then the gunman stepped in.

Gun*woman.*

He stopped breathing as Vera dragged an unfamiliar man in behind her and closed the door.

The room fell quiet. Every head turned. No one was breathing.

She aimed a Glock at Alejandro's face, who had pulled his own gun the moment she came in.

He stood close enough to knock the weapon from her hand. But he wouldn't. Because her other hand held a goddamn grenade. The pin was gone, her tiny fingers white-knuckled around the spoon. If she dropped it, they were all dead.

Luke scanned the room, confirming that only

three people were armed. Alejandro, Vera, and the man she'd brought in.

What the fuck was she thinking? She was supposed to be gone and calling in backup. Goddamn her for not listening.

And God love her for showing up.

He should've known. This woman didn't run. She fucking fought.

Rifles and ammo hung from her shoulders and hips. Beneath the heavy artillery, she wore a bulletproof vest. Her bare arms and neck showed multiple spider bites and signs of swelling. But there were no visible holes in the vest. No signs of gun wounds.

How had she made it in and out of the armory and all the way here without getting shot?

No matter. She was here, and he couldn't have been prouder of her.

"I fucking told you she wasn't dead," Alejandro growled at his brothers.

"Easy, Vera." Miguel didn't move, his accent losing its smooth charisma. "Put the pin back in."

"I dropped it outside." She shrugged, rattling the rifles on her back. "Whoops."

"Romero." Marco glared at the skinny man at her side. "What are you doing?"

"She held me at gunpoint, *jefe.*" Romero gripped a huge phone, his gangly body weighed down by more guns and ammo belts than Luke could count. "She broke into my room and… I'm so sorry, *jefe*. She was going to kill me."

Who was this kid? He didn't look like a coldblooded cartel member.

"What did you do, Romero?" Marco asked dangerously.

With Alejandro's gun trained on her, she returned the aim with her Glock. "He shut down the cameras and sent the coordinates of the compound to Restrepo. If you listen hard, you might hear the choppers overhead."

Luke's pulse burst into a sprint.

Except Matias only had one chopper in the States. Maybe she assumed there would be more? Or maybe she was lying through her teeth.

His anxiety reached an all-time high as she waved the weapon through the room and pointed it at Silvia.

Did she even know how to use a gun? Could she shoot accurately under pressure?

"Unshackle him." Vera scowled at Silvia's naked body. "So help me God, I'll pump your skank ass full of lead, starting with your tits."

"You're not shooting anyone." Miguel stepped forward.

She swung the Glock toward him. Until Omar called her name, and she turned the gun on him.

Luke's mouth dried as he watched her finger bounce all over that trigger. With any luck, she wouldn't shoot *him.*

"How did you get in here?" Omar asked. "Only the people in this room have access."

"I used your sister's key."

"Then whose key…?" Silvia's face paled, and she shot a deadly look at Luke. "Oh, my God. You swapped it on the veranda. That's why I couldn't get into my room tonight."

"This is bullshit." Omar charged toward Vera.

With one hand on the grenade, she adjusted the gun's aim on him, let out a screech, and squeezed the trigger.

Nothing happened.

Omar froze, and the room went still.

"Well, shit." She rattled the Glock side to side. "Is this thing on?"

The brothers erupted in mocking laughter.

She laughed nervously with them, sobered, and retrained the gun.

"Just kidding." She fired off a shot with a yelp of surprise.

Holy fuck. Luke jerked as if he could dodge the bullet.

It missed him, missed Omar, too, and hit the concrete wall. The men moved, rushing at her, and she fired again. Over and over, rounds pinged through the room, until one finally hit Omar in the chest.

Silvia wailed as he hit the floor, dead before he dropped.

The beautiful part? Vera had shot him without letting go of the grenade.

She's incredible. Ferocious. And mine.

Outrage and grief poured off Marco and Miguel, but it was Alejandro that kept Luke's attention. The only reason the muscle head hadn't fired yet was because of that grenade. But if he inched close enough, he could wrestle it from her hand. If she shot him, he would shoot back, to hell with the grenade.

Luke burned with the urge to shout commands at her.

Don't take your eyes off Alejandro.

Keep Romero beside you.

Don't let anyone take the kid's weapons.

The Glock only has one bullet left.

Don't drop that fucking grenade.

But she was already doing everything right. For someone who hadn't been trained for combat, she was killing it.

There was only one problem.

Alejandro.

"Give me the grenade." He stepped toward her, gun aimed, patience gone. "Right now!"

TWENTY-SEVEN

I don't know what I'm doing.

I don't know what I'm doing.

Oh, Lord Jesus, what the hell am I supposed to do?

Vera's pulse bellowed in her throat, and her hands grew clammy around the gun. It was hard to think with all the screaming coming from Silvia, who lay prone across Omar's dead body.

The weapon that Alejandro aimed at her head didn't help her focus, either.

She couldn't even look at Luke and his position on the table. Or the strap-on on the floor. She was going to kill that fucking bitch. But first, she had to deal with Alejandro.

He pressed forward, forcing her to retreat.

"Stay at my side, Romero." She veered, angling toward Luke without a plan in sight.

Romero clung like velcro, souring her inhales with his fear. The computer whiz kid had been reluctantly instrumental in helping her get here. He also served as her pack mule. She could only carry so many guns, and she expected a war.

Silvia hadn't left Omar, her wails grinding into blubbering sobs as Marco and Miguel crept closer.

"Get back." She waved the pistol between them and Alejandro. "Move to the wall."

Holy shit, they were angry, their expressions crimson, veins bulging, hands flexing at their sides.

Good for them. She was pissed, too. And tired. Her fingers quivered around the grenade, and her arm flagged from training the gun one-handed.

When she reached the steel table, she glanced at the restraints. Latches on the chains. A key jutted from the locking mechanism on the handcuffs. Easy peasy.

Except she had no spare hands.

"Romero." She jerked her chin. "Free him."

"If you do," Alejandro said coldly, "you're dead."

"Remember my promise, Romero. Your tech skills are destined for better things. You're too smart to make the wrong choice here."

"She's out of bullets and won't be able to fire those rifles one-handed." Alejandro sneered. "She can't protect you."

"Oh." She played dumb, knowing she had one left in the chamber and a loaded Glock wedged in the back of her jeans. "Romero, I'm going to need you to get moving on those shackles now."

Her heart went ballistic as she waited for him to obey. She only had one chance at this. One try.

Aim at the chest. Don't let go of the grenade.

Romero shifted. Alejandro turned his gun toward the kid, and she fired.

A direct hit in the chest. As he stumbled back, she dropped the empty Glock, grabbed the second from her back, and sprayed bullets in the direction of Marco and Miguel.

Don't drop the grenade. Don't drop the grenade.

She silently chanted the reminder and counted off the rounds as she fired through the room. Mostly, she missed her targets, but at least two of the shots were fatal. As Marco and Miguel slumped to the floor, Silvia's ear-splitting shrieks rent the air.

Vera spun back to Alejandro. *Too late.*

His gun boomed, and her thigh buckled beneath explosive, scorching pain. The dizzying cloud of agony stole her balance. She held tight to the grenade, but she couldn't stop her fall.

Luke's roar shook the walls, penetrating her haze.

I've been hit.

I still have a gun.

Two bullets.

She squeezed off one as she went down. And missed.

Alejandro sprawled on the floor. Blood on his chest. Gun in his grip. Hard eyes locked on her.

She fired again, dropped the empty Glock, and clutched the grenade with both hands.

The gun slid from Alejandro's limp fingers. Two red holes, side by side, bloomed on his chest, his head lolled at an awkward angle. Dead.

She blinked, snapping out of a suspended fugue, and that was when the real pain kicked in. All at once, it crashed into her like a vengeful flood, slamming her teeth together and bowing her back.

The room spun in a cacophony of chaos. Fists pounded on the door. Silvia wailed. Romero unshackled Luke, and through it all, she clung to that grenade.

"Vera!" Luke's voice grew closer.

Then she felt roaming hands—on the grenade,

her face, her leg. Oh, God, her leg.

"I need to tie this off." His breaths came in bursts. "Can you hold the grenade?"

"Got it." She clenched her teeth, tasting blood.

"We knew all along!" Silvia screamed from across the room. "We knew when you chose her in the basement that you were with Restrepo, you lying, miserable, limp-dick murderer! You're dead. You're so fucking dead!"

She was coming, her voice announcing her approach.

"Deal with her." Vera pulled the grenade against her chest, blinking through tears of pain. "I've got this."

Luke's beautiful face turned to stone. Cold. Brutal. Lethal.

He stood, gloriously nude, and just as Silvia reached him, he punched her screaming mouth.

She went down, and he followed her, caught her by the throat, and wrenched her close, nose to nose.

The cartel continued to bang on the door, shouting and ramming the steel frame.

He ignored it. "I came here to free Vera Gomez, kill your brothers, and destroy the cartel. I'm part of a vigilante group. We annihilate monsters. People just like you." He bared his teeth in a terrifying smile. "I fell in love with Vera the night I saw her fight. You, on the other hand, have repulsed me from the moment we met."

Her head hit the floor as he dropped her. Then his fists flew. One punch after another, he bludgeoned her face. She made no noise, no attempt to fight him. Soon, the sounds of wet smacks gave way to crunching bone. He didn't stop.

Vera recognized the torment in his eyes. The rage.

The haunting nightmares. Silvia had raped him, and she hadn't been the first. Vera's heart broke as she watched him unleash eight years of memories in the harrowing drive of his fists.

He hammered strike after strike, raging in a gruesome trance, long after Silvia was dead. Long after Vera could stomach the macabre sight of blood and bone splattering beneath his blows.

Romero sat in a huddled ball with his eyes clamped shut.

"Luke."

He didn't hear her.

"Luke. Luke! Snap out of it and look at me! I need you!"

He stopped, stared at his bloody hands, and met her eyes.

"Time's up." Her body felt like ice, her head squishy with fuzz. "I'm losing blood, and you need pants."

He looked down at himself, brows knitting as if noticing his lack of clothes for the first time. Rising to his feet, he didn't give Silvia another glance. He strode directly toward Marco's corpse, stripped off the suit pants, and dragged them on.

By the time he returned to her, the blood was gone from his hands. He appeared composed, hawk-eyed, and laser-focused. One-hundred-percent Luke.

"Romero." He snapped his fingers. "Stand up."

"Don't hurt him. He designed the cartel's security system. Really smart kid." She felt herself fading, her fingers slipping on the grenade. She readjusted her grip. "I promised him amity and protection. He's coming with us."

A period of murkiness flickered in and out,

disorientating her. Seconds passed. Or minutes? She was losing her sense of time and awareness.

Luke was bent over her, his shirtless torso bulked up and strapped with weapons. Expression hard, eyes aglow with green flames, he looked like a rogue soldier, armed and ready for a revolution.

"Let me have it, baby." His hands were wrapped around hers, keeping the grenade safe.

She released the locked grip of her fingers and watched through blurred vision as he passed the small missile off to Romero. Then he removed the heavy artillery from her body.

A necktie appeared in his hand, one that Marco had worn. He tied it tightly around her thigh above the bullet wound. She cried out and pressed a fist to her mouth, shaking through the unholy pain.

"I'm so sorry." He kissed her face and pulled her hand away to kiss her mouth. "I'm getting you out of here."

"For the second time." She tried to smile, but her lips were numb.

"For the last time."

As he bent to lift her, an explosion rocked the foundation. The ground shook like an earthquake, and the atmosphere charged with electricity. He spun, grabbing the grenade from Romero's hands.

Her ears rang, and the boom lingered in her chest. When the tension released, overpowering relief swept in.

His team was here.

As the dust settled, Luke turned to her, thunderstruck. "Tell me that was our guys."

She looked to Romero for confirmation.

"I hooked your friends into my phone's GPS so

they could track us, and vice-versa." Romero removed the device from his pocket and tapped on the screen. "They're on the south side. All the activity is there. We should be able to escape out the main gate."

"I can't wait to hear how the two of you pulled this off." Luke grinned.

Romero might've been a genius, but his story wasn't much different than hers. Poor Latino boy supporting his poor family. A wealthy, powerful man strolled in, offered him a high-paying job, U.S. citizenship, and a slew of other empty promises.

She'd learned about him through the gossip of the girls in the estate. The cartel kept him sequestered away from the guests, but with Silvia's key card, she'd been able to enter his room and take him by surprise.

Romero wasn't really a bad guy. He'd made some mistakes, the same as her. Now they were both working toward redemption.

"The pounding on the door stopped," she said.

The explosion had drawn the crowd away.

Luke glanced at the grenade in his hand, then at the wall near the exit. "What's on the other side of that door?"

No way could he carry her, a grenade, and aim a gun at the same time. He must've been thinking the same thing.

"A garden." Romero looked up from his phone. "Lots of foliage to hide anyone who might be waiting for us to come out."

"Stay here." He strode toward the door, opened it with Marco's key card from his pocket, and chucked the grenade.

Seconds later, it detonated with a chest-rattling bang.

Well, there was no one waiting out there now. But more would come.

She didn't know how he planned to carry her to the gate without taking gunfire. But the pain in her leg was eating away her ability to worry about the endless details.

The persistent pull to close her eyes was grueling. She wanted to sleep, needed it desperately after being awake all night. But Luke probably hadn't slept, either, and his night had been much, much worse.

"Here we go." He crouched over her, gun in hand, more guns strapped to his back, and lifted her into his arms.

She bit back a scream as her leg jostled and burned with a vengeance. "Remove my vest. It's bulky. Too heavy."

"Not a chance. Hold on."

She tried, but the universe was spinning around a black curtain. Daylight speckled in through moments of darkness. Gunfire sounded off and on, muffled pops, as if passing through wads of cotton.

Then there was nothing.

"Vera."

"Huh?" She woke with a rumbling vibration beneath her and a rumbling voice beside her.

"Vera. Wake up."

She rubbed her eyes and found herself in the luxurious leather seat of a fast car. Like really *fast*. It flew down a barren road, hugging the turns and growling through the gears.

Behind the wheel sat the most beautiful man she'd ever seen. Red hair glinting in the sunlight, shirtless chest boasting strength and hard work, and powerful hands that knew how to maneuver high speeds, deliver fatal punches, and touch a woman until her eyes rolled back in her head.

"We're alive," she said in wonder, watching trees blur by. In the distance, clouds of smoke billowed on the horizon. "Is that the compound?"

"Yeah, it's burning. We hit them hard and fast. There will be nothing left by the time the authorities show up."

"How did you get us out?"

"Your badass haul of guns. I had enough firepower to clear a path to the car. Romero's safe. None of us were hit."

"What about the girls?"

"Rounded up and protected. This is what we do. Trust me, they're fine." His green eyes cut to her and returned to the road. "How are you doing?"

"I'm in shock, I think."

"It's the blood loss. And the adrenaline dump. You single-handedly took down all four of Hector's sons."

"I had help."

"You're a goddamn warrior. The fucking bullet is still in your leg." His hand clenched on the steering wheel. "Restrepo's doctor is waiting on the plane. You're going to be okay."

She believed him.

She loved him.

How could she not? They'd been through hell and back together. Sacrificed their lives for each other. Witnessed each other at their lowest, most degrading points.

Funny how the threat of death opened a person's eyes. Without tribulation and strife, a woman could go her life and never truly understand the meaning of love.

Had Vera spent enough time with Luke without all the danger, she would've eventually fallen for him. But after everything they'd been through, time had no bearing. After meat hooks, spiders, metal dildos, jealous bitches, and gunshot wounds, their relationship had been tested more in a short period than most couples experienced in an entire lifetime.

They'd already proved they could overcome anything together.

"Luke."

"Mm?"

"I have something to tell you."

"I know."

"No, you don't."

"I love you, too."

She grunted a breath that tumbled into a pain-laced groan. "You ruined it."

"You can still say it. Go ahead."

"But now you know what I'm going to say. It's lost its impact."

"Jesus, Vera, don't you know that every word that passes your lips impacts me? When you say *those* three words the first time, the next time, and if I'm lucky enough to hear them more times than that, they *will* have an impact, profoundly, significantly, in every way that matters."

She couldn't feel her injury. Or her legs. He was the cure for pain, pushing it into extinction and replacing it with sublime, soul-deep joy.

She let her head roll toward him and waited for his gaze. "I love you."

He didn't smile. Didn't repeat the words back. But it was all in his eyes. The coming together. The collision of souls. The brilliant shine.

The *impact*.

The force was so great she felt it everywhere.

"Eyes on the road." Her lips quirked.

Sprawled in a seat that seemed to be made for him, he shifted through gears with the confidence and fearlessness of a race car driver. He was in his element, driving too fast and taking too many risks. The car suited the man. Sexy as all hell.

"Is this Marco's sports car?"

He made a choking sound. "It's a *hyper*…car. A Koenigsegg Agera. Fastest car in existence."

As if to prove that, he opened the gas and tore down the road at dizzying speeds.

There was no one in front of them, but the side mirror revealed a long trail of hypercars behind him, glimmering in every color. She recognized them from Marco's collection.

"Where's Romero?" she asked.

"In the Lambo." He flicked a finger at the rearview mirror. "Those are my guys. I doubt they'll keep up, but they know where we're going."

"Where are we going?"

"Home. Colombia. To see your sister." He gripped her hand. "We made it, Vera. Just hang on a little longer."

She wove her fingers around his and squeezed.

For him, she would hang on forever.

TWENTY-EIGHT

Vera lay on her back on a plush sofa in Matias Restrepo's personal jet. With her head propped on Luke's lap and a heady flow of pain killers circulating through her system, she floated on a cloud.

This is what freedom feels like.

Voices whispered through the cabin. Jet engines hummed, and Luke's warm hand kept a constant, hypnotic rhythm along her arm, lulling her deeper into tranquility.

This is what love feels like.

He spoke quietly with two lethally handsome men who sat across from him. They'd introduced themselves as Tate Vades and Cole Hartman.

Lucia Dias, sister-in-law to the Restrepo capo, reclined beside Tate with a leg hooked over his knee. The beautiful Latina worked silently on her laptop as Tate absently stroked her inner thigh.

More vigilantes filled the seats in the front of the plane. Others had stayed behind to sell Marco's cars, relocate the girls, and clean up loose ends. They were also looking for Tomas. He hadn't contacted anyone since last night.

Picar, the cartel's doctor, hunched over Vera's exposed thigh, putting his final touches on the wound. She'd already received a blood transfusion and IV fluids. It was no surprise that the aircraft was equipped with the personnel and supplies to treat injuries. Cartel business was bloody.

At first, she didn't think the old doctor's cloudy eyes could see past his own nose. But he'd had no trouble locating and treating all her spider bites, removing the bullet, and stitching her up with tiny thread.

Speaking of stitches, the man who accompanied Picar wore a smile that had been sewed shut with heavy black thread. Add in his frizzy fluff of black hair, stark white complexion, and dark smudges around his eyes, and the man looked downright ghastly.

Luke had referred to him as Frizz and assured her that he deliberately sewed his own mouth closed.

She tried not to stare.

"All done. You need rest," Picar said in Spanish, straightened—as much as he could with his crooked spine—and waddled toward the front of the cabin.

She wished her sister was here. But since La Rocha had been looking for Tula, she'd been forced to stay in Colombia.

Romero seemed to relax now that he was on the plane and away from La Rocha. He sat on the other side of Luke, talking through the events leading up to the interrogation room.

"If you had access to all the cameras," Luke asked, "how did you not see her enter your room?"

"I was asleep."

"And I only had to dodge two cameras between the pond and his quarters." Vera shifted on the couch, seeking a more comfortable position with a better view of Romero, Luke, and his friends. "I know the location of every camera and their blind spots. It took me a long time to skirt around them undetected. But once I reached Romero's door, I knew I wouldn't have to deal with the cameras again."

"I woke with this woman straddling my hips." Grimacing, Romero scrubbed a hand over his black short-cropped hair. "She jabbed the barrel of a gun under my chin, with her eyes all feral, clothes and hair soaking wet, and—"

"It was an empty beer bottle, not a gun," she said.

"I didn't know that at the time." Romero dropped his hand. "She started making demands and screaming in my face. I knew immediately she was the girl who won all those fights. I thought for sure she was going to kill me."

Luke's hand never left her, his fingers tickling her neck and gently working the tangles from her curly hair. She drifted into a peaceful place, listening to Romeo explain the rest.

He was the hero, after all. Without him, she wouldn't have been able to enter the armory or move through the compound undetected. He'd manipulated each camera they'd approached so that the guards in the monitoring room wouldn't suspect a breach.

"I'll be honest," Romero said. "Her plan scared the shit out of me."

"It was reckless." Luke gave her hair a scolding tug.

"Shut up," she mumbled. "It was brilliant."

"You saved us a lot of time." Cole leaned

forward, arms braced on knees.

The vertical frown lines between his eyes were more prominent than the downturn of his lips. His thick brown beard did a good job of hiding the subtleties in his expression, which was probably a calculated effort. But no amount of hair could conceal the beautiful symmetry of his features.

"When you contacted us," he said, "we were at least two or three days away from isolating your location. You saved a lot of innocent lives."

"And ended a lot of evil." Luke's fingers tightened in her hair.

"It was all her. I was just doing what she asked." Romero blushed, looking sheepish. "She was pretty convincing once she started talking about how I could earn back my freedom by joining a movement against human sex traffickers. When I got involved with La Rocha, I knew they were criminals, but I didn't know about the girls and the slave buyers and everything that went on at the compound. I really had no idea what I was getting into until it was too late."

He told them about his family in Mexico, their poverty and sickness, and his desperation to help them. He'd been naive, just like her, and they'd both paid the price.

Romero had been imprisoned in his concrete room at the estate for two years, designing and maintaining the proprietary technology that secured the property. Only Silvia and her brothers had access to his room.

Vera would bet her last dollar that Silvia had raped the poor kid. Frequently.

"They threatened to butcher my family," he said. "I left my parents two years ago, promising to send them money. They haven't heard from me or seen a single dollar since I left."

"We'll take care of them, kid." Lucia looked up from her laptop and winked. "You're one of us now. *Tu familia es nuestra familia.*"

Your family is our family.

Vera felt that in her bones, and it made her eyes heat and dampen. Luke was taking her to her sister, bringing her into his tight-knit family, and giving her a home.

He was offering her a world of tangible dreams and possibilities.

"I'm sorry it took me so long to show up." With her head in his lap, she reached up and cupped his scratchy, chiseled jaw. "Romero and I didn't come to an agreement right away. I didn't trust him not to use one of his devices to notify the cartel."

"And I didn't trust her not to smash in my skull." Romero released an anxious laugh.

"We eventually worked out a fragile truce. Then we spent hours ironing out a plan." Guilt riddled her. "I took too long."

"You showed up." Luke slid a thumb across her cheek.

"Not soon enough."

"I'm alive, Vera. With all my body parts intact."

Her throat tightened at the memory of Marco holding pruning shears when she'd charged in.

"I saw the instrument Silvia used on you." She lowered her voice. "You should let the doctor examine you."

"What instrument?" Tate asked.

"Strap-on." Luke met his friend's eyes. "It had been a while since..."

"Eight years, man." Tate blew out a breath. "It's not easy to relive a second time, is it?"

"No, but I remembered the training, everything Van taught us. It helped."

"Are you injured?"

"It's minor. I'll heal."

She watched their interaction, recalling everything Luke had told her about the captives in Van's attic. The nine of them shared such horrific memories, but she found comfort in the ease in which they could talk about it.

Lucia set her laptop aside and crawled onto Tate's lap, wrapping her arms around him and nuzzling her face in his neck.

For a group of vicious killers, their empathy was palpable, their deep friendships undeniable. Vera respected them for that. Quite frankly, she was in awe of how these proud, dominant males could undergo such trauma and not lose themselves on the other side of it. Some victims never recovered.

"I betrayed you, Vera." Luke's roughened voice drew her gaze.

"What?"

"Silvia…put hands on me. Her mouth." His jaw went rigid. "My body reacted. I couldn't control—"

"Did you want her? Did you give your consent?"

"No. Fuck, no. But I wasn't strong enough to—"

"Don't forget who you're talking to, Luke." She pushed herself up to meet him at eye-level. "I was raped for three years. You don't have to convince me you didn't want it. I've been there."

"Yeah, I know." His eyes hardened. "*I* raped you."

"I forgave you. You don't have to forgive Silvia.

In fact, I'll be royally pissed if you do."

"Dayyy-um." Lucia grinned. "I like her. It's about time someone put you in your place, Luke."

"When her leg heals, my place will be standing behind her upturned ass while I blister it red."

"Promises, promises." Vera lay back down, returning her head to his lap.

She slept off and on through the duration of the flight. During moments of alertness, she listened to them wrap up the details of the mission and discuss the status of another one Camila was running in Mexico.

But mostly, they talked about Tomas.

Cole asked a lot of questions about the email, its origin, and Tomas' childhood. Luke and Tate didn't have the answers. Tomas had never told anyone he'd loved and lost a girl. He'd certainly never told anyone he'd been writing to her ghost all these years.

It sounded like they were going to give him a week to make contact. Then Cole would fly back to America and go after him.

"Who are you?" Vera cringed at the rudeness of her question. "Sorry. That came out wrong. But seriously. You're not one of Van's captives. You're not related to them by blood or marriage. You're not a Restrepo cartel member. So… Who are you?"

Cole flashed her a wolfish, bearded smile, all teeth, and no answers.

"If you ever figure it out…" Luke stroked the curve of her hip. "Tell the rest of us."

TWENTY-NINE

Vera spent the next week in a blur of recovery and acclimation. She'd been dug out of hell, dropped into a brand-new life, and she embraced it with her entire being.

The Restrepo Cartel headquarters in Colombia was even more lavish than *Casa de La Rocha.* Nestled in the Amazon rainforest, it boasted top-notch security, freedom to roam without consequences, and the best part? The cartel didn't traffic humans. They sought and destroyed those who did.

Matias and Camila were in Mexico right now, running another mission. But she met the rest of the crew. Liv and Josh, Van and Amber, Kate and Tiago, Martin and Ricky. And Tula…

Her sister had greeted her on the helicopter pad, arms wide, black hair whipping in the turbulence, and tears streaking down her face. They cried together, blubbered their regrets, and reconnected for days.

Tula's guys, Martin and Ricky, had greeted Vera with warm, hard-muscled, masculine-scented hugs.

Then they hung around, listening to her and Tula exchange questions and reminisce for hours. They were good-looking men. Attentive. Devoted to her sister. But dangerous.

Everyone she encountered vibrated with ruthlessness and menace. A sense of danger hung in the air and lurked around every corner. But not like it was with La Rocha. The danger here wasn't directed at her.

Luke's friends protected their own, followed their own laws, and viciously destroyed anyone who threatened their loved ones. She felt it in every handshake, embrace, and flinty-eyed look.

For the first time in her life, she felt safe among criminals.

Tula monopolized her first week here, showing her around the fortress and introducing her to everyone they passed. Vera hobbled along on her crutches as Tula shared the brutal details of her time in prison. But when she spoke of Martin and Ricky, her eyes lit up, and her cheeks rose with a goofy smile.

Love.

Vera sympathized with that ailment.

Luke was giving her space to catch up with her sister. He was using that time to work on a strategy with Cole, who was leaving tomorrow to return to the States.

Tomas still hadn't made contact.

So she stayed out of Luke's way and formed a delightful friendship with Tiago's wife, Kate. The pretty blonde only stayed here part-time. She was shadowing Picar, learning medicine, and working toward her degree. She wanted to be a doctor.

She didn't have the experience to treat Vera's wound, but she always accompanied Picar, absorbing his broken English while he examined Vera. Then she hung around after, chatting and sharing stories about her captivity with the Venezuelan crime lord, Tiago Badell.

Everyone here had a story, and Vera loved learning about their survival, their triumphs, and how they all interconnected.

There was so much she'd yet to learn about Luke.

She wanted to know all his quirks and complain about them. She wanted more Klondike and rap-song moments. She wanted to bicker with him over nothing and whack him with a pillow when he snored. Because that was what couples did, right? They drove each other crazy.

Crazy with Luke was going to be crazy amazing. She couldn't wait.

She missed him.

"Do you love him?" Tula pushed her sunglasses to her forehead and squinted in the afternoon sunlight.

"Yeah. Terribly." Swallowing a sip of beer, Vera stared out across the crystal-blue pool. "I've barely seen him all week."

"He's busy. But you're sleeping in his bed, right?"

Every night, he tucked her against his chest, kissed her everywhere, touched her over her clothes until she was wet, and… "No sex."

"Well, hello? You were shot. With a bullet."

"In the leg. Not in my vagina."

Tula burst into laughter. "Haven't you figured out that these guys are different? They're not like those selfish, abusive boys back home. They want us healed and healthy and begging for it before they beat us."

They stared at each other, biting back smiles.

"Never thought you'd crave a fist around your throat, huh?" Tula gave into her grin. "Or a stinging-red ass, bite marks, bruised thighs…"

"Never in a million years." She leaned back on the lounger and sighed. "It's been a rough road for us, you know?"

"Don't you feel like the hardest part is behind us?"

"Yeah. Even if it isn't, the hard stuff feels a lot less hard with someone you love at your side."

"Or two someones."

"You're such a whore." She knocked the sunglasses off Tula's head.

"A happy whore." Tula chuckled.

"Who's a whore?" Amber strolled up to their loungers.

"Your mama," Tula said.

"Doubtful. She spent a lot of time clutching her pearls. Can I join you?"

Tula dragged over another lounge chair. Meanwhile, Vera couldn't take her eyes off Van's wife. The woman radiated head-to-toe beauty, from her shiny chestnut hair and rosebud lips to her flawless, hourglass figure on full display in a tiny black bikini. Good God, she was gorgeous. Beauty queen gorgeous.

It was hard to imagine her with a man like Van Quiso. Vera knew their story and couldn't help but resent the man for everything he'd done to Luke and the others. She also knew they'd forgiven him.

He was among their kindred, which meant she would learn to accept and forgive him, too.

"I'm just going to put this out in the open." She shifted on the lounger, adjusting her injured leg before meeting Amber's eyes. "Your husband terrifies me."

"Me, too." Amber moved the coasters around on the small table beside her, arranging them in neat groups of four. "He's meaner than piss."

"With you?"

"Hmm. Why don't you ask him yourself?"

"No, that's—"

"Van!" Amber leaned to the side, shouting toward the open door of the veranda. "Come here!"

"Oh, now you've done it." Tula groaned. "You call one of them out here, and they'll all show up."

Sure enough, as Van ambled into the pool area, Joshua and Ricky trailed behind. They wore swim trunks and carried beers. Sunglasses and sexy hair. Shirtless and shredded with stacks of muscle. Where was a camera when she needed one? They belonged on a vigilante calendar. She would call it *Freedom Fighters, the Weapons of War edition.*

Van paused beside Amber, gazing down at her, and his smile stretched the scar that curved from his mouth to somewhere beneath his shades. As he leaned down to kiss her fully on the mouth, his hand swiped over the coasters she'd arranged on the table.

When he straightened, her eyes zoomed in on the mess he'd made.

Apparently, Amber's OCD was a work-in-progress.

"Vera wanted to know," Amber said, without looking away from the scattered coasters, "if you're mean to me."

"Nah." He removed a toothpick from his pocket and set it between his teeth. "I'm a big sappy baby."

Joshua laughed as he stepped into the pool. "He's an asshole. With everyone."

With an unapologetic shrug, Van rolled the

toothpick to the corner of his smirk. "Anything else you want to know? Like if I'm mean when I suspend my wife from the trees out there?" He nodded at the rainforest. "When I whip her and welt her pretty skin? Or when I bring her to orgasm, and she screams so beautifully everyone in the estate can hear her?"

"No, I…really didn't want to know that." Vera squeezed thighs against the warmth that rushed between them.

During that brief and disturbingly hot exchange, Amber had discreetly started moving the coasters back into symmetrical groups.

Van tossed his toothpick next to her busy hand. Then he kicked the table, just enough to jostle her attempt at order.

"Excuse us." He grabbed her, tossed her over his shoulder, and walked straight into the pool, submerging them both as she screamed.

Vera shook her head. "Well, that was…"

"Typical Van." Ricky took Amber's chair, stretching out his legs and closing a hand around Tula's knee. "You'll get used to him."

Not likely.

For the next few hours, she hung out with Tula, Ricky, and Joshua. Van and Amber stayed in the pool until Van started removing her bikini. Then they disappeared, taking their foreplay elsewhere.

Beer flowed. Platters of food arrived, and the air buzzed with laughter and conversation.

Until Tula started harping on Vera for hiding the magnitude of their mother's medical bills. They both had regrets and hashed it all out over multiple beers. Then Tula revisited the topic of Luke.

"He hasn't fucked her in a week," she said to

Ricky.

Vera gave her the stink eye.

"She has a gunshot wound." Ricky scraped a tortilla chip along the bottom of a salsa bowl and crammed it into his mouth. "I'd be the same way. A wound like that needs time to heal."

"That's what I told her. You're all so overprotective."

"Okay, first of all…" Vera picked at the gauze on her thigh. "I'm not a sex addict. There's more to Luke than his body."

Tula snorted. "You're in the honeymoon phase of your relationship. It's *all* about the fucking. I mean, the guys and I still go at it like rabbits."

"You're wet just thinking about it." Ricky winked.

"You know I am."

"Not helping," Vera muttered.

"Go to bed naked." Joshua arched a brow and reclined back in the chair. "Trust me. All chivalry will fall by the wayside the moment he reaches over and finds his woman laid out and bare. It'll trip the wires in his stubborn head."

That night, she took Joshua's advice. No t-shirt. No panties. No bandage on her leg. She slipped beneath the covers, wearing only her skin, and shut off the light.

Luke hadn't come in yet. He'd been tied up with Cole and Tate all day.

As she started to drift off, the door opened. He crept in quietly and removed his clothes in the dark. Then the mattress dipped.

Lying on her side with her back to him, she held her breath, her blood heating in anticipation.

His hands went directly to her ass, as they always

did. Only this time, they froze on contact.

Keep going, Luke. It's all bare.

Slowly, his clever fingers slid up her spine and back down, questing, hunting for more nudity. His breaths grew shorter. His body inched closer. Within seconds, his hands were everywhere, trailing along her neck, molding around her breasts, and dipping between her legs.

"Killing me, Vera." Panting against her shoulder, he reached the vicinity of her gunshot wound and stopped. "Where's your bandage?"

"Don't need it." She wriggled her backside against the iron proof of his arousal. "Just need you."

He groaned hotly against her nape. "I don't want to hurt you."

"Denying me hurts me." She shifted onto her back and found his gaze in the moonlight. "If your hesitancy has to do with what happened with Silvia, we need to talk about it."

"No." His eyes widened. "I haven't thought about that once. It's your leg. Picar said you need to go easy on it."

"Go easy on it." She pulled off the covers and spread her thighs in a wanton display. "But don't go easy on my pussy."

In a flash, he was up, stripping off his underwear and straddling her hips. His mouth came down on hers, his tongue pressing in. He kissed her maddeningly, passionately, unleashing the depths of his need.

"I missed this." He rocked against her as he ate at her mouth, dragging his erection along her stomach. "I love you."

"Love you." Pre-come smeared her skin, and she basked in the sensation, reaching down to caress the heavy sac behind his cock.

He grunted against her lips and leaned back a few inches to stare at her. His hand caressed her face, clearing away the hair that had fallen over her cheek. Then he dipped his head and attacked her mouth again.

They kissed like teenagers, grinding, groping, and making out with tongues and teeth. Then he turned his attention to her body, licking and biting every dip, working his way down her breasts, down her belly, down through the slit of her cunt to burrow into the wetness between her legs.

She moaned guttural sounds and writhed against his mouth. He spread her apart and lapped at her flesh, fingertips flirting and rolling alongside his wicked tongue.

When he finally sank a pair of fingers inside, she cried out, clenching, and that was all it took.

She came instantly and with wild abandon, bucking and trembling and screaming, "Luke! Luke! Luke!"

"Christ, you have a magnificent cunt." He dipped his fingers in and out of the pooling moisture, making her shudder and ache all over again. "Swollen and pink. Primed for my cock."

"Fuck me, you redheaded sadist."

"In good time." He crawled back up her body and slid his nose along hers. "How's your leg?"

"Same as the other one. I need you between them."

He grinned, and she whimpered, knowing he had every intention of making her wait.

As he leaned in to kiss her, she took a mental picture because damn, he was sexy. The way he rolled his tongue past his parted lips just before their mouths collided… It got her every time.

That irresistible tongue felt so perfect against hers. So warm and controlling and *him*. She loved everything about him—his kisses, his touches, the heat of his body, and how it made her feel when he was moving inside her. She would never tire of this. Never tire of him.

He made the world a better place, and he was the only place she wanted to be.

His mouth left her lips to kiss over her face. Then he straightened on his knees and shifted until his sculpted thighs bracketed her head.

She devoured the sight of him towering over her, a powerful symbol of sexuality. His crowning glory jutted outward, bobbing above her head, thick and swollen, and tipped with a fat bead of pre-come.

Her inner muscles convulsed around nothing, throbbing to be stretched and pounded by that long, beautiful cock.

His hand wrapped around the root and slid up the broad shaft. He watched her, eyes smoldering beneath hooded lids, as he glided his palm around the head, gathered the moisture, and began to stroke with vigor.

Erotic didn't begin to describe the sight of this man pleasuring himself. His brawny legs trembled. The bricks of his abs contracted. Veins bulged in his forearm, and his eyes…

They were predator eyes, molten green, bold and hungry as ever, deadly dominant, deadly overbearing, just plain deadly.

He smacked the plump crown of his cock against her mouth. Then he did it again. And again. When she gasped, he shoved himself in, past her lips, her teeth, and straight to the back of her throat.

Her hands flew to the granite globes of his ass as she relaxed her tongue and breathed with his thrusts.

He gripped the headboard, bracing the cant of his body, while his other hand fisted in her hair. He held her head immobile, fucking her face with the frenzy of a mindless animal.

But he wasn't mindless, his gaze too alert and watchful. He never looked away, penetrating her with his eyes as deeply as the plunge of his cock.

It was that constant, worshiping eye contact that turned her on more than anything else. She savored the salty taste of him, the feel of his balls grinding against her chin, the way his body moved in a sensual dance. But God almighty, she loved the way he watched her.

He was language without words. The devotion-forming capacity of nature. The spirit of adventure and love. A humanist at war with monsters. And a carnal beast in the throes of pleasure.

His breathing deepened, and his honed physique flexed and dampened beneath her hands. She indulged herself, tracing all his grooves and indentations while sucking and licking the furor of his hardness in her mouth.

He gritted his teeth, his masculine features straining as he battled against completion.

"Fuck." He pulled out and squeezed the base of his erection as if trying to ward off a demanding release. "Your mouth feels too good, baby. I almost came. Not going to last a minute once I'm in your hot pussy."

"Good thing you have supernatural stamina. I'm expecting a long night with you."

"How about a long life with me?"

"That, too."

"Stay there." He shifted down her body, curling his warm, hard muscles around her uninjured side. Lifting her good leg, he hooked it over his hip while keeping her wounded thigh flat on the bed. "Don't move or fight against me. I don't want that leg straining."

They'd both been tested by the doctor. They were clean, and she was on birth control.

"No condom." She quivered at the feel of him sliding along her drenched slit from behind.

"My first time bareback." He leaned over her face, mouth open and panting against her lips as his cock teased the pulsing ring of her opening. "I'm so in love with you."

"Same." She gripped his nape and pulled him down for a kiss. "Please, Luke. Fuck me."

He pushed in his tongue. Then he pushed in his cock, sinking both with a shuddering, body-trembling groan.

With her lying on her back, he hiked up her good leg, holding it against him while guiding the movement and angle of her lower half as he plowed into her from behind.

The position allowed her injured leg to rest on the bed and away from the piston of his hips. It also gave him access to her mouth and a view of her jiggling tits, of which he took full advantage. He kissed her. Stared at her body. Kissed her again. Bit her nipples. He was everywhere, over, under, and inside her at once.

Lying on his side while holding her leg in an arm lock didn't affect the rhythm or force of his thrusts. Nor did it stop him from reaching a hand to where they were joined to add another layer of stimulation.

He played with her clit and stroked the flesh that

squeezed around him. Then he pushed two fingers inside, entering her alongside his cock. Triple-penetration. She nearly came undone.

"The silk inside you feels unreal." He licked at her mouth, trying and failing to keep their lips sealed. "The sensation is so much hotter, softer, fucking wetter without a barrier. Christ, I'll never go back to condoms." He held her gaze and slammed into her with cock and fingers. "I want to put a baby in you."

She laughed blissfully around his hungry tongue. "Let's practice for a while. Lots and lots of practice."

He moved his hand to her breast and got to work, fucking her with shocking endurance. His deep, frenzied strokes delivered a religious experience, the heat of his kisses an empowered sense of rapture. He injected wonder into reality and transformed the world into electric hues of elation.

Making love to him was a cosmic explosion of body and mind. A splitting of atoms. Nuclear fission.

Energy released around her, sparking a chain reaction, rapidly multiplying the sensations plummeting through her, and sending her over the edge.

She came so violently she screamed, gasping for air and choking out his name. Pleasure burst in a starscape of light, crashing through her nerve endings and sucking all her strength.

Complete and total surrender.

"Vera." He saw it, felt it, and went rigid, groaning and jerking and succumbing to his own breathless release.

A warm rush flooded into her as an expression of gobsmacked adoration overtook his face.

"What are you thinking?" She cupped his hard

jaw, laughing and wheezing.

"No words." He tried to catch his breath and lowered her leg. But he didn't pull out. "It's indescribable."

"Yeah."

"We're not finished." He thrust lazily inside her, testing the rigidness of his cock.

"I hoped you'd say that."

"You're not getting rid of me."

"Not even when we fight. And we will. I'm going to challenge everything you say and do. Can you deal with that?"

"I fucking look forward to it."

His mouth covered her lips. His hips rocked against her, and their bodies came together, unshackled in love and united in war.

THIRTY

Luke circled the Koenigsegg Agera, admiring its low profile, aerodynamic lines, and metallic silver paint. It used to be the sexiest goddamn thing he'd ever seen.

That was before he rested his eyes on Vera Gomez, who was currently naked and bent over the hood.

"Luke." She rubbed her pussy against the front wheel well, no doubt leaving streaks of moisture on the paint. "If you don't finish this soon, I'm going to take care of myself."

"Be quiet." Fucking hell, he was hard. Painfully, miserably rock-hard. "I paid a lot of money for this view."

All of Marco's hypercars had been sold, but this one. Luke had personally funded the shipping expenses to transport it from California to Bogota, Columbia.

For one reason only.

He wanted to fuck the world's sexiest woman on top of the world's sexiest car.

Never in his wildest fantasies did he think he

would be standing here, in the middle of a forest outside of Bogota, taking in this view.

Her heart-shaped, upturned ass bore the welted marks of his spankings. Her skin slicked with sweat. Arousal soaked her thighs. He'd been playing with her in this position for over an hour.

"This is the pinnacle of my life." He grinned at her backside. "Nothing will ever top this."

"Don't say that, you fucking asshat. What about marriage? Kids? Grand—"

"Nope. This is *my* fantasy. One I've dreamed about for as long as I can remember."

"You fantasized about beating a woman's ass when you were a kid?"

"Beating the *sexiest* woman's ass on top of the *sexiest* car." He unzipped his jeans and freed his cock. "I can't even tell you how many times I shot my load with this image in my head."

"How's the reality holding up?" She wriggled her hips.

"Fuck." He gripped his cock, trying not to come. "It's better. The reality is so unbelievably sinful. Wish you could see it."

She moaned, stretching her arms out over the hood and rocking her hips. "Come on, Luke. I *ache*."

He stood still, committing every glorious detail to memory. Then he prowled toward her, kicked her feet apart, and sank himself into her throbbing wet heat.

His hands traveled over her delicious curves. His heart raced with the unfettered force of his thrusts, and she gripped him, clenching, with a tight, greedy cunt.

He wanted it to last forever, but she was already there. His body, completely attuned to hers, followed the sounds of her blissful cries, climbing with her, fusing, crashing…

Impact.

He drove savagely into her, spilling his seed as she found her own release. His head fell forward, his mouth sucking and biting her shoulders, his senses exploding in ecstasy.

As they settled down, he tucked himself away and pulled her limp body into his arms.

She stared up at him, and he kissed her dazed smile, lips gliding, and hearts pounding a single tattoo.

"I have a surprise for you." He brushed her hair from her face. "Get dressed."

He stepped back, admiring the view of her tight, sexy body as she dragged on jeans and a t-shirt. "What's the surprise? Go ahead and tell me."

"Vera." He clicked his tongue. "Don't start."

"I just want to know."

"You want to argue."

"No. I just don't like surprises."

"Too bad."

She growled under her breath. "You're so annoying."

"You're so beautiful."

Her dark eyes softened. Her lips turned up, and he considered riling her up again, just so he could savor all her expressions.

An engine sounded in the distance, and a moment later, a motorcycle emerged on the winding road through the trees.

"Expecting someone?" She joined his side.

"Yep." He removed the Koenigsegg key from his pocket.

The motorcyclist pulled to a stop in the clearing and turned off the engine. The man had been thoroughly vetted, the deal already negotiated. Luke expected no trouble.

"Mr. Smith?" The man removed his helmet, revealing a bald head and a silver beard.

"Yep." Luke held out the car key.

"She's a beauty." Eyes on the hypercar, the man shrugged out of his backpack and handed it over. "It's all there. In small bills, just like you asked."

The heavy weight of the bag promised a clean transaction. While the man checked out the Koenigsegg, Luke opened the backpack and counted the money.

"What are you doing?" Vera stood over him, her fists anchored on her hips. "You're selling that car? Why? It's your dream car!"

"Shh." He continued counting.

She fell quiet, waiting for him to finish.

"It's all here," he said to the man. "We good?"

Better be. He was selling that car for a fraction of what it was worth.

"All good." The man grinned. "The second helmet is on the bike."

Luke strapped the backpack onto Vera's shoulders and kissed her stiff lips. "Let's have some fun."

"I can't believe you sold that car."

"I have everything I want right here." He kissed her again. "Come on."

Then he put her on the motorcycle, tucked her close behind him, and hit the road.

As much as he enjoyed the hypercar, it didn't compare to the feeling of an engine between his legs and Vera's warm body wrapped around his back.

He opened the throttle, startling a yelp from his girl. Then she laughed, clutching his waist and squeezing her thighs around him.

This is heaven.

He took her to a small town on the southern outskirts of Bogota. Not the safest area, but they wouldn't stay long.

Zipping along the crumbling streets, he veered toward his destination. When he arrived at the old hospital, he turned off the engine and lifted Vera from the seat.

"What are we doing here?" She scanned the dilapidated building, the broken wrought iron on the windows, and the overall gloom shrouding the place.

"We're spending the money." He grabbed the backpack and hooked it over his shoulder. Then he grabbed her hand, pulling her along. "Twenty minutes. In and out."

"Okay, but isn't this a hospital? What are we buying?"

"Smiles."

He couldn't stifle his own as he led her through the front entrance and down a dank, unkempt corridor. There was no security here. No visitor protocols. Nothing to stop them from entering the first room.

An elderly woman lay in the hospital bed, her arms and chest hooked up to a chirping, outdated machine. There were others in the room, presumably her family, sitting on the floor and standing along the wall.

"Luke?" Vera squeezed his hand. "Do you know these people?"

"Nope. Reach into the backpack and give them a gift."

Her forehead knitted. She glanced around the room at all the silent, staring faces. He watched the realization widen her eyes and swell in her chest.

She pressed a fist to her mouth, nodding as tears welled along her lashes. Then she reached into the backpack.

And so it went.

He followed her from room to room as she passed out money, speaking rapidly in Spanish, trying to convince each patient that she expected nothing in return.

When she lingered too long at a bedside, he quickly dragged her to the next one, keeping her moving.

They were in a dangerous neighborhood, riddled with poverty and crime. He wanted all the money gone before they drew too much attention.

By the time they reached the last room, her smile was blinding, contagious, and worth all the hypercars in the world.

She was happy making people happy, and he knew without a shadow of a doubt that she would thrive as a Freedom Fighter.

He couldn't stop staring at her, at the majestic glow that shone in her eyes, her tears, her constant smile.

"What?" She walked beside him through the parking lot, watching him watch her.

"You know the fantasy I had with you and the hypercar..."

"And my glowing red ass?"

"Yeah." He stopped at the motorcycle and hauled her against his chest, smiling against her lips. "You just topped it."

"*We* topped it. Thank you for that, for what you did in there." She raked her hands through his hair and kissed his mouth. "I love you."

Impact. Direct shot to the chest.

"I felt that." He rested his brow against hers.

"I'll say it again if you stop for ice cream on the way home."

"Klondike bar?"

"Three boxes." She wedged on the helmet and flipped up the visor. "Variety packs. All the flavors."

"One box." He straddled the bike and pulled on his own helmet. "Six orgasms."

She started to argue until she registered the last part. Then she grinned, slapped down the visor, and climbed on behind him.

"No stops." She rested her chin on his shoulder and hugged his back. "Let's go home."

The DELIVER series continues with:

DOMINATE (#8)
Tomas' story

COMPLICATE (#9) - *the final book*
Cole's story

LOVE TRIANGLE ROMANCE

TANGLED LIES TRILOGY

One is a Promise

Two is a Lie

Three is a War

DARK COWBOY ROMANCE

TRAILS OF SIN

Knotted #1

Buckled #2

Booted #3

DARK ALASKAN ROMANCE

FROZEN FATE

Hills of Shivers and Shadows #1

Cage of Ice and Echoes #2

Heart of Frost and Scars #3

DARK PARANORMAL ROMANCE
TRILOGY OF EVE
Heart of Eve
Dead of Eve #1
Blood of Eve #2
Dawn of Eve #3

STUDENT-TEACHER / PRIEST
Lessons In Sin

STUDENT-TEACHER ROMANCE
Dark Notes

ROCK-STAR DARK ROMANCE
Beneath the Burn

BILLIONAIRE REVENGE
Dirty Ties

OLDER WOMAN / YOUNGER MAN
Incentive

DARK HISTORICAL PIRATE ROMANCE
King of Libertines
Sea of Ruin

New York Times, Wall Street Journal, and *USA Today* bestselling author, Pam Godwin, lives in the Midwest with her husband, cats, retired greyhounds, and an old, foul-mouthed parrot. She traveled the world for seven years, attended three universities, married the vocalist of her favorite rock band, and retired from her quantitative analyst career in 2014 to write full-time.

Her interests veer toward the unconventional: bourbon, full-body tattoos, and tragic villains. Equally peculiar are her aversions to sleeping, eating meat, and dolls with blinking eyes.

EMAIL: pamgodwinauthor@gmail.com

www.ingramcontent.com/pod-product-compliance
Lightning Source LLC
Chambersburg PA
CBHW020457310726
48979CB00016B/2689/J

* 9 7 8 1 9 6 6 5 3 7 0 1 4 *